FOREVER

BETTY LOWREY

ISBN 979-8-9901548-5-8 (paperback)
ISBN 979-8-9901548-4-1 (eBook)

Printed in the United States of America

CONTENTS

PROLOGUE

L IFE RESUMED IN THE CAPE. Ellen Anderson finally married Daniel Gates and as her four year old was prone to say. "Daniel married us, me and Momma and we are going to live happy ever after and I'm going to ask God if He will send us a new baby because Momma says God works in mysterious ways."

In spite of Matthew Langley's parent's not liking Ruthie's best friend, Marigold; Matt and Marigold married, and in the proper length of time little Matt came into their lives, but not without considerable stress. Marigold forego medical treatment thinking the signs she was seeing in her own body happened to all pregnant women and if she let them be known everyone would realize she and Matt were secretly married; all because she wished to give the situation between her and Matt's parents *time to come together*. Foolish thinking, she learned can get you in trouble.

It was a long and wearying story, hers and Matt's, but Marigold found her birth mother through the ordeal and what she dreamed would be a wonderful reunion hadn't happened. She envisioned a fairy tale setting with the sun shining and music playing as they glanced up and knew each other instantly; thus, an end to her search after the accident took the lives of her adopted parents but she was in for a surprise when it was Harriet, the neighbor down the block she locked horns with on every occasion; the one she tried to please to find *more was always* expected. The first onset of realization that Harriet Becker was her mother had not been met with elation but more like trepidation.

Then, there was Bitty, Ruthie's sitter, as Ruthie explained, "She used to be a widow, that means her husband died and she was never going to marry again but Captain Mayfield told her it was a sin to live alone when there was someone loved her and needed her to marry him. So now, Bitty married him and lives in the house me and Momma used to live in and I still get to see her almost every day." Yes, a whole lot of change had happened in the lives of the four friends. Harriet's search for the daughter she gave up at birth ended two doors down, with the impish girl she dare not understand, her birth daughter, "It didn't matter that they had been mean to each other," Ruthie explained. "Once they were lost but now they were found."

Ellen had taken in Anne during the beginning of nurses' training; when Anne struggled without funding and found herself suffering through each ordeal her ex-husband laid upon her, the most hurtful was his deceit in gaining custody of their son. Although she agonized through each shenanigan Andrew presented she was now on decent speaking terms with him. But Anne never knew if Andrew's actions were a carefully planned ploy for his own benefit.

Group conversations started with "remember so and so and ended with I would never have believed it." New people entered their lives as they moved on the block and Marigold brought them together. Happiness and tragedy intermingled and they worked through each situation. Ruthie, ever in tune with everyone's lives seemed to keep record of the happenings and now she was concerned with Andrews plans to move out on his own, away from the people who had "taken him in and turned him around," as Bitty was prone to say, but there were more problems, *the family who had taken him in* had a daughter coming home who had been in *a lot of trouble*.

A four year old can only comprehend so much but Ruthie had the gift. That's what Momma and Bitty called it, a gift from God that must be used wisely, as Bitty often reminded Ruthie. "I agree with your Momma, "It is not to be taken lightly, nor is it to be boasted, it is simply a gift the Lord has given you." Ruthie loved Bitty and listened to her advice but the news Andrew mentioned in conversation was that his benefactor's daughter might be a *hand full*. Ruthie let the words roll around in her head; *a hand full. Benefactor.* She had to ask Momma what those words meant. She didn't know *Andrew's* benefactors, but she had seen them. She smiled. It would be a happy time for them, with their daughter coming home. If I meet Haley, Ruthie decided, I'll tell her when she feels sad or whatever that word is, rebellious, all she needs to do is listen to Jesus.

Ruthie really didn't have time to worry over Andrew. Momma and Daniel's twins were *a handful,* too. Momma said God worked in mysterious ways and it was best to let Him take care of everyone's problems and when it was her job to watch over the twins she could use all the help God could give her.

Based on her up-bringing, Ruthie believed God would love her forever and the group of friends that surrounded her life would be there forever because God loved them and Ruthie knew she would love them all forever, especially Jesus and his Heavenly Father. Forever.

FOREVER IS THE FOURTH BOOK in the series of Ellen, Bitty, Anne, Harriet, and Marigold. It is the author's wish that you have read Forgiven, Forbidden and Forsaken, as the lives of the women unfold and their friendship blooms. You are invited to join the author on her daily blog; Forgiven by Betty Lowrey on Facebook.

DEDICATION

To our Heavenly Father, first
To Those Who Encourage and care
Always to BJL, Forever, and his kids
Thank you to the one who edited
Thank you to Tori and Bliss Photography for the image of Ellen

QUOTE:

No man is an island,
Therefore never send to know for whom the bell tolls;
It tolls for thee.

Excert: John Donne 1572-1631

CHAPTER ONE

T HE PLANE DESCENDED BANKING RIGHT as a line of buildings appeared on the horizon, tiny dots that neither resembled anything she had seen before or wanted to now. They'd left Oklahoma's holding tank four hours earlier where overnight she'd been checked from head to foot to verify there was nothing wrong with her. Physically, she mused, for there were innumerable things wrong in her head.

Never in her wildest dreams would she have found herself ready to enter the doors of a women's prison. "State your name. Your age. What's your number?" The questions had become routine and one thing she realized, Federal Prison was nothing like living in the County Jail where friends could visit and you were near family, if you wanted to see them.

They'd lied. Everyone lied. The Judge, the Federal people who took her statement and promised leniency and said, "No, you won't go to prison. Just tell us what you know and we'll see to that." And there'd been Mom and Dad. Hadn't Daddy said, "I won't let you go, baby. No matter what you've done, we'll get the best lawyers but you got to straighten up, baby."

In her heart she knew she was responsible. She had brought this on herself. She'd run with the wrong crowd, done things no one should do and now she was going to pay the price. Bubba paid too, didn't he? But where was Race? She heaved a deep sigh. It still hurt. Bubba was dead, had been gone two years now and all she could think was she wanted to see him, see him and tell him she was sorry. Sorry they'd quarreled. Sorry she didn't take his advice when he said,

"Sis, you gotta straighten up. You see what it's done to me. Get off of it. You're not that far in. Look what I've done to Mom and Dad; you don't want to hurt them more."

Bubba, her brother, born Grant Harper Gipson, died from an overdose and the sad part of his dying was he wanted to die. He tried but he couldn't kick the habit he'd been doing since he was fifteen years old. Seven years of needles in the arm, foul tasting drugs that turned his insides against him and the doctor's words, "you've developed leukemia due to the state of your body breaking down from the drugs." Whatever else the doctor said was lost after he said, "Young man, I wish I could help you and while there's always hope, it will take a miracle. If you can walk a straight line, stop using, I'll do my best to help you." She was with him that day at the doctor's office,

"Why'd you ask him to level with you?"

Those sad eyes had pinned her in a heart wrenching stare. "I needed to know, sis. You think my body hasn't been telling me this all along? If I don't have much time left, maybe I can do some good, with you."

Grant's last months of life had torn the life out of her. He'd moved back home with his childhood room becoming a tangle of hospital equipment, tubes running in and out of his body and a machine that clicked as it brought air into his lungs. For all the world knew, Grant Harper Gipson had been borne with a serious defect, but the family knew it was the aftermath of drugs. Vicious and demanding drugs sucked the life out of her brother. He had explained to her a million times, "Let go, Sis, drugs are not for you and neither is Race. He'll never amount to anything."

She wiped a smudge of tears from her cheek, hoping the Marshall escorting her was asleep and had no insight to how frail and vulnerable she felt at the moment. Chains between her feet, the orange suit a dead giveaway that she was his prisoner, she had no choice but to follow. Fat chance she could dart away when her feet could only slide a foot forward as she walked behind him.

They walked to the front desk. A lady in a brown uniform was waiting. The Marshall handed her over. His work was done. She was now in the hands of East Coast Women's Prison, made famous by

Martha Stewart, famously called the hand tap for the rich. But they were wrong; Haley Marie Gipson wasn't famous at all. She was a twenty year old air head, her face blotched with sores and her body trembling from withdrawal. She had never sold drugs. Never. But Race had persuaded her drugs would help.

She lived through induction, dealt with the groupies and formed her own alliance. Three bunkies later and too many nights sleeping under the bright lights meant to bring her to submission she finally came to rest on an upper bunk that she fell off when dreaming of Grant one night. In the dream she'd been trying to save him but the struggle had been such, she in tossing and turning fell six feet to the floor.

She cried. No one cared. The one in the bunk below moaned, "For goodness sake, Gipson, tone it down. It's just a fracture to your tailbone. I got yard work tomorrow. I need my sleep."

Haley sucked in the waves of nausea that swept over her. There must be more wrong than what the doctor said. She had the same symptoms as Taylor, when they were ten years old and Taylor slept on the top bunk when Haley spent the night. They'd said Taylor had a concussion. Bouts of nausea and head ache had lasted for months after she fell from the top bunk and landed on the concrete floor. Now here she was, twenty years old her head felt like it was splitting in half and her vision was blurred and all they could tell her was she fractured her tail bone.

She was allowed a call home. "Mom." Hearing her mother across the miles, Haley began to sob. The call was nothing but listening to her mother's voice and then Dad crying as he said, "we love you, honey."

Those in charge made her take classes. For those classes she received certificates. "If you don't get in trouble, this may shorten your stay," the instructors explained. Like they cared; boring and in full charge, they stood there daring you to look cross eyed at them so they could take away your privileges.

Here, a forgotten society existed. Women in brown uniform answering roll call, sitting through classes meant to make them better citizens when they were introduced back into the realm of public domain. She missed her phone and computer. Neither were allowed and only certain television stations.

Haley hated lunch room duty. It was a thankless job, on your feet eight hours a day listening to fellow inmates complain. The food was cold. There were no salads, only fattening choices and what was that meat? They called it zoo food, fit for animals but offered for human consumption.

She found a niche in landscaping. Whether it was the freedom of being outside where clouds appeared bluer and the grass greener, she didn't know but she liked working with old Timms. He probably wasn't more than fifty or sixty, lithe and moved well enough but it was his kindness drew the girls to him. Timms would say, "I got me a girl like you uns. She's twenty, just finishing up her last year at college, going to be a psychiatrist." And they'd all laugh. "We could use one," they'd reply. "Maybe she'll apply for a job here." Then he'd laugh.

"All right, Harper, you did right well sculpting that hedge. I hope the warden likes Mickey Mouse 'cause I believe that's what you were aimin' at, wasn't it?"

The girls would snicker. They were nicer outside the walls. Numbering five or seven to a group, depending on the day and the weather they followed Timms out with their weed eaters and trimmers. "Now don't even think of tryin' to run away," he'd say. "Nothin' pleases the folks here about more than takin' off after a Camp Cup Cake escapee. The ransom's pretty good for people who have to scratch out a livin' in these mountains."

Her *folks* mailed four hundred dollars a month until she had full supplies, then the amount became two hundred dollars she counted on to keep her sane. The uniforms were issued but she had to buy her work boots, twice, because someone stole the first pair knowing if they were caught time would be added to their stay. There were bullies. Life in the prison was intensified by not knowing who you could trust and for that many a mistake was made. Haley Marie Gipson decided to put her nose to the grindstone and get out of there as quickly as she could.

Much to her amazement she took up knitting classes. Everyone knit. Needles clacking, purl one, "oh, no, you mean I got to rip that whole row?" Crocheting was easier with one needle, two needles required skill. Often she glanced around, hunched shoulders, hair curtaining around faces, the women concentrated on the task, there was nothing else to do and they filled the extra hours with skeins of thread. Had they been weavers the tapestry would have told a million tales, instead they knit head bands, gloves and bags of many colors.

Haley blinked. She'd been asleep, reliving her humble beginnings at Camp Cup Cake West Virginia Women's Prison. She was on a bus, dressed in gray sweats, her belongings in a crocheted bag she'd made herself. Her parents had mailed good clothes, shoes and a coat but the warden's goolie informed her they'd sent it back. "You knew you couldn't receive anything." The scolding last until the woman ran out of breath and ended with, "You got to make do with what you have."

Maybe she wouldn't attract too much attention, but then again why wouldn't she? Even the poorest on the bus wore jeans and jackets, while she sat there shivering. She was thankful two years had passed and she'd served enough time to be released. But she couldn't go home. She was on her way to a half-way house. If she got a job, they'd think about her returning to her parent's home. If she didn't, she would sit all day eating candy, soaking up the foul smell of the others detained who neither wanted nor cared if they found employment. She knew because her friend told her what to expect.

The bus pulled into McCoin's car wash. Down the street flashing lights pulled her attention to The Go-Go Girl's Club. Now that was a thought, if regular employment wasn't available. For the first time she smiled. She doubted the half-way house would accept that as a job and Mom and Dad certainly wouldn't. A man wearing a black leather jacket was coming toward her. Inwardly she shrank.

"You Haley Gipson? Haley Marie Gipson?" He repeated as he glanced at a card that probably bore a photo of her. She studied him, cautiously. He was over six feet, appeared to be into weight lifting if the wide shoulders and thick arms meant anything and he wore a silver stud in his left ear. The fact that his head was shaved reminded her of Bruce Willis at a younger age. He was taller and should've been handsome but she wasn't into shaved heads. "Now that you've examined me," He said sarcastically, "Are you Haley Gipson?"

"You're the one with the photo. Aren't you supposed to show me your credentials?"

He pulled a leather holder from the pocket of the black jacket, flashed a Marshall's badge and a photo of himself with dark hair. "I like the hair, otherwise you look like a ninja turtle," She'd seen his name and the gun holster when he flashed the badge. Bodie. Mentally, she filed the name away. W.F. Bodie.

"I see they didn't take the vinegar out of you." He turned toward a mud- caked jeep. "Follow me."

"What? No chains or handcuffs?"

He turned for a minute, stared at her and resumed walking. "You're supposed to be beyond that."

She crawled into the passenger side of the jeep, fastened a plastic screened window and looked for a seat belt. They'd warned her, try to remember what the law requires so you don't get off on a wrong foot. "Where's the seat belt?"

He leaned across her, fumbled around a bit and came up with an equally mud encrusted belt.

"Smells like dog."

"Exactly. I carry two of them around with me but tonight they were tired, been out chasin' down detainees."

"I saw the gun. Did you have to use it?"

"No. But that's none of your business."

She settled into the seat, bracing her feet as he swung out into traffic. The roadside landscape appeared barren. "Where would a person run to in this mess of concrete?"

"Don't even think about it. No one has ever left the camp."

"Until today," She smirked, her words sounding sarcastic.

"They didn't try their stunt while at the camp. They were supposedly job hunting and went the wrong way. When we found their car on the side of the road, abandoned, we knew it was either car trouble or an attempt to go home."

"So, if you have a car, you can drive it around looking for a job but you can't go home?"

"Don't sound so amazed. They'd been here awhile but they don't know the territory. It was pretty stupid deciding to strike out across the marsh to get to the camp. That's why we used the dogs."

"I'm still hung up on being trusted to drive one myself to find a job."

"It's all in the process of being allowed to go home. Get a job. Keep the rules; watch who you associate with and it will happen. You know the rules." He glanced quickly her direction. "Time is the key word and trust turns that key."

"Poetic, aren't you?"

"Still a brat, aren't you? I read the report."

"Hope you liked what you read."

"I didn't. I'm on to you, Gipson. Don't try anything funny."

Yes, sir."

The marsh was alongside the highway, nothing but brown grass growing in the flood plain, no doubt inhabited by wildlife. They wouldn't find her traipsing through that muck and mire. She was afraid of snakes.

It took the guard an hour to check her in, assign a room and examine every item she owned in the bag. "You'll be rooming with two other girls. Keep your nose clean. Don't give us any trouble and you can be out of here in no time. Finding a job will be the first step."

She met the girls. Elise and Yolanda. Elise was petite and wore a shag haircut. Yolanda appeared mixed. She was dusky eyed, tall and beautiful. They eyed her for what seemed forever before they held each other's glance and said together, "She'll do." Yolanda continued to stick her wily hair beneath a silk night cap while Elise was brushing her teeth. "Bathroom's in there. We share." Elise pointed to one end of the room. "You can tell which bed we've chosen and you got full privileged to any of the rest. But if you get too close to the bathroom there's an odor and the one by the window is cold and rain blows in on those days."

"There are guys here," Yolanda added. "But they won't bother you. They're a lazy bunch; don't even go out to hunt for a job, just sit here waiting for the next meal. What you in here for, anyway. I mean, I know you been to prison. So have we but what did you do?"

"You first." Haley was unpacking the bag, wondering whether to use the key to a locker the guard out front had given her or just sit everything on the nightstand next to her bed. She noticed the door beneath the drawer and decided to store more below.

"I beat up my boyfriend." Yolanda said, "You might say I nearly killed him and he pressed charges."

"And got away with it? I'm surprised."

"He's the chief of police son," Yolanda paused as if to ask for understanding, "back in Mississippi."

"You're a long way from home."

"Yeah? But they ain't no distance goin' to be that far when I go home."

"Mine was drug dealing," Elise admitted. "But I'm workin' on stayin' clean."

"Same here." Haley said it easier than she'd thought she could. "They got me for drug trafficking but I didn't."

"Bet it was the boyfriend," Elise sided onto her bed. "My story, too. I took the rap for my boyfriend."

"If I did I didn't intend too." Haley glanced out the window to the darkness of night. "He says I didn't."

"But someone's responsible and you got caught. Nobody believed you, did they?"

"Nope. Not a soul and Race, well he conveniently left the country."

"Race?" Elise tilt her head waiting. "What kind of name is that?"

"Nickname for Rutherford Alexander Cooledge. He's been wearing it since school days."

"Sounds like high ups, to me." Elise pulled the covers up to her chin, settling in to sleep. She yawned. "I'll talk to you in the morning. That walk through the marsh wore me out. Goodnight."

"So you were the ones. The Marshall told me someone walked through the marsh."

"That'd be Bodie. He's all right. Comes on strong first time you meet him, but he mellows if he sees you are really trying." Yolanda snickered. "Elise was scared to death there were snakes in the marsh but it was her idea we cut across. Once you get into that mess it stretches for miles and you lose your way."

"So? Did you see snakes?"

"Yeah. Water moccasins'. But I didn't tell her."

SHE SKIPPED THE SHOWER, ALL she had done was ride the world's transit system with an assortment of non-descript travelers, who she suspected bore stranger and more fascinating stories than her own. After thirty minutes of tossing on the mattress that made sounds that resembled the rustling of dry corn stalks, she thought perhaps she should have taken a long hot shower. Her body refused to rise and her mind wouldn't shut down. Crossing the bridge over the Mississippi brought back memories of the time she ran from the Cartel. She had thought Race dead; the mock funeral had shaken her to the bone. Now the truth of the matter slapped at her through the midnight hours. Usually when dawn arrived she wasn't certain what part had been dream or if what she remembered really happened the way it played out in the dark. Before prison, before the trial, she had run, scared for her life and alone. Pulling the regulation blanket up to her neck, she slipped back into the dream's dialogue.

CHAPTER TWO

*S*HE CROSSED THE BRIDGE INTO *Tennessee leaving Missouri behind. Beneath the giant structure of man-made steel the waters churned in turbulent unrest. My life is like that water.* She gave no signal, turning quickly onto Front Street, with a fast glance in the mirror; the non-descript black car that had followed her across the state line, drove past the exit. She knew that car was carrying members of the drug cartel Race was involved with. They would hunt her down. What was she to do? Her mind became a frenzied mass, stalling, growing numb; she couldn't think for the moment. Making a quick left, she entered the street that led to the convention center, another right turn and she was inside the underground parking lot, searching. Searching parking that might conceal her vehicle and give her time to decide what she must do. There, between two pick-up trucks; pulling forward to the concrete barrier; no, leave room there was a job to be done. A car drove past; she hunkered down, sweat beading on her brow. It was red, no worry.

She had seen the screw driver in the console, wondering why? Now with heart pounding, she removed the license plate from the rear of the car and hurried to the front of the Denali truck to exchange plates. Her whole body was shaking as she stooped between the truck and the barrier praying no one saw her and if there were cameras they were pointed another direction. Hands fumbling she set the screwdriver on the head, dropped the screw driver, retrieved it and gave one last turn. There. Now to put the truck's plate on her car; a cotton boll with the words beneath *grow more cotton*. If she could hide out inside the building where no one knew her, she had a chance.

The license plates exchanged, she entered with a crowd of people. "You have to register, miss." A man wearing a red vest with a logo front and back Farm Show was motioning her towards a booth. She stepped in line behind a burly man with three children in front of him and a scraggly looking woman she supposed to be the children's mother, his wife. Banners hung from the ceiling; Farm Show. Letting out a deep breath of air, she realized just how scared she'd been driving those two hours, her body tense as a fiddle string. "Here, you go, Miss. Fill in the lines." Accepting the clip board she did as told and received a tag with her name Laurie Stokes, *except it wasn't her name.*

"This is a brochure explaining where each exhibit is housed and the row of five stickers are for you to have stamped at each booth, which gives you a chance to win the grand cash prize or lesser and your name can be drawn for the puppy. Now, write your name right there. It's needed, puppy or cash."

"Puppy?"

The lady smiled. "Every year they give away a puppy. It is one of the highlights of the show."

"I could use the cash, but I don't know about a puppy."

The woman smiled and pat her hand. "They are adorable. We have all looked at them. You'll see."

It took only a few minutes before she realized she was dressed wrong for this event. Fleeing the cemetery dressed to the nines in respect for Race's love of flair she had not known she would end up running for her life. Now amidst the long line of machinery and people wearing denim, she stood out like a sore thumb. Off to one side of an exhibit she perused the brochure they'd handed her. Family living on third floor advertised the latest in farm wear. Climbing the stairs, a hand reached out, "Miss, do you have a name tag? It will be with your material, there." The hand reached for the map, raised it, and beneath pointed to the tag. "You have to wear it." With the name tag bearing Laurie Stokes name, she proceeded on and found the denim booth. Twenty minutes later she stepped out of the rest room wearing faded jeans and a gray fleece vest with a cotton boll insignia. She managed to salvage her own black sweater and boots. The suit she had worn to the funeral was neatly folded in the black and white bag that said *grow cotton*. Nothing would do the owner of the booth but she stamp the first ticket on the list of five. "Honey, you may even win the jackpot and if not that you could win that sweet puppy."

Down the aisle she found a booth sporting sunglasses, caps and sun screen, everything *you need for outdoors.* An amused smile touched her lips; these farm people must need everything for *outdoors.* She made the purchase, sunglasses and a short billed cap touting more *grow cotton* and a chunky silver bracelet. Now she was a blend with the women around her that she suspected were farmer wives. She had no idea why they were on the shopping floor, whether to socialize or escape boredom but as she observed the group around her there was a mix of frizzy and high maintenance. Frizzy was in majority.

She wandered the aisle, aware many a man eyed her curiously. She had to think why when there were other women but it did occur most of them were either with friends or men she assumed were their husbands. "Could I interest you in a tractor?" She glanced up to where a blonde Neanderthal wearing an amused grin was eyeing her with interest. Six four she guessed, broad shouldered, looking more like a football player than a tractor salesman. He was waiting for her reply.

"No," she practically stuttered wondering what one said when you knew nothing about tractors.

"No, I don't interest you or no, you don't need a tractor?" He was humoring her.

"I don't know the first thing about tractors."

"So, what are you doing here at the Mid-South Farm and Gin show?"

"Tell me your story, before I tell you mine." She studied him, her chin slightly raised, her eyes holding in a slight sarcastic hold he couldn't see behind the shades. "You don't really know much about tractors, do you?"

"Well, I know this is the latest thing off the line, green and mean. Power everything, right down to the seat control. Want I should show you? Just climb right up that ladder and have a look out over the crowd."

"And what will you do while I'm climbing that ladder?"

"Why, sugar," he said in his best southern drawl. "I'll be right there with you. I'll go first if you wish."

It would be a good way to check out who was in the crowd, though she didn't think in a million years her followers would consider a farm and gin show worthy of her attendance or theirs. "All right," she surprised him. "Let's have a look- see who's in the crowd." Glancing over the suns, she said, "You first."

Top of the steps, he stopped and stood to one side. "I don't think you want me in that cab with you and frankly my height doesn't help matters any." He reached for her hand. "Here you go, my lady, try out that seat."

She slid onto the bright yellow leather, placed her hands on the steering wheel to examine the cab as he'd called it. "Whooie," she let the air out behind the word, slowly. "This thing has everything but a refrigerator." Now he leaned across her pointing. "You're kidding; a tractor has a refrigerator, too?""

"Maybe not all." He saw her stiffen. "Did you find a rough spot on the steering wheel?

She shuddered; they were there, on the floor below, the escalator visible over the half wall of third floor. She saw them climbing the stairs, impatient and not waiting for the escalator to do its job. They glanced her way, stopped climbing, one of them motioning toward where she was sitting. "Kiss me," she said. Startled, the Neanderthal turned to face her, puzzlement written on his face. He opened his mouth to ask if he'd heard her say something when she said, "Please, just lean into me like you like me and kiss me. My old boyfriend is watching. The jerk, he stepped out on me. Please. He said no one would..."

"Oh, I get it." Without a moment's hesitation, he leaned in and placed his mouth over hers. Her arms went around his neck. What was going on? She was talking as he was mouth to mouth close. He listened. *Smile?* And when he turned around he was smiling like a love struck goon, holding her hand and helping her down the ladder.

From the corner of her eye she saw her followers shaking their head. She could hope they were saying, it isn't her, surely that was their opinion as they turned at the top of the escalator and took the other side back down. But Neanderthal had his eye on a cowboy dressed in too much silver, his hat pushed back, his eyes narrowed staring at her. It was then she noticed Neanderthal's eyes were a beautiful shade somewhere between blue and green and she just knew they deepened with emotion.

"Is that him?" Neanderthal asked. "The one with the big silver buckle and the cowboy hat?"

"Yeah," she lied, but Neanderthal took off, covering the distance between where she stood and where the cowboy seemed to be taking it all in. "No, wait," she called after him. "It's all right. He's not worth it."

"Ma'am?" She looked up into the face of an equally tall white haired man. He had to be the father.

"Yes, sir?" She replied meekly, feeling as though he was going to give her a good tongue lashing.

But he was laughing. "Did Jeremy put you up to this?" He held out his hand. "I'm his father. He was supposed to be minding the store for me, instead I return to find him kissing about the purtiest young lady I've seen today," He grinned, "And believe me, there are some pretty southern beauties down here." Looking directly into her eyes, he handed her the sunglasses she hadn't known had fallen to the floor. "Jonathan Southern at your service ma'am. We're here with our dealership to show off this new machine. What do you think of it?" He was reaching for the tickets and stamping the second one.

Blushing, she stuck the sunglasses in the black and white bag. "I think it's pretty impressive."

"Come over here, let me explain the mechanism of this wonder of art." He took her on a tour around the green machine, pointing out different features while she was aware of Jeremy the Neanderthal standing with his arms folded staring at her with animosity in those blue green eyes.

"My goodness, that is impressive." She said. "I don't believe I've ever had anyone explain the workings of a machine to me before." She extended her right hand. "Thank you, Mr. Southern." He was beaming down on her. She had to smooth her way past him because his son was approaching with a distinct irritableness in his demeanor. "I think I'll walk on, Mr. Southern."

She had only walked a short distance when the Neanderthal stepped by her side, taking her right elbow firmly in his hand, he glared down at her. "What was that all about? The cowboy said he'd never seen you before in his life and he was just admiring you from a distance."

"Well," she trembled at the firmness with which he was gripping her arm. "It was worth a try. I needed to distract two men on the escalator. I hadn't meant to lie to you but I kind of got my tail in a crack there." She felt the pressure slacken, then he stopped in the middle of the aisle, glaring down at her in that take control way she had already recognized. "Do you always manhandle women you meet?"

"No, but they usually don't beg me to kiss them and then lie to me, either." He turned her around to face him. "So what's going on?"

"You don't work for the FBI, do you?" The way he was commandeering her, the black bag seemed alive. It moved with her movement and with his controlling her walk down the aisle, the bag was busy.

"No." Indignant, he wanted to shake her. "I'm in the process of deciding exactly what I'm going to do with myself. And you."

"Well, you do have daddy, already established. I'd say your future is secure."

"That's a bit sarcastic, isn't it? For someone who needed diversion and my assistance you do seem unappreciative." He was pulling her down the aisle, towards the escalator, his eyes hooded and threatening her not to make a scene.

"Where are you taking me, I mean dragging me, too?" She was becoming annoyed with his firm hold on her arm. "I'm a big girl and I don't need you anymore. Besides, I haven't had all these tickets stamped for the grand prize drawing."

"Ha." He snorted more than laughed. "Using that for an excuse to walk away after I threaten a cowboy?"

"I could use the money."

"All righty, we'll see about that." He veered toward a booth selling anhydrous ammonia tanks, with two grinning salesmen on their left. "Hey, guys. Andrew, Seth. My friend here needs the stamp. I think she's going for the puppy." The one called Andrew reached for the tickets, stamped a logo on it and gave the Neanderthal a knowing glance while Seth raised an eyebrow, nodding approval. "See you fellows."

She had the urge to run, but he would not loosen hold on her arm. Second floor held the Family Living booths and a display of signs that read; **Give Us Your Words** and we will turn them into your advertisement. "Hey, Bill, this little doll wants you to sign her ticket. She's in the run for the money."

"That was smooth," she muttered under her breath as he turned her toward the escalator that look in his eye saying, keep your opinion to yourself until we see this thing through, which she did. The last ticket was stamped by a toy dealer with every imaginable piece of miniature equipment; tractors, disks, and machinery she was at a loss to identify. Finally, unable to restrain herself, she said, "Are we through?"

"No, we've just begun. There's a lounge for those with displays. We are going in there and you are telling me your story. It's plain to see; you have more than your tail in a crack. You are in trouble."

They pushed through heavy black curtains into a large room with comfortable chairs and a few upholstered u-shaped sectionals drawn to one side as if set up for quick conference among the retailers. However, he was leading her toward a table on the far side with seating for two, where a low blend of piped in music could be heard. "Have a seat," he said, sliding one chair out and waiting as she slid into it. Taking the chair opposite, he leaned across, his elbows on the table. "Let's hear it."

"The truth will sound so far-fetched you won't believe it." She set the bag on the floor by her feet, and the prize tickets on the table between them, which she quickly had forgotten.

"Try me."

"My boyfriend," she sighed, "at least he was my boyfriend." For a moment she was lost, how could she explain something she was involved in when she wasn't sure herself how it happened. She glanced uneasily to where he waited, his eyes on her, unwavering. "Race, his nickname, became involved in drugs, I've only recently found out he was selling, too. Well, we have a new prosecutor in our county who is determined to attack the drug problem head on. He is only part time, currently and most folks think he is looking for full time employment and the drug issue is a way to prove himself."

Jeremy the N was listening.

"Race's father is a Judge in our court system." She sighed. "I think he's honest but this is his son." He nodded. "First the county picked up Race. I wasn't with him that night. Then he was released. But two nights later when we were having dinner, a group of his friends drop by our table, they ask if he will go outside for a minute to discuss a project they apparently need …" She sighed. "I don't know what he had to do with the project or if there was a project. Long story short, Race did not return. I pay the bill and leave; on my way home a friend calls and says they have Race charged with selling and he is back in jail. It all went from bad to worse." She dropped her head to stare at her own hands folded in her lap.

"What are you doing in Tennessee?"

"I was at a funeral, actually standing at the gravesite when I saw these two men, dressed in black suits, wearing sunglasses." She shuddered, remembering. "They were watching me and I don't think they were friends or family of Race because I have never met or seen them before."

"Who do you think they are?"

"Either Feds or part of the drug cartel." Her eyes filled with tears. "I shouldn't be telling you this."

"Why would they be after you?"

"Race warned me, they have questioned him if I was part of *the package,* as they called it, you know, part of his team selling."

"Drugs?" She nodded. "Were you?" She shook her head. "Whose funeral were you attending?"

"Race's." The tears ran down her cheeks. "Anyway, I'm told it was Race. I don't know. It was closed casket. I only saw him one time after they picked him up the second time and that's when he told me to be careful and watch my step, and a few other things." He handed her his handkerchief. "His parents were terribly upset. His mother kept saying she couldn't believe he was gone and his father was stoic."

"Did he speak to you?"

"That's all. He spoke and asked me not to reveal anything I knew about Race until he got to the bottom of it. He's a Judge. Rather stern and foreboding but I always wondered if I felt that way because I knew his official capacity and some of my friends went before him in court and it wasn't good."

"What's your gut feeling as to who's following you?"

"I'm afraid it's the drug cartel's people. I think it would take the Feds more time to move, don't you?"

"I don't know how the system works in Missouri." His expression was stern as he asked, "Have you been in trouble, before?"

"A few times." She sighed. "I admit, I have a bit of a rebellious nature. But not on anything illegal."

"Where are you staying?"

Alarm ran through her body. She hadn't considered that. "If I don't win the money, my car," she replied, blanching at the thought of a night on the street in Memphis, Tennessee. She had watched to many cop shows that showed the seedier side of town, but then her small city had the same problems.

"You drove all this way, with no funds? Did you stop for gas, or anything?"

"I did, but I was careful. They were always visible in my mirror and I took advantage of the big trucks. As to money, I have a debit card, but its limited and I think I have fifty or so dollars in cash in my purse."

"What's in the sack?"

"The reason I don't have much money." She sighed. "I didn't fit in here and I bought these denims, my suit made me stick out like a sore thumb. Remember, I was at a funeral. In a cemetery."

"So you have a few pieces of clothing in that sack, maybe fifty dollars and no idea where to stay?"

"Yes." She drew herself up, suddenly wary of his questions and where this conversation was headed. "I hope you are gentleman enough to keep what I've told you in confidence. It could mean my life. Don't worry about me, I'm a survivor. I can take care of myself."

He whistled, rising with her. "I bet you can. From what I've seen you are doing a good job of it."

"Now who's sarcastic?" She glared across the table at him. "I'll be going. Thank you, I guess."

The loud speaker blared in the outer halls, "Ticket number." They heard the announcement. He cast an amusing glance her way as she studied the stubs in her hand. "When did they announce the other drawings?" She asked. "He said this was drawing number five, isn't that for the grand prize."

"While we were talking," he replied. "Your tickets were lying there, on the table between us and I noticed, but none of the numbers were yours." As if to soften his words, he said, "But let's step out into the hall and see who won."

She heard the numbers over the loud speaker and listened as they were repeated. Jeremy, the Neanderthal was biting his lip, his shoulders hunched forward, as he was reading the numbers on her ticket. "You won." He whispered.

"I did?" She blanched. "I can't make myself public. What if they're still here, they'll see me."

Relieving her of the ticket, Jeremy waved his arm above his head, and started towards the speaker. "Wait here," he said. "I'll tell them you are unable to come to front, but they have to know your name."

Struggling a moment, she tried to remember, and then trembling said, "Laurie Stokes." Searching for the name tag, beneath the gray fleeced vest, she said, "It's on the ticket, isn't it?" He examined the ticket and nodded.

Her heart was pounding in her ears. Did she really win the jackpot, or was there some mistake. She glanced around. If the guys in black suits were in the building, they might be drawn to this floor, thinking she was in the crowd. She didn't see them and breathed a sigh of relief. How could she cash in the money? No doubt it was in paper form, not cash, a check with Laurie Stokes name on it and she had no proof. *They would ask for* proof. Another mess, she'd gotten herself into by lying, but part of it was his fault pushing her along to where his acquaintance manned the stamp booths. What should she do, run?

Then he was there, standing in front of her, holding a whimpering little puppy all chocolatey brown with eyes that stared solemnly at her as it trembled. "Ah, hmmm," he said, "I believe this is your prize, the best prize, notice the word best, not the grand prize."

Disappointment sank to the pit of her stomach. "A puppy? I can't have a puppy. I'm running for my life."

He pressed the animal into her arms, a look of disgust on his face, as he extended his arms out. Yellow stains of animal pee ran down the left arm of his shirt sleeve and on his torso, matching stains. "Now, your little pee-ball is smelly and if I'm not mistaken so am I."

"He is not my pee-ball." She thrust the puppy back into his arms. "You should never have accepted him. There's no way I can take this puppy with me."

"Are you Miss Stokes?" A lady with a camera aimed her direction was asking the question.

"No. I'm not."

The lady appeared confused. "I'm supposed to take a picture of the person who won the puppy."

"Then, take his picture. It's his puppy."

Neanderthal laid his arm around her shoulders drawing her close to his body. "Darling, you can have the dog. It's all right. I'll just have to learn to live with it. Now let's kiss and make up. O.K. Sweetheart?" While performing all his loving attention on her he was winking at the photographer. "We had a little falling out over the puppy. She's always wanted one but I said all they do is pee on you."

The photographer loved it. "I'll just snap a picture of the two of you. It will be in several of the leading farm magazines." She was snapping away. "Aren't you Jonathan Southern's son? I think I was at your father's display yesterday." She oozed with words as her eyes caressed the Neanderthal.

"I bet you were, "he agreed, smiling as he hugged Laurie Stokes tightly to his body. "But try to erase those pee stains off my shirt, will you, hon?"

I think she would do your laundry and kiss your butt while she was doing it, Laurie Stokes, the alias, was thinking as she dug her fingernails into Jeremy Neanderthal's lower arm. She felt him jerk as he nearly choked the life out of her. She dug her nails deeper.

"This girl just can't get enough of me." He was grinning, but Laurie the alias knew he was feeling pain.

"Thank you, so much," the photographer gushed. "Oh, my word, I hope I find someone and we can be as happy as the two of you. I just can't wait for my boss to see these pictures. Bye now and thank you."

"You are welcome and we wish you a good life. Be careful now driving home."

CHAPTER THREE

S HE AWAKENED FROM THE DREAM. It was so real. She
could only imagine the Neanderthal wondering if she had slipped
off the side of the earth, and she.........well, she wondered about
him, too. Had he married that little southern belle his father mentioned? She could not linger on what would never be, Jeremy was
engaged, his parents loved the girl, she was an intruder in their lives
although they had welcomed her that week end before the Feds
found her and demanded, no not demanded, physically in handcuffs
returned her to Missouri, and from there she had done due penance
and arrived here at the camp.

"Gipson, you better rise and shine." It was the rich voice of the
one named Yolanda, she had met last night. Now hands were on the
blanket, lightly shaking Haley's shoulders. "Crawl out, Gipson. It's
just another day at the camp Many-Me-Ha, affectionately called by
those who leave the pristine social impairing camp for the federally
incarcerated Marsh hill complex."

"I thought it was the opposite of impairing," the second voice
chimed in. "Aren't we here to build us up and slowly but surely slip
us back in to society's blighted stream? We will be the light in the
dessert, the hope of the world."

"Shut up," Haley pulled the blanket up around her ears. "I
heard all this at Camp Martha."

"Girl, you picked a good one. Did Martha Stewart really get
good mattresses for the bunkies?"

She shrugged the covers away. Peering through morning eyes at
her roomies; she saw they were already dressed and wearing make-up,

of which she had none. "So what's the big rush? What do you do here that got you out of bed?"

They turned to stare at her. "Did you sleep late at Camp Martha?"

"No, I did not. By this time of morning I was out wielding a weed eater across the rolling landscape." She yawned. "I thought it would be different here."

"Only if you want a few more days added." Yolanda came to sit beside her on the bed. "Here's the deal. You want out of here, go home to that nice boyfriend, or yo' Momma, you get up show these people here at Camp MMH you want to do better, go to town find a job, act like you are their poster girl for reintegration!"

"Wow," Elise paused from combing through her hair to stare at Yolanda. "Where do you get those words? And do you know their meaning?"

Yolanda laughed. "I do the cross words on a daily basis. It means restoration." Now she arose, taking Haley's hand and pointing toward the bathroom. "Go, do yo' thing, get dressed and report to Bodie." She snickered. "He ain't so bad, that white boy with the shaved head but he likes to look tough." She strut around the room, "Wearing his black leather jacket, flashing that badge and running those dogs."

Thus began Haley's reintroduction to society by way of Marsh hill and Federal Marshall W.F. Bodie.

"What's the W.F. stand for?" She was sitting in his office which contained a desk, a file cabinet and two chairs, his and hers. He was studying her file. Today his shirt was startling white against the black vest and she noticed his teeth were that white, too. "I've not got toothpaste," she said, as though he cared. "No clothes to speak of and no make-up. Can I call my Mother?"

Drawing himself up from studying the file, he took a deep breath. They were all this way. Just once he would like one that was different. Silently he studied her. She didn't look bad for one who had traveled cross country on a bus, had maybe five hours of sleep and awakened to a world of need at his camp. She seemed drawn to study his shirt and his teeth. That was new. The file implied she had been caught with drugs she said she was unaware of in her vehicle.

The boyfriend was the one they were after but then there was incriminating evidence to a new prosecutor for the county determined to cut out drug traffic and he didn't care who the perpetrator's family happened to be; she was part of the problem. But it had risen up to bite him where it hurt when the main lead was the Judge's son.

"I said, can I call my mother?"

"You may call your mother after a few stipulations are discussed." He glanced back at the file. "Now, here's the way it works at Marsh hill. These are our expectations and you already know what's required of you. You didn't spend two years at Camp Cup Cake for nothing did you, Gipson?"

"No, sir, I didn't." She studied the papers he handed her. "I can do all this."

"You will get a job. You will call before and after you visit each stop you make. You will report back to camp at the designated hour. There will be no use of drugs." His voice droned on as he wondered if she were listening. The drill was the same, only the recipient made the difference.

"Yes sir. She wore a serious expression. She felt the need to make him believe her. "Now, when can I call my mother? And can I really leave here and have my own vehicle?"

THE CALL CAME THROUGH AT nine in the morning. "Mom, I'm back. Got in about midnight and they wouldn't let me call you. Can you come over today?"

"Where are you?" Dorothy clutched the phone. "Marshhill? Never heard of it. You mean there's a half-way house within two hours' drive of us and we've never heard of it?"

"You don't travel these paths, Mom." Haley rolled her eyes. "I know, neither should I but I'm here. Can you come?" She sighed. "I need things. Shall I give you my list?"

ANXIETY CHURNING HER STOMACH, DOROTHY called Harper. "The call came just after you and Andrew left. Haley's at a place called Marsh hill." She listened as Harper repeated the word. "You haven't heard of it, either?" They talked a few minutes. "I can make it," she assured him. "I know you need to stay on the job. It's o.k., honey. I'll find out when you can see Haley."

She wasn't as confident as she sounded. She wished Haley's dad could accompany her. There'd been bad words between them. But Haley was lost to the world at the time and it was the drugs talking. "I hate you, both of you," she'd screamed at them as the officers of the court drug her from the courtroom. They had heard her cries for help down the hall way. "Daddy, you promised. Mom. Mom. I can't go. Don't let them take me, Daddy." Dorothy had wept openly, not caring who observed. That was her baby.

Gathering the items she thought would be allowed, she filled the cosmetic case, closed the lid and opened a suitcase. Surely Haley would fit in her jeans and t-shirts. "All I've done is work with a lawn crew," Haley had written. "I can weed eat with the best of them. Why, Mom, I could weed eat your and Dad's whole neighborhood, but I can tell you one thing, I'm muscling up like a boy. If my shoulders get any wider I'll have to step up to the next size in my shirts."

Then there was the letter saying she'd had to do lunchroom duty. "I'm on my feet all day, ten hours. You think they care? No, they'd like to see me fall on my face." Dorothy wondered who they were. In a brief moment she wondered if Haley had learned to cook, learned anything? Then came the day they allowed her to start making phone calls if she had money in her account.

Sinking onto the bed, Dorothy supposed her daughter had learned something, losing phone privileges the first month because she refused to clean the toilets like they'd told her, Haley was reduced to writing letters. "Now, I can call once a week, Mom, if you keep money on my account."

In the beginning, Dorothy had been embarrassed, having to take cash to the nearest vendor who serviced the prisons, wiring money to the Federal Bureau of Prisons who then put the money on the prisoner's account, no matter where the prison was located. Lines of people collected behind her as she filled in the blanks, Dorothy felt paranoid they were reading the information over her shoulder but they weren't. No one cared. Maybe the lady behind the counter sympathized; she was always kind. The man on the other hand was brisk and rude; evidently all his children had grown through the years with flying colors. "Fill this out," he'd bark. "No, that's not right." She would be wringing wet with sweat by the time she left the building and had actually called the store to find what days the woman would be behind the counter.

Dressed in a pair of taupe slacks with matching sweater, Dorothy tied a mingled scarf of rust, gold and turquoise around her neck; selected a brown jacket and studied herself in the mirror. She didn't want to appear overly dressed, nor be wearing too much jewelry; as the saying went Dorothy wanted to blend in, brown purse, brown shoes that should do. She changed the items in the bag she'd been carrying to a nameless piece of brown someone had given her one Christmas and was ready to leave.

She couldn't install the address of Marsh hill, evidently it was a new camp and not yet on GPS. Her heart beat with anticipation. She hadn't seen her daughter in over a year. The one trip she and Harper made had upset them all to the point Haley had resignedly asked them to forego another trip, it had taken her days to overcome the realization she could not visit her parents without supervision, and that visit was limited to fenced off grounds and the one room visitors hall with all the other in mates and their families. There was no privacy and still Haley had wrapped her arms around her parents in a hug that said it all. Leaving had torn the heart out of her and Harper. She would never forget the tears that ran down his cheeks as he trod down that hill path back to the car stationed a safe distance away. They had lost their son and now their daughter was incarcerated. A better word, she thought, was locked away.

The drive by-passed the town, edged by the college and side tracked onto a second main highway. Swampland lay alongside the pavement, a scatter of side roads and few houses until she reached a small settlement and then the camp. Cameras were on each corner of the building. There were limited parking spaces and only two cars on the grounds. It was obvious loiters were not permitted. They just as well have a sign up that read do *your business and leave.*

She entered the building and was met by a stern looking lady in brown attire, a name tag on the upper left pocket, who asked her to state her business. A sign above the desk read NO VISITORS BEYOND THIS POINT. The woman motioned to a row of four seats. "I'll bring your daughter," she said.

Haley burst through the door, grabbing her mother before Dorothy was fully standing and knocked them both back into the chair. Haley recovered and pulled her mother up. "Mom." She lay her head on her mother's shoulder, her arms wrapped around Dorothy's waist. "Oh, Mom."

When they had both settled, Haley motioned towards the door. "We can leave, Mom. But today I'm on trial, we can go to a restaurant and shopping at one place, but that's it."

Wiping tears from her eyes, Dorothy replied. "Sounds good. Now, where do you want to go?"

"I need things, Mom." Haley's voice was wistful, reminding Dorothy of when she was a little girl, that long time back where a little girl held her hand and glanced her way with trust in her eyes and her heart. "I have a list. I have to have a phone to call in and it can't have internet or any of the bells and whistles."

"Tell me where to go first."

"Goodwill." Haley saw the surprise in her mother's eyes. "They taught us, we are in transition and we shouldn't rush out and buy the best even if some of us could afford it. We are to choose wisely, think frugally and remember this is our first stage."

"But Goodwill, Haley?" Dorothy's troubled gaze rest on her daughter. "I don't understand."

"Mom. I don't know these people. Some may have very nice things... clothes, but some may not have a penny to their name and some steal. So they told us, don't put a lot of money in what we need while we are here."

Putting the car into reverse, Dorothy backed out the drive and onto the road. "This is new to me, Haley."

"Me, too, Mom." Haley settled back into the seat. "Oh, Mom, this is heavenly. I love you, Mom."

CHAPTER FOUR

ANDREW CAME TO DINNER WITH Harper and Dorothy that evening. "You two are unusually quiet. What's wrong?"

"Nothing's wrong." Harper glanced at his wife. "You just as well tell us how the meeting with our daughter went."

"Or, if you had rather not discuss family business in front of me, I'll apologize for asking."

Dorothy lay a hand on top of his. "Andrew, it is no secret. Haley has been transferred back to the camp about fifty miles from here and today was the first time I've seen her in almost two years."

He whistled. "So she is out of prison, so to speak and there for reentry, rehab, of sorts. Right? To bring her back into society."

"Exactly."

"So, how did it go?" Harper asked.

"Confusing. You know how Haley loves to shop?" Harper nodded and Dorothy continued. "Well, she said for us to go to Good Will, which we did and she actually found some nice things there." When Harper frowned, she added, "Freshly laundered and laid out as if in a boutique."

"Couldn't you take her own things to her?"

"I did take a few things and her cosmetics and such." Dorothy grinned. "And she hugged me, a big old bear hug that knocked me off my feet and back down into the chair where I had been sitting."

"What's next?"

"She has to get a job and when she does it is possible they will give her a pass to come home, maybe on a weekend but we can't have anything other than a regular phone, no television or I-phones available when she comes here and they will send out an official to inspect to be sure we aren't hiding anything."

"What about my work phone? I can't run a business without a phone."

"Then you will have to check in at the office." Dorothy's hand clenched Harper's wrist. "Do you want Haley to come home, or not?"

"What is this business with the phones?" He glanced at Andrew. "Do you know?"

"I'm sitting here listening, glad the judge turned me over to you. I would suspect it is for them to have the best recourse to check on your daughter and no means of warning her when they plan to do it."

"We haven't been through this before." Harper's voice was gruff. "We have no idea whether she's changed or if we have the same disrespect to look forward to." Sadly he let his head fall, chin to chest.

"I'll get the rest of my things out of your guest room, this week end." Andrew's grin spread across his face. "That's a good thing, isn't it? Now the Judge says I can live unsupervised. The apartment is supposed to be empty this week. You turn me loose and get a new person to work with, your daughter."

"I hope you won't be a stranger, just because you'll have your own apartment."

Andrew's laughter was joyous. "I have you two to thank for so much that has happened in my life. Who knew you could turn me around?" Dorothy was holding up her hand. "No, Dorothy, I've got to say this. I was rebellious and in deep trouble. If Harper had not intervened with his friend the Judge, I would have gone to prison. Not to say, I didn't continue to give Anne a lot of trouble over our son, but thanks to the influence you and Harper showered on me, I finally did a turn around and now, wonder of all wonders Anne and I are engaged. She lets me share our son, and even Harriet, who I thought was a mean spirited, not to mention rich old lady, has come around and given me her blessing. So I've said all that to say this, give your daughter every chance, she will come around if she hasn't already. With you two, she can't miss."

As Andrew stood to kiss Dorothy on the cheek and then shake Harper's hand, she couldn't help but remember the night Andrew's skin had come alive with the insulation debris he had worked in that day.

"What's funny?" Harper rose up from is chair at the table. "I can tell our boy, here is leaving, but you must have something else on your mind.

"Only the night the insulation caused him such pain, after he worked sleeveless and it got under his skin. Then there was the night he left with the truck and you knew all the time."

"I am learning the trade, Dorothy. No more shirtless forays into the job, when I'm hot. But I will tell you this; I'm torn. Harper wants me to consider the construction business and the counseling and helping people in need of a lawyer that the Judge made me do, have me floundering as to which direction I'm going to take for the rest of my life."

"Can you not do both?" Harper asked. "I really need you to stay in the business with me."

"I have to retake the bar exam. In fact, I have a bit of studying to do this evening after I see Anne and Andy. We are taking it slow, this time. After all I put Anne through; I want her to trust me." He sighed. "Now, I see what could have happened to her and our son if Harriet had not taken her in."

"How is Mrs. Becker?"

"Well, you've heard, no doubt, the girl who moved two doors down from Harriet turned out to be her daughter. Harriet had given her up for adoption at birth and then spent years trying to find her."

"How unreal is that?" Harper sighed. "I suppose there's hope for us. You know the girl's husband came to us for a job, if I have the story correct, the girl, Marigold had lost her parents and moved here. She did find out when her parents died that she was adopted and the birth mother was from here."

"But," Andrew took up the story for Dorothy's benefit, "the other part of the story that's amazing is when she and Matt Langley fell in love they married secretly and lived apart because his parents disliked her. Her thinking was; if they knew her, in time they would accept her. They lived apart, until she was pregnant and when Matt found out he put his foot down. He said his parents might never change."

"All our lives have twists and turns," Dorothy replied. "But the truth is, God knows every turn we make and he knows the hardships we will encounter and how we will work through them."

"I'm beginning to think you know the story." Andrew said. "You have led me to believe in him."

"It is the Savior I know, Andrew. And I'm a firm believer; those who believe should be baptized. It is not the act that saves them. Believing and asking God's forgiveness is what saves us, but we are baptized to show we agree with His teachings. We commit our life to Him, in accordance with his teachings."

Andrew grinned. "I've come a long way, too, Miss Dorothy."

"But you haven't made the complete commitment."

BODIE EYED THE TRANSFORMATION. THE Gipson woman was a knock out. He sat there studying her and contemplating whether she was capable of following the rules if the camp allowed her to start looking for a job. The requirements to move off camp grounds began with a job, the home or place where she would locate to being examined and his opinion of her meeting the stipulations; no contact with the people from her life previous to prison and certainly not the boyfriend, mainly those who had felonies.

"So?" She eyed him, face on. "Do I pass?"

"You pass."

"What do you have in mind? I read the papers." She sighed. "There are a lot of rules and regulations. Do you really expect me to keep all of them?"

"Only if you want to stay around; the same bus that brought you in can take you back. It's up to you."

Haley stood up. "I want to stay. But how am I going to get a job if I don't have transportation?"

"You will have to take that up with your parents."

"Then, if they agree, I can bring my car on grounds and you won't confiscate it?"

"I thought we covered this before."

"But you didn't tell me how soon I can have it."

"Go with the girls in to town today and see if there are any job openings. Then, we'll decide."

"I get it. It's a set-up, to see if I'm going to run or whether I apply myself. Right?"

"Something like that, all part of the protocol."

"Well, it stinks." She headed toward the door.

"That may be true, but it is what it is, isn't it?" He stared at her. "It's a step toward your freedom.

"YOU GOT MONEY, GIPSON?" YOLANDA'S mouth was set in a definitely demanding way. "Cause if you have, yo' going to have to buy our gasoline, today. There's just enough in the tank to get us to the station."

Elise giggled. "You pull this on every newby."

"I don't see you with a hand out. Now, do you two want to go to town or not?" Hands on her hips Yolanda stared at them. "Quicker we find jobs the sooner we leave Camp Many-Me-Ha. I got no money but I got the wheels."

"I have money." Haley was climbing into the back seat of a car from the eighties with torn seats, springs obviously gone and a familiar odor. "What's that smell?"

"Bodie borrowed my car when he had a flat. It's against regulations, I bet, but he's the Marshall."

"It smells like dog."

"Here, spray this and you can make it for a while and then you spray again." Yolanda handed her an old bottle with a blue mix in it. "It's thick. Sometimes you just take the lid off and smear it on the seats."

Elise smirked. "You think that clothes softner works, white girl?" Shaking her head, she watched as Haley tried to spray the liquid to no avail. "Here, try my perfume."

It was interesting, riding along in Yolanda's old clunker of a car, listening to the two in front talk. It was obvious they had developed a friendship through sharing lives, why they had to go to prison and what their plans were for the future. The perfume had helped but she had a feeling she was about to up-chuck the breakfast the camp served. It wasn't that she didn't appreciate it, but the food had been greasy and now Elise's perfume was circling her head and her stomach was rumbling.

She thought about her mother's arrival at the camp. "It scares me," she had whispered to Haley.

"It's all right, Mom." Haley found their roles reversed as she comforted her mother. "Everything will fall in place. I don't know how long they expect me to stay here." She sighed, staring at the piece of tissue in her hands. She had twisted and torn it until it was ready to fall apart. "Did I tell you I'm glad to see you?"

Dorothy gave a laugh that came out more a sob. "You did and I'm happy you're back."

"Well, back here doesn't mean as much as it will when they let me come home." She searched her mother's expression of sadness, feeling remorse she had caused her parents pain. "What can you do about the phones and the television and the computers, Mom? They said I can't be released to you, if you have all that."

"Remove them, I guess."

"But Dad needs them for his business."

"We'll work on it, Haley." Her mother's hand had gripped her own. "Don't worry, we'll see to it."

"Bodie will send someone out to check over your house, Mom. That's what they do."

She had come this far to be so far from home. Haley watched the marsh slide by from the window of Yolanda's car. Bodie said she could have a car for transportation. She told her mom not to bring her own. "They'd think I was a rich kid, Mom. Ask Dad to find me something else. You understand?"

"Yo?" Yolanda's eyes in the mirror held with Haley's. "You day dreaming back there?"

"No, I'm just enjoying the fine scenery along the way and soaking up the fragrance of your car."

"HOW'D IT GO?" HARPER LAID his cell on the counter, going to where Dorothy was stirring something in a pan on the stove. He placed a kiss on her cheek and turned her around. "Let me see your eyes when you tell me." His mouth settled into a grim line. "That bad, huh?"

"They have you wait in this outer room while they collect her. They talked to her but I couldn't hear." Dorothy sighed. "Let's set the table while we talk, before Andrew arrives."

"He won't be here, tonight. Something the Judge expects him to do." Harper washed up at the sink. "So it was troubling?"

"I didn't know what to expect. The Marshall examined the car, from under the hood, the floor mats, and probably the exhaust pipe. John said they always look for drugs. How would he know?"

"Hon, it's happening in families everywhere, every day, now. That's why I sent John with the car for Haley and Brandon to pick him up. It was on the way to pick up supplies. It worked out."

"It's embarrassing, Harper. Now our men know where Haley's been and that she's in a half-way house."

Harper pulled her into his arms, nuzzling her neck as he said, "Hon, you are going to have to quit worrying about what people know. They've got their own skeletons in the closet. And we've got our chore set before us." Turning Dorothy loose, he turned toward the table. "What do you think? Is she going to be a hand full or has she learned anything?"

Tears rimmed Dorothy's eyes. "I'm hoping the clothes from Goodwill and not wanting her own car mean something. You're sure the car John drove over will be all right?"

Harper's expression couldn't bely his own concern. "So what did our girl think of the car?"

BODIE FINISHED THE PAPERWORK, GLANCED up at Gipson and asked, "What do you want, now?"

"Keys to my car and permission to go into town and look for a job."

"You understand, Gipson? You call each time you leave location and limit yourself to three businesses."

"Yes, sir, Sir." Haley saluted, clicking her feet together. "I got that down pat, through Yolanda and Elise."

Bodie shook his head. "Someone needs to take the salt out of you, Gipson. You didn't learn enough at Camp Cup Cake and it does not bode well."

"I learned it all right." Haley met him head on. "You are too stiff, Bodie. Someone needs to take the starch out of you." She leaned across the counter, staring down to where he sat at his desk. "What's your story, anyway? Couldn't they use you in Washington?"

Anger reddened his face. His eyes mere slits, he stared at this insolent female hanging over the counter. "You're out of line, Gipson. Stand back. If you want my permission to do anything, go to the bathroom, wipe your tail, run to town on pretense of looking for a job, then show restraint of your smart mouth and respect those in charge of your future." He stared hard at her. "You got that? I'm one of them."

Yolanda and Elise stepped around the corner. "Can we ride with you, white girl? Bodie done give us permission." She stopped talking and stood still. "What? What? You and Bodie locking horns, again?"

Showing bravado she wasn't feeling at the moment, Haley replied, "He thinks I have a smart mouth."

"Here's your keys." Bodie rose up from behind the counter, eyeing the three. "Don't make me come after you. I just might enjoy it too much and if I do, that adds time on to your stay here."

"Lookee, here." Yolanda opened the door and slid into the front seat, Elise in the back. "Ain't this just the cat's meow? Your folks done good. What you call this, besides a Chevrolet? Vintage?"

"My aunt had one of these." Elise patted the seats. "Your Daddy even had the inside cleaned, white girl."

CHAPTER FIVE

THE SECOND WEEK PASSED AND Haley was into the third. It was three in the afternoon and she was discouraged. Sunday, locked up in Camp Marshhill was no fun. As Bodie allowed she had made the rounds looking for a job. "I need to go home," she lamented, to no avail. "Why would you want me to find a job near the camp if I'm going home in a few weeks?" Bodie had only stared at her.

"What's up? Why you layin on that bed like a sick and dyin female?" Yolanda stood looking down on her. "Get up."

Haley stuffed the pillow over her head. "Go away. It's Sunday. We can't go anywhere and I'm sick of looking for a job. You know the local people have taken them, already."

"Listen, white girl you got more hope in you than that. Now get out of the bed. That's a sign of depression and you don't want Bodie seeing that."

"I don't care what Bodie sees. Who does he think he is?" Haley jerked to a sitting position, anger hot in her veins. "I thought I was allowed to spend weekends with my parents."

"It's kind of a catch twenty two," Yolanda replied, sitting gingerly on the edge of Haley's bed. "You get a job; you can pretty much do a regular life. Your problem is you need to get along with Bodie."

"How do I do that?"

"Watch your mouth. Go along with him." She caught Haley's expression. "No, no, no. Nothing sinful, just try to be respectful. What you got against him, anyway?"

"He's a man." Haley flounced out of bed and began to walk the floor. "He irritates me. I irritate him."

"Honey," Yolanda's voice mellowed. "It ain't Bodie. You're mad at that rich boy, you don't know if he dead or alive and you're taking it out on Bodie." Yolanda slipped back in to the roots of growing up in the South, her voice a rich timbre of the blood that ran through her veins. "Me? I got the same feelings." She sighed. "The Chief of Police, his son loves me, but his daddy know I got mixed blood, he ain't havin' me in his family. It causes a lot of trouble in the family."

"That could happen anywhere." Haley's mind caught up with Yolanda's slow speaking words. "I thought my life was settled. I went to college two years. Race had finished. He accepted a good job, traveling, yes, but home most weekends. Then I begin to notice he had money. I asked where'd it come from and he said his job. But that kind of money was not from a regular job. Then my dad warned me. I can hear him now, 'that boy is going to get in trouble, Haley, and take you down with him.'"

"I got college." Yolanda nodded, understanding. "You think I'm uneducated, white girl?"

"Stop it." Haley stomped her foot. "You demean yourself with that nonsense, calling me white. You're white. If you are educated," she stared hard at Yolanda, "then stop putting yourself down. I'm not impressed."

Yolanda gave a deep throaty laugh. "That's more like it. You stay out of bed and I'll clean up my speech, but right now, here in the camp with two of the guys from down south, it pays me to keep this profile. Now, Bodie knows I been looking for a job and my time here's almost over, then I'm let go."

Haley flopped down onto the bed, again. Running her hands through her hair. "What am I going to do to get out of here?"

"Starting tomorrow morning, you go before Bodie in a nice girl way and speak with respect. He's the boss, here, girl. You got to transform that rebellious spirit and learn you are not the only individual with a problem in this camp and don't take it out on the people around you."

"What have I done to you?" Haley stared at Yolanda. "I don't recall being mean spirited with you."

"Not me, honey," Yolanda pat her hand. "You just got to get that chip off your shoulder in order to reenter society." She laughed again. "Between you and Bodie, we all get a bit tense."

HALEY DECIDED TO TRY YOLANDA'S advice. Elise had gone home and she knew Yolanda was next, job or no job with her pleasing attitude Yolanda would be back in the South leaving Haley to sit in a room with a bunch of males that neither looked for a job nor cared where there was one. They would serve their time, a scourge on society taking what was free until they were turned loose, then they'd adapt.

It worked. The very day Yolanda was scheduled to leave, Bodie called Haley to the office.

"Gipson, I'm going to trust you to your parents care this weekend. Smothers has checked out their home. They've removed the necessary items that will allow your presence." Leaning back in the chair that squeaked and groaned under his weight, Bodie stared up at her, his eyes questioning while his words of requirement droned on. "You got it, Gipson? You think you can follow the rules?"

She nodded again, hugging Yolanda and listening to her advice. "You watch your mouth, honey," Yolanda pulled back to stare into her new friends eyes. "You're a good person, now behave and let other people say their piece and let them help you. Forget that rich boy. Find a nice hard working man you respect. You don' have to have the last word, honey. Listen. You'll learn more that way."

The drive was uneventful. The car ran like a top and she suspected for all the flakes of paint on the outside her father had everything under the hood in rare condition for its age. There were no modern conveniences, no GPS or Sirius radio but there was an air conditioner. Maybe she could find a job opening over the weekend and then Bodie could wish her good bye, or vice versa.

The front door was open. She walked in to sniff the fragrance. This was home, clean and comfortable. She was so thankful her eyes teared up and she hastily brushed those tears away. Her parents would never know how she cried when she landed at the women's prison, nor how many nights she snuffled away the sound lest the women cry out, "shut your sniveling, Gipson. You did the deed now pay the price." She sit her suitcase by the hall door.

"Mom?" She walked through the rooms, coming to Grant's. A man's suit hung on the silver groomer she had given him. He was nineteen, dressing for a date, his clothes on the bed *when he said, 'surely there was a better way for Mom to lay out his clothes,' and that weekend she and Mom had found the stand at the new Gifts and More boutique. It can be your gift to your brother for his birthday, Mom said.* She hadn't known she'd feel this pain coming home. It felt like yesterday and the pain was turning to anger that someone else dared stay in Grant's room. "Mom."

The back door squeaked shut and footsteps brought her mother into the house. "Haley. Welcome home." She stopped short, seeing the expression on her daughter's face. "What's wrong?"

"Whose stuff is in Grant's room?"

"Oh, that?" A perplexed frown crossed Dorothy's brow. "I don't really know how to explain Andrew."

"Andrew? Who?"

"Your dad brought him home last Christmas. He was about to be sent away. Your dad intervened with his friend the judge's help and we became Andrew's guardian, so to speak."

"A child does not wear a man size suit, Mom."

Dorothy laughed. "He is a man, Haley." She reached out, "come, here. Let me hug you."

For a moment she wanted to resist but it was good being home and that privilege could be taken away. She went into her mother's arms and before she knew it she was clutching her mother to her body. "Oh, Mom." She lay her head on her mother's shoulder. "Oh, Mom." The tears came unbidden.

Dorothy was leading her into the living room, settling them onto the sofa. "Don't cry sweetheart. It's not what you think, letting

Andrew stay in Grant's room. At first, I couldn't stand the thought, but you know, having Andrew with us helped. He's a little older than Grant was then and he had serious problems, too."

"It hurts to think you would do that, Mom."

"We can't eulogize Grant, Haley." Dorothy wiped her own eyes. "He will always live in our hearts but he's gone and we can't bring him back."

"But we could keep his room sacred, Mom. Not let some stranger come in and desecrate it."

"Grant was not an idol, Sweetheart. He was flesh and blood that made mistakes that took his life." Dorothy sighed. "I think if Grant could tell us, he would be happy for us to help someone and save them from the price he had to pay." She squeezed Haley's shoulder. "Think about it, Haley. Let's not let your brother's precious years of life be in vain. If we can help one person…" Her voice trailed off.

"I won't have to meet this kid, will I?"

"He's no kid, Haley, and yes, you may have to meet him. He has a few things he will be by to pick up."

"I just hope it's not while I'm here. I don't think I can handle it." She rose to go to her room. "It's all bittersweet, Mom. Even if it's done in pink, it's still my room and after where I've been, it's a haven."

"You settle in and I'll set the table and put ice in the glasses for tea. Everything's ready."

"Will Dad be home soon?" With her mother's nod of the head, Haley felt better.

"BABY." HARPER GAVE A LOUD whoop and rushed toward Haley who was running toward him from the hall. "I missed you, girl." He had her crushed to his chest in a bear hug as her legs went around him like she did when she was a little girl. He was nuzzling her neck with his whiskers and laughing joyously. "Baby, let's don't ever go through this again. It almost killed me and your Mother."

"Dad, I'll do everything in my power to stay out of that place." She grinned, laughter bubbling to the surface. "I missed you, Pops. Thought time would never pass and I could get back home."

"Feels good, don't it?"

"Better than that." They all heard the door bell.

"I'll get it." Harper hurried to the door; swung it open and revealed a handsome young man standing there. Stretching out his arms, he boomed, "Come in here, meet our daughter. Haley, this is Andrew.

Andrew stuck out his hand, not amiss to the cool stare Harper's daughter was giving him.

"Come have dinner with us," Dorothy invited. "I've made plenty of Haley's favorite foods."

If Harper noticed his daughter's aloofness, he didn't mention it. He and Andrew kept up the banter throughout the meal and as Haley helped her mother clear the table, they discussed business, but when Haley went directly to her room after the dishes were finished, he realized something was wrong and said so. "What's wrong, Dorothy? Is she sick?" And when Dorothy hesitated, Andrew stepped in.

"I think whatever is wrong is directed at me, Harper," Andrew said. "I'd bet it's because she found my things in her brother's room. Let me collect them and I'll be going. Dorothy," he paused, smiling. "You are the best cook in the country. Not only do I miss you but your good cooking, too."

"What about me?" Harper feigned sadness.

Andrew cuffed him. "You old dog, I hate to admit it, but your gruffness makes me feel warm and fuzzy." He glanced from one to the other. "If there's anything I can do to help, please tell me, I'll try."

"You don't know where there's a job opening, do you?" Dorothy's appeal was not without concern. "If she finds a job, she can stay at home and check in with the camp, otherwise she has to return."

"A job?" Andrew considered. "I don't, but I'll keep my eyes open. You never know. I'll ask around."

CHAPTER SIX

H E DROVE TO HARRIET'S HOME. Thankful Harper allowed him to use one of the company trucks, but he wondered if he could find an automobile on the money he had saved. That amused him. He, who had driven a BMW and Walden's little gem, reduced to this. Stealing Walden's car was the beginning of his complications. His former boss might be a problem later, but for now Walden was in prison for killing the police officer, Sima. Andrew hoped they threw away the keys, but then he had to look at himself. He could only shake his head, not with remorse but with the wisdom he had learned. Now, that Anne was back in his life, happiness was no longer judged by his clothes or what he drove but by his sincerity.

They had experienced a miracle in Andy's speaking again. Seeing his child laying on the street after the hit and run incident had nearly killed him and when Andy was unable to speak for months thereafter he had prayed to know Anne's God, to understand the faith she seemed to instill even as she was there by his side and for Andy's sake kept up the appearance of a united front. Now, finally, they were the parents God intended for their son. He still wasn't sure how it had all come about.

He knocked on the door and faintly heard Harriet telling him to come in. She was sitting in her favorite chair and motioned for him to take the one opposite. "What have you been up to?" She asked.

Sighing, Andrew let his body unfold. "Let me think." He gave her a mischievous grin. "Other than working four hours with Gipson Construction, serving three hours under Judge Michael's jurisdiction," he paused, "That was a full day, but I just come from the Gipson's where I picked up the last of my belongings and I have one last appointment."

"How are the Gipsons? I don't know much of their story but the little I've gleaned from listening to you time to time as you talked about the family, their son died, and a girl that was in prison. Is that right?"

"Well, she's home. Not permanent, yet, but as soon as she finds a job she can begin life anew in community." A concerned expression came into his eyes. "Where's my family?" He glanced toward the bedroom hall, wondering why Anne and his son hadn't come to greet him.

Harriet chuckled. "They ran over to Bitty's for a minute. Andy's a bit keyed up. We planted petunias in hanging pots this evening, but I'm sure Andy will be looking out the window for your truck.

"Harper's truck," Andrew corrected. "That's something I have to work on, finding my own transportation." Grinning, he brought his attention back to Harriet. "Harriet, who would have known three years ago you and I would be sitting here having normal chit-chat together."

"You were definitely sour grapes then," she acknowledged. "When Bitty and I visited Anne in the hospital we were afraid to leave her there alone with you in the room." Her smile matched his, "But as Ellen says, God does work in mysterious ways."

"Yeah, I'm learning that. I'm working with a couple who have two kids. The parents got on drugs a few years back and now Family Services have the children. If the parents don't quit dealing drugs, the state can place their children permanently."

"Isn't that enough to turn the parent's around? No one wants their children farmed out to another family, do they?" Harriet remembered all the years of searching for her own child.

"Drugs rob you of reason, Harriet." He shrugged, his shoulders cupping around his body. "I know from first-hand experience. Thank God I didn't get in any deeper than to test the waters. The people I knew who did have suffered, considerably, health wise, financially and broken spirits."

"Tell me, do you feel you are completely finished with that life, not just because of the Judge's decree, otherwise you would go to jail?"

"Harriet, not many men get a second chance. It took all that to show me what a wonderful woman Anne is. I'll spend the rest of my life, loving every moment, trying to make up for the hurt I caused."

The door burst open with Andy flying into his father's arms. Anne followed, serene and comfortable with Andrew's presence. Harriet could only remember the trials she suffered at Andrew's hands. Now, if things remained on the right track, perhaps the ring Andrew had placed on Anne's engagement finger would find new meaning. It would be wonderful if the three could be a family again. "Andrew," she said, "Tell Anne about the Gipson girl and her needing a job."

GLANCING OUT THE WINDOW, MARIGOLD changed hips with baby Matt. He was fussy, perhaps due to teething, she wasn't sure. She was new at this mother thing. Mostly she fret right along with him, trying to do her best according to the doctor's instructions. 'He's just a baby, Marigold. You aren't going to hurt him. Don't worry. With your schedule, you are going to have to trust him to the baby sitter and get on with life."

True. Her schedule was hectic. Maybe it was time to open her own shoppe. Matt was supportive in that but right now, he was on his way home from the store with the groceries they needed and when he arrived she could get dinner on the table. She longed for a hot soaking bath. Who knew throwing a baby into the mix could create more havoc to an already full schedule.

"Babe," he came in with arms full of sacks. "I think the formula is in this sack right here." He leaned to kiss baby Matt on the head and then planted one on Marigold's lips. "Got a sassy kid, huh, Mom?" He exchanged the last bag for his son. "Let me see if I can get him settled, then I'll help you with dinner."

"I can manage. If you are able to get him to sleep, go ahead and take your shower, because I want to sit in the tub and soak for an hour. I'm that tired and Harriet says I'm too young to be this tired." She paused for a moment, meeting Matt's concerned eyes. "But, my opinion is, she gave me up, so how would she know how tired a mother gets?"

"Still a bit of animosity there, babe. I imagine the worry in what she had done was more health affecting than actual work caring for a baby. It's these other jobs you have wearing you out. Two, too many."

"Let's discuss that later."

Matt grinned, would that be at the table or while you soak in the tub?" The empty sack, she had scrunched into a ball hit him in the center of his back as he headed toward the big rocking chair. "Just wondering," he called back. "Food for thought, you know."

Marigold began the preparation of dinner. Last night's left over chops, green beans, and the mandarin salad would tide them over. She was sitting the plates and silverware, when the phone rang.

"Marigold, its Anne." Anne's soft voice always reminded Marigold of Anne's sweet nature. "I'll keep you a minute. I saw Matt's truck go by and I know you are busy. That's what I called about, Andrew and Matt's boss. Well, actually, the Gipson's have a daughter, looking for a job. She's not trained to work in a doctor's office, so I can't help her. Got any suggestions?"

"Let me think on it. Matt is putting our little pumpkin down for a nap; before we sit to eat." She yawned, "Sorry about that, I didn't mean to yawn in your ear. How long does this teething thing last?"

"IT'S SETTLED." MARIGOLD SETTLED OPPOSITE Harriet' as she sat holding baby Matthew. "We talked it over and I'm going to use the insurance money I received from Mom and Dad's accident to open a business."

"Maybe it will be easier on you than holding down three jobs. You know I would be glad to help you with expenses, if you'd just let me."

"No, we've had this conversation before. I kept the three jobs because I enjoy each one, but I'm so busy running to and fro I hardly have time to breathe and Matt's been after me to quit one or two."

"Will the Insurance money be enough?" Harriet was placing the baby on her shoulder to burp him after his bottle. Catching Marigold's tilt of the head and expression she used when she was repeating the phrase, '*haven't we discussed this one before, also?*' Harriet gave her a non-plussed shrug. "I'm trying to help you, if you'd let me."

"I know, but I have to see what I can do on my own, with Matt's help, of course." Sitting clean bottles on the counter, finishing unloading the dishwasher, Marigold turned to hold her birth mother's attention. "If, I can pull this off, would you feel comfortable, or even want to help on Saturday's by keeping the pumpkin?" She had spent considerable hours thinking the matter over before she asked.

Harriet drew the pumpkin closer as she grinned. "I thought you'd never ask but we've got to come up with another name to call this precious little boy than Pumpkin."

Marigold giggled. "I know. It gives Matt pride to have his son called after his name, but it's confusing."

"As you say, let's think on this." Glancing down she sighed. "Our baby is asleep. Maybe the gums won't hurt for a while. Since you won't let me help you, I guess I'll slip back across the lawn and check on Andrew and Anne. When I left they were building a tower out of Legos with Andy."

"Tell her, if my plan goes through, I may have a job for that Gipson girl but I should meet her first."

HALEY RETURNED FROM A WEEKEND at home. Bodie was waiting. "I have to check your car."

"For what?" Haley's indignant reply burst from her lips. So much for trying to win Bodie over. "I mean, what do you think I have, other than an extra set of clothes?"

"You did go to Camp Cup Cake on drug charges, I believe. Scoot." He motioned her out of the car and then held his hands out for the keys.

"I never sold drugs."

"So you say." He was pushing the seat back, ready to slide in. "I'm not your judge and jury, Gipson. That's already happened. I'm here to see you follow rules and don't go back."

The week was terrible. Haley went into town on the days scheduled to look for a job, attended counseling on Tuesday and studied the paper work on Fridays. Without Yolanda and Elise, the camp was bleak, the guys ogling her all day, except one. Jensen wasn't so bad. He said he was from Alabama, owned a trucking business and couldn't wait to get back to it, if it was still there with his family in charge of operations.

"What do you mean, trucking business?" She asked.

"Logistics. You know, cargo, hauling across country. I thought you would identify with trucking easier."

"Oh, like the suppliers send products to stores and such? I got it. So where do you run?"

"Wherever there's a profit to be made."

"So…how did you end up here? Is this your territory, where you base your business?"

"I'm on the line." He laughed. "Seriously. Walk out my front door I'm in Missouri, but if you go out the South side door and walk fifty feet you are in Arkansas. Fortunately there's a river marks a pretty good boundary, so we don't stray far." He sobered. "To answer a question, why I'm here, I'm ashamed to say I was going through a divorce, my business suffering and before I hit bottom, I tried the drugs to tame me down but everything went in reverse, then I hit rock bottom."

"That's interesting."

"Which part, the divorce or how I got caught?"

"Both. If you want to explain." She held her hands up, "If you prefer not to, that's all right, too."

"Long story short, I was on the road, a lot. She had too much time on her hands. My best friend told me he was checking on her to be sure she was all right. He was checking on her, all right. Not a best friend, it turns out. They are married now. I never see them, don't want too."

"Sorry."

"What's your story?"

"I don't have one. I'm looking for a job, near my parent's home. There seems to be a shortage."

"What's your first name? All I hear is Bodie calling you Gipson."

"Haley." She smiled. "I think Bodie gets a kick out of being the boss.

And Jensen, first or last?"

"Jamie Jensen," he stuck out his hand, "Proud owner of J and J trucking. Logistics." He grinned. "I won't be around much longer. They've struck a bargain, I'm to take a lot of classes. Anger management, the usual drug one's and can you believe they'd tell me I need to go to church and find structure?"

"The government can't tell you that."

"Bodie's side kick, Lucinda, the cook did." His grin was infectious. "I forgot to mention, the anger management is because I beat the daylights out of my *use- to -be* -best friend when I found out. Then I left."

"Wow. Do you have those bouts of anger on a regular basis?"

"Nope, just that one time and I think it cured me. I couldn't believe he pressed charges. He didn't think his broken nose and smashed face looked as good, after I finished with him. I'm done with all of that."

"I just might make it through another week, here, if you can keep the stories coming," Haley said, laughing. "I'm about to go out of my mind." The laughter faded away. "It's like treading water. I'm going nowhere and I'm ready to start over but I have to admit I still have a lot of hostilities to deal with."

"Are you going home this weekend?"

"Yeah, but Bodie's making me wait until tomorrow. How am I supposed to find a job in one day, and it being Saturday no one will want to take time for me." She sighed. "I know most time you just fill out a form, but to get the job there has to be an interview."

"How are things at home? Is it hard to readjust?"

"I really don't know. Yeah, there are situations that are upsetting, that I can do nothing about."

"WE'RE GOING TO CHURCH, TOMORROW," Harper said, his eyes on Haley, as they sat at the dinner table.

"Oh, Dad, so soon?" Haley's countenance fell. "Do you really want to stir up gossip?"

"Haley, you have to meet folks, sooner or later. Church folks will be the fore runner to your return."

"I don't think so, Dad. Sometimes, they are the worst of all. Maybe we could change church?"

"That's ridiculous." Harper reached for Dorothy's apple pie. "Isn't it?" He stared at his wife.

"If it would ease Haley's feelings," she turned to Haley. "Where do you have in mind?"

"We could attend the one with the glass dome. I always wanted to see what it looked like inside." She wasn't sure they would accept her choice when they looked at each other as if there was a reason not to. "It's all right," she gave in. "I just don't want to face the questions from everyone that knows the story."

"That's a good choice." Harper busied himself with the last few bites of pie on his plate. If it were true, Dorothy's opinion that Haley hadn't liked Andrew, they'd have to watch where they sit, because it was his understanding Andrew was now attending Christ Church with the girl Harper talked to on the phone, Andrew's ex-wife. He knew Andrew had given her an engagement ring, hoping they'd try again.

HARRIET WAS A BIT FLUSTERED. She preferred arriving on time, rather than an entourage down the aisle with baby Matthew fussing over his swollen gums. She explained to Marigold, "You can leave him in the nursery. They have good workers."

"Harriet." Marigold's stern countenance locked on her mother. "I am not leaving my baby in the nursery for some toddler to bite, take his bottle or give germs to. Now that's final. Pumpkin sits with us."

Matthew grinned and patted Harriet on the shoulder. "It's all right, Harriet. You said your piece and lost. Now let's play church." When she gave him the evil eye, Matthew hugged her right there in the middle of the aisle before she slid into the pew next to Bitty and her chief of Police."

"What's wrong?" Bitty asked, grinning. "You look like you got your feathers ruffled. Did they make you ride to church in the feathered van?" Ruthie, sitting between the captain and Ellen and Dan, pushed out of the cushioned seat and came to stand in front of Harriet.

"I need to hug you, Aunt Harriet. When Momma says my feathers are ruffled, she hugs me."

Accepting Ruthie's hug, Harriet whispered, "How old are you, really?"

Ruthie grinned. "You know I had my birthday party with five candles on it." Ruthie pressed in front of Harriet to stand between Marigold and Matt. "What's wrong, baby Matthew? You got teeth hurting you?" She tickled his tummy. "You a pumpkin baby?" Baby Matthew laughed and Ruthie giggled. "The twins are in the nursery. They have one room for little babies and another for the walking babies. Momma said if they got to going out here, no one would hear a word the mininister says."

"Minister," Marigold corrected.

"That, too." Ruthie agreed.

Sweat was running down Marigold's cheek. "They have a different room for the babies, Ruthie?"

"Yes, and those women in there just love to hold babies. They reach their arms out for the twins."

Marigold was rising. "Show me where to go, Ruthie, and we will let them keep our Pumpkin." She leaned forward. "Ellen, is it all right if Ruthie shows me where the nursery is located?" Relieved when Ellen nodded, Marigold said, "Good."

Matt glanced at Harriet's raised eyebrow as if to say, she listens to a five year old? "It's all right, Ma," he whispered.

Harriet gave him a smirk as she whispered back, "Listen, buster, I'm not your ma." But she grinned, pleased with this son in law that seemed never to lose his cool and watched whatever happened with a modicum of amusement. "How did you ever pick this girl to be your wife?"

"Who? Tinkerbell?" Before Harriet could answer the organ pealed its first note. As service began Matt glanced toward movement in the aisle to see his boss settling across the way and with Mrs. Gipson and perhaps the daughter he heard rumored back from a trip abroad. He could only wonder that he had not seen the Gipson's before at Christ Church. Marigold and Ruthie returned, with Ruthie going on down to sit with her parents as Marigold slid between Matt and Harriet. "That's my and Andrew's boss over there," Matt whispered, "But don't look just yet, they will see you."

"Who's the girl?"

"I figure the Gipson's daughter? I heard she's been away since her brother died."

CHAPTER SEVEN

"TODAY'S SERMON," BROTHER JOE BEGAN, "will be about a bird." He smiled. "Yes, that's right, a bird." He paused. "And yes, worry and how to go beyond that when we seek God's plan for our life. May we stand for the reading of God's Word. Matthew chapter six; verses twenty six through thirty four."

"From the New International Version of the Bible: Look at the birds of the air: they do not sow or reap or store away in barns, and yet your heavenly Father feeds them. Are you not much more valuable than they? Can any one of you by worrying add a single hour to your life? And why do you worry about clothes? See how the flowers of the field grow. They do not labor or spin. Yet I tell you that not even Solomon in all his splendor was dressed like one of these. If that is how God clothes the grass of the field, which is here today and tomorrow is thrown into the fire, will he not much more clothe you—you of little faith? So do not worry, saying what shall we eat, or what shall we drink or what shall we wear? For the pagans run after all these things, and your heavenly Father knows that you need them. But seek first his kingdom and his righteousness, and all these things will be given to you as well. Therefore do not worry about tomorrow, for tomorrow will worry about itself. Each day has enough troubles of its own."

Matt found listening to Brother Joe's explanation of the scripture always carried him through the week. It gave him something to think on. "Let us take this a little out of context and say you are the bird. Now if you were a worrying bird, what does scripture say? Before we have a need; our heavenly Father knows what we need.

Then what's the solution to worry? Let us say we have something weighing heavily on our mind, how do we handle that problem?"

"Read verse thirty three and thirty four as we discover in seeking His righteousness, faith has entered, *that habitual little ritual we exercise, or don't exercise in our daily lives.* The essences of these scriptures are to put our hearts and minds at ease, if we believe in God. Let us say we have something we are praying about, we need answers. Are we anxious? Do we fret? Or, do we pray and listen for God's answer? True, this scripture only promises God will provide our need while it emphasizes our God's power but who do you want on your side? You are the bird, except you are busy- busy, trying to get ahead in life. Or, perhaps you are just starting out. Or, restarting. You've given up on the past, you are moving forward getting on with life. Who do you need? That's where verse thirty three comes in. Seek first, the kingdom of God and His ways and these things will be added to your life."

Marigold listened. Was she fretting about the busyness of her life? Maybe she was. She had become sharp tongued, at times, when stressed out over trying to work, take care of Matt and the baby and yes, she was stretching herself thin over the scurry to three jobs. Something had to go.

Harriet was listening to Brother Joe and thinking back on the worry she had gone through trying to find her daughter. Now she was fretting over how to ease their lives into a normal every day working situation. They still rubbed each other the wrong way, as the old saying goes.

On the other side of the aisle, Haley Marie Gipson struggled with the message. True, she had messed up, but to stand on faith; that if she kept God's ways he would watch over her, allow her the basic needs and allow her to go forward in her life. As the old saying went, the rest was up to her.

Brother Joe was closing his Bible. "In closing, this morning our last song will be by Mr. and Mrs. Daniel Gates. The song, appropriately is, "His Eye IS ON the Sparrow." Listen to the words and if you have a burden of the heart and wish to approach the Lord, please come to the front and let us pray together."

Matt felt happiness within his heart. God was blessing him and Marigold every day but he realized there was a decision to be made. Then his thoughts strayed to those around him, wondering if they, too, had decisions requiring God's blessing. Daniel and Ellen were finishing the song as Brother Joe rose up to end the hour of worship.

"Jesus never condemns us for asking, but this scripture makes plain, it is not a means to obtain possessions; it is trusting Him to supply the basic need and our job is to seek His plan for our lives, live accordingly and realize, the God who cares for the birds of the air and the lilies of the field cares more for His children."

Services over, there was the usual hustle and bustle of people down the aisle. Today many lingered to comment to Daniel and Ellen on their singing. "We are stopping off at the new restaurant," Anne told Harriet. "Do you want to join us?"

Harriet glanced up as Matt and Marigold discussed whether Pumpkin would be too fussy for the public. "But I haven't anything prepared at home," Marigold said, and that seemed to clinch the deal.

"All right with you if we go with the group, Harriet?" He grinned. "I almost called you Ma. We've got to settle on a name. What shall I call you?" His grin was breaking down Harriet's usual primness. "How does 'M' sound to you, you know, as in Double O'Seven's 'M'?" He knew he was treading seriously gray waters, and Marigold was taking it all in. "She's always going to be straight-laced," his wife had said.

"Anything sounds better than Ma." Harriet's eyes met Marigolds. While Marigold had asked her if she had made up her mind to be her mother and Harriet consented, yes, her daughter had never called her anything other than Harriet, which was all right too, she supposed if you called your son, Pumpkin.

They arrived as a group. "We only have one table left," the waitress said. "Do you want it?"

"Of course, we want it." Daniel silently counted heads. "We will need two booster seats and a bed."

The waitress laughed at his joke. "For the twins, I'm thinking."

"Yeah," Daniel agreed. "This eating out with your arms full is quite an experience, but we can do it."

"This table will hold four more," the girl with the name tag Ashley, was handing out menus, "But you can put your purses in them, ladies and my boss won't say anything. It's an unusually busy Sunday for us."

"No purses," Ellen replied. "We are traveling with a diaper bag. How about you, Marigold?"

"Same here." Marigold was busy sliding into the chair Matt was holding for her, after he seated Harriet. Whispering to Ellen, Marigold said, "Either my hormones are raging or I'm sweating like a Trojan." She pressed a sleeping pumpkin to her breast. "I hope he sleeps through the whole lunch."

"Trojan gone to war, right?" Ellen squeezed her friend's hand. "This motherhood thing is quite encompassing isn't it? And I remember it last through the two's. Ruthie was such a quiet little one and now I have these two and there's a definite difference. If one cries, the other joins right in."

"You are holding up, it seems," Matt said to Daniel. To which, Daniels raised eyebrows raised question.

"I'm glad it appears that way." Yawning, he took the chair across from Matt, a baby in the bend of his arm. "We'll see how this works. It's like check-check, bottle, diaper, binky, check the diaper, install bottle. You know what I mean? At least you're ahead in the game."

"Just wait. There's teething." Matt glanced up to see the head waiter perusing the crowd. She was shaking her head. "Say, Dan, you think we could squeeze in three more, that's my and Andrew's boss waiting to be seated." At Daniel's nod of consent, Matt raised his arm, motioning and pointing at their table. "Send word down the table to Andrew that our boss is here, Daniel."

Haley was reluctant but her father was hungry. "Why don't we go home, Mom? We can eat peanut butter on bread." Harper turned to give her a disbelieving glance. "Oh, Dad, you don't change. Always hungry. I guess you still get up in the night and eat a cookie."

"Yes, I do," Harper replied. "But today it's Sunday and these fine folks are offering us food and company, let's take them up on it." He led them straight to the table. "Hey, there, Matt, it's kind of you to share your table." Introductions were made as the waitress appeared with the first groups drinks, ready to take their orders. "What're you drinking, Dorothy? Haley? Sweet tea for me," he said.

"So this is your daughter, Harper." Matt leaned forward to make eye contract. "Mrs. Gipson, how are you? I don't think we've officially met but I have seen you stopping by the work site, now and then."

"Harper has told me about you, Matt and that you have a precious little baby boy." She turned to her daughter. "This is Haley." Dorothy smiled. "Thank you for sharing your table. I'm afraid I didn't have lunch cooked at home."

"It's all we can do to make it to church on Sunday, since we have our boy," Matt turned to Marigold. "Hon, you need to meet my boss and his family." Glancing down the table, he noted Andrew and Anne were in discussion with Bitty and the Chief. "You know Andrew from work," he said to Harper, "But this is my wife, Marigold."

All eyes were on Marigold as she smiled; acknowledging Matt's boss but her eyes lingered with the boss's daughter. There was something amiss there. "How are you?" She asked. "I'm trying to keep this one asleep, as he has a new tooth coming in and is cranky." She gave a self-conscious laugh. "I had thought I'd keep him in the Sanctuary during worship hour, but when Ruthie explained they had separate rooms for baby-babies and then toddlers, we took him to Nursery." The daughter just sat there. "I don't believe I remember your family in our worship service before."

Dorothy explained, "We don't normally attend Christ Church, but it was very enjoyable and the people are very accepting." She reached for her daughter's hand. "Marigold, this is our daughter, Haley. She has just returned to the Cape and she is seeking employment. Perhaps you would know someone in need of a helper."

"I'll give you my number and you can call me. I may know of something." Not intending to be rude, she introduced Harriet to Mrs. Gipson. "And this is my mother, Harriet Becker."

"Harriet Becker?" Harper's voice boomed. "Why, I knew your husband, Mrs. Becker. We did business."

"That's the way you re-enter society," Harper stated, turning to Haley in the back seat, as they were driving home. "Now aren't you happy we stopped off for lunch, instead of peanut butter sandwiches?" Now he met her glance in the visor mirror. "I know. I know. You are skeptical whether Matt's wife will call. What's her name? Margo?"

"Marigold." Haley supplied. "That's a different name." Haley paused. "I don't know why, but I think she saw right through me. I wasn't away on vacation or to college, I was in prison and I didn't just hop into the conversation and explain." Her voice lost softness, taking on an edge. "I'm the out sider here, but one thing's for sure, they feel comfortable among themselves."

"Those were very nice people. Maybe we will change church attendance for a while, if that makes you feel better, Haley." Harper's eyes turned somber as they met his daughter's in the mirror again. "Would that help?"

◆

SHE WAS IN HER ROOM when the phone rang. "It's for you," her mother appeared at the door. "Just pick up. I'll shut the door and give you some privacy."

Haley glanced at the plain black phone installed for her convenience, once she was approved to move back home. "I'm sorry, Mom. I'm not used to phone calls. It's just another adjustment I have to make." She picked up the phone from the small bedside chest. "Hello." She sighed. "Hi, Marigold. Yes the timing is good."

CHAPTER EIGHT

"THAT ABOUT DOES IT, GIPSON." Bodie handed her a file of papers. "Report back to us, each Tuesday. I'm being very lenient with you, allowing you to come in after five. That means I have to stay over, for you."

"I'm flattered." Haley's smug expression brought a flush to Bodie's face. She remembered instantly Yolanda's words. *'You gotta get along with Bodie, girl. He has a hand in your future.'* "That was mean," she said, quickly. "I apologize."

"For your own good, Gipson, get a hold on that sarcastic tongue. Keep it to yourself."

If he only knew; she alternated between sarcasm and sinking into despair so deep she thought it would drown her. Her personality was not out-going as her father's but she wasn't the sweet honey type of her mother, either. She often wondered if Camp Cup Cake had killed her spirit. The warden's warning sounded in her mind. *"You have to accept the fact you messed up, Gipson. No one else makes your decisions. We're big on facing our own problems, here at Camp Cup Cake. We teach you to examine yourself, realize where you went wrong and that no one but yourself brought you here."*

"I said you are dismissed. You can go."

"I need your permission." He was scrutinizing her, waiting. "It's about the job. Tell me what I can do and what I must not." She was to call before she went anywhere, when she arrived, and upon leaving.

She was going home. She had a job. She wasn't clear, exactly what the job was about, but it was a job. The girl, Marigold, she figured was near her age. *With a baby.* Haley's mind flit to Race. *But*

Race was gone. Then there was Jeremy, the Neanderthal, the one she met briefly in Mississippi and left behind to marry his southern belle, whom she had not the privilege to meet. *"She's away with her Momma on a cruise," he explained.* Otherwise, she very much doubted good old Jeremy would have taken her home to meet his Mother, since she already met Jon Southern at that strange farm and gin show in Memphis.

She still remembered Jeremy's kiss. Strange that she should. He was hiding her face from the Feds. Completely in the dark as to her situation, Jeremy was the kind of man that would help a female in distress and she had been in dire stress, not knowing if the men in black suits were Fed or drug cartel. A deep sigh escaped as she paid closer attention to the landscape along the road side. Birds flew up from the pavement where they were busy pecking at an animal carcass, run over, pancake size. She lingered on the sermon from Sunday's church. Or was it the song the couple had sung? *His eye is on the sparrow, therefore he watches over me. Birds neither sow or reap or stow away, their heavenly watches over them.* Where were you when I needed you, she questioned. Were your eyes on me?

Hadn't she dreamed of this day? Then why the dark shroud that continually enveloped her mind? She vowed nothing within her power would take her back to Camp Cup Cake but it wasn't easy returning to the world she had left behind for two years. *Do not worry about tomorrow for tomorrow will take care of its self, seek first his kingdom of righteousness and all these will be added, as well.* The scripture teased her conscience; causing her to wonder the truth in the pastor's message. *Your Father knows what you have need of.* If, only, it were really that easy. Maybe, the response of her childhood when she walked down the aisle and gave her heart to the Lord had not been enough. Maybe she didn't know who He was, after all. Those nights, away, lying in bed, staring at the ceiling, questioning weren't much different than now. Nothing was stable; the friends she met in the camp were moving on, was she?

MARIGOLD SAW BITTY OUT IN the yard. Hurriedly throwing a blanket over little Matt, she was out the door striding toward her neighbor. "Bitty, hold up; I need to talk to you."

"Well, let's go inside." Bitty, checked out baby Matt. "You are growing like a weed, little boy."

"Is Chester home?"

"Not yet, he called and said he had an appointment. He would explain later." Bitty opened the door, motioning them inside. "Let's sit in the kitchen. Maybe you would like something…"

"No, I want to know what you thought of the family that joined us for lunch, Sunday. I think I hired the girl. Did she seem quiet to you?" Bitty was reaching for the baby. "Here you go Pumpkin, go to Bitty."

"Hired her on the spot?" Bitty seemed to question that action. "Do you know her story?"

"Only that she has been away two years and needs employment."

"There's a bit more to it, than that." Bitty knew her information must be true, coming from Chester, the Chief of Police. "I'll tell you what I know, but don't pass this on to anyone else." Marigold nodded and listened. "That's all I know, but Chester would probably feel better if it's not repeated, elsewhere."

There was a knock on the door, Bitty called out, "come in," and Harriet entered. "Well, hello, Pumpkin," Harriet's voice carried the warmth only a grandmother knows in seeing her grandchild. "I didn't know you were here. How's my boy?" Baby Matt leaned toward her.

"Here you are stealing my thunder, again." Bitty handed little Matt over to Harriet. "I must say he knows you." The baby settled into Harriet's arms, immediately attracted to the necklace she wore.

"Marigold, we have to find a name to call this baby besides Pumpkin." Harriet tilt her head, staring at her daughter. "I can't imagine introducing him to my friends as Pumpkin.

"You don't have that many friends, so don't worry about it." Marigold said, grinning. "If I say Matthew, both my husband and my child are confused. What do you suggest, Harriet?"

"You should have thought of that before you named him after his Daddy."

"Well, I can't change it now. Besides, it made Matt happy. So what do you suggest?"

"This sounds like the old days," Bitty said, "You two bickering. I thought you had given that up."

FROM THAT CHANCE MEETING, MARIGOLD found someone she could train to help with Jack's Party Supply and the Art Gallery, but she had not mentioned to Melissa anything about Haley until she was certain the girl met all requirements. There was one last test. If Haley was drawn to Ruthie, as she had been, then Marigold knew she had found her partner.

"There's someone I want you to meet," she said to Haley, as they were hanging the last oil on the wall of the Gallery. "A friend will be dropping her off, shortly. This person and I are dear friends. She was one of the first people I met when I arrived at the Cape."

"Fine with me," Haley replied. "But these days, not a lot of people are drawn to me." She sighed. "You know my story. I had to tell you, if I hadn't and something comes up missing you know the first finger would be pointed at me."

"You know what I remember?" Marigold climbed down from the ladder, handing Haley a hammer and folded the ladder for storage. "You seemed so withdrawn that day at lunch and your mother tried very hard to bring you out of yourself, but you weren't having it."

"Moms are like that, aren't they? I didn't know if any of you knew I had been in prison and were making suppositions about me. It will take a while before I loosen up." They both turned to the sound of the door opening. Marigold's face brightened at the sight of Ruthie. Haley took the ladder to put it away.

"Why, Ruthie, look at you, wearing our favorite tutu." Marigold hugged Ruthie, then Bitty. "Haley, do you remember these two from our luncheon the day you and your family visited Christ Church?"

"We were on the far end of the table and really didn't have a chance to speak," Bitty said. "But this one, she remembers everyone."

"You were sitting by the big guy in Police wear," Haley replied. "I remember him. I felt a bit intimidated."

"Intimidated." Ruthie let the word roll off her tongue. "Does that word, intimidated, mean you liked him?"

Stooping to be on a level with Ruthie, Haley said, "I believe, Ruthie, it means I was a bit overwhelmed, maybe even unsettled. A uniform signifies authority and until you know the person, you are uncertain…"

"But Uncle Chester is really nice," Ruthie's eyes were serious; pinned to Haley's somber expression. "He won't hurt people. When I was lost, he found me and put his arms around me and took me to Momma."

The two continued their discussion. Haley was listening to Ruthie's praise for Captain Mayfield.

"How are you and your new assistant working out?" Bitty and Marigold had moved a discreet distance away. "And how are you, leaving baby Matt with Harriet and Hattie?"

"Question number two, first," Marigold grinned. "I know we will have one spoiled child. Those two women dote on my little Pumpkin, but lest he grow up with that name, they still call him baby Matt. And it looks like they conned you into doing the same. Am I right?"

Bitty laughed. "Yes. Now, for the second question; the assistant is working out?"

"She just passed the final test. I knew if Ruthie trusts her, we had a good one. Look at them."

Animated, Ruthie was retelling Uncle Chester finding her after *that* woman *dragged* her through the fields and it was cold and she was wet, *but Uncle Chester took her to Momma* and everything was good.

Five o'clock arrived, Marigold and Ruthie prepared for dance, ready to leave for Melissa's Studio. Haley gathered her purse and keys, as she asked, "The friend you wanted me to meet, didn't come, did she? I know you wanted her to check me out and give you an opinion, didn't you?"

Marigold grinned. "Yes, she came and the two of you had a nice talk and you passed with flying colors."

THE MONTH PASSED WITH HALEY reporting weekly to Camp Marshhill. "How much longer must I check in?"

"You find us that repulsive, Gipson?" The usual squint eyed scrutiny accompanied his words. "Two months, ten percent of your wages and phone calls before you leave location, when you arrive destination and keep your nose clean, then I'd say you will be on your own, though I may write in your report I want to see you on a regular basis."

"Do you really have that authority?" The words slipped out, defiant as always, when she met up with him. "And just tell me why you are entitled ten percent of my wages?"

"You read the rules and regulation form, Gipson. The camp operates off of that ten percent. You're lucky there was a camp to come home to…"

"Some home."

"It's not my money, Gipson." Bodie sighed. "You know, Gipson, you somehow *always* manage to get on my last nerve."

"It's mutual."

She left without apologizing but down the road as the marshland fell behind, she thought of him. He wasn't a bad guy but she wondered what he was doing stashed away in some little forgotten corner of the earth like Marsh hill. Wasn't a United State Marshall supposed to be a job of glamor and distinction? The weekly three hour drive there and back cut into work. It didn't seem to bother Marigold as she trained her in the various tasks of the Gallery, but it was the Party Supply Haley liked best. Helping Jack set up for family celebrations lent a festive air and somehow calmed Haley's heart to know there were people who cared about such things as birthdays and anniversaries.

Marigold mentioned she was actively seeking a building to start her own business. "I'm trusting the Lord to bring the right one to my attention," she said. "Thus far, nothing meets criteria."

There was that word again. *Trust. Trusting the Lord.* She was finding her whole life centered on that one word, and she was trying to maintain everyone's expectations. No way, did she want to return to Camp Cup Cake. There were times she felt so tense and distraught over the prospect that the tiniest little mistake could happen to send her packing back to that place of dire restriction and its lack of freedom. Inside, there was a longing for the unrest to settle, but how did that happen?

THE GROUP WAS HAVING LUNCH again, on Sunday. This time, Bitty had prepared. Marigold wandered through the rooms, observing Bitty's own particular brand of decorating; nothing too precious, but good wholesome furnishings. "You know, Bitty," she called out, "You've got something amazing going on here, but a few of Matt's paintings as focal pieces would bring your rooms to life."

"Can I afford him?" Bitty came to stand beside her. "He hasn't become so famous that his price is out of my reach, has he?"

"I heard my name." Matt appeared in the doorway, Pumpkin riding on his arm, taking it all in.

"What do you think, Matt? Don't Bitty and the Captain need a few paintings to make their décor come to life?"

"You tell me what you want, Bitty, and it's yours. If I'm doing something a person wants, that just ignites a fire in me and I would love to do something for you and the Chief."

"If you let me pay you," Bitty gave him a worrying glance, "If I can afford your oil paintings, that is."

"I'll let you down easy." Matt grinned. Baby Matt was gurgling his agreement for all to hear.

"It's a deal. Now come on, foods on and everyone's ready to gather at the table."

"I'm thinking with Bitty's country style, that painting we have at the Gallery of the man behind the plow would work great in the foyer. Are you surprised she decorated country?" He nodded. "Me, too."

"Where in the world did you find double high chairs?" Ellen was tightening belts around the twins as Marigold placed Pumpkin in a matching single. "They are stunning, custom made, aren't they?"

Bitty grinned, pleased. "Dan, you sit across from Chester, Andrew on his left, Dr. Silverman by Harriet and the rest of us will find chairs by our men." She laughed suddenly, "Well, as we can. Mercy, I did sit enough places, didn't I?" She sighed. "I thought about asking the Gipsons, too, and I will the next time."

"Anne, after we say grace, would you bring the rolls from the oven?" Bitty was in her element, taking care of everyone. "My, Ruthie, you and Andy are so grown up and being so nice while we get settled."

Ellen's heart skipped a beat as she glanced from Ruthie and Andy to the Captain, suddenly very aware there was a graying to his skin tone. He is not well, she thought. Oh, dear Father in Heaven, are you giving me a message? Please, no, not our captain. How can I deal with this? Backing away from what she knew was truth; Ellen listened as the Captain began the blessing before they all partook of the food.

Later, as they were in Daniels Escalade, once he backed out of the drive and was on the road home, he glanced back to see both children sleeping. "Was there a reason you turned quiet?" he asked.

Lest Ruthie hear, Ellen glanced to the back as she replied, "I'll tell you when we are alone."

Two miles and ten minutes' drive brought them to their home. Each carrying a baby, Ruthie walking by Ellen they lay the children down for an evening nap and found themselves finally alone in their own room to sit in chairs that looked out onto the back yard where Daniel's landscaping had become a thing of beauty. Ellen sighed, content, as Daniel reached for her hand.

"Now, tell me, why you became so quiet. Did something happen?"

"You know, sometimes the Lord gives me these messages?" Those serious eyes questioned Daniel. "And I'm supposed to approach the person to whom they are directed?" A sadness crept into her expression. "It's the Captain. I don't know what's wrong, but his color is gray and he didn't have his usual energy. Did you notice? Now this."

"I did notice he seemed tired but I thought he was working on a case and possibly midnight hours."

"I'm supposed to ask him to see his doctor and I know it isn't for another month because Bitty told me."

He squeezed her hand. "Do what you have to do. Shall we pray about it?"

Ellen nodded. "Will you?"

"Father in Heaven, we thank you for a good day with our friends, for a service that gave us your word and instruction to live by. But Lord, now we come to you with troubled hearts. Our friends have found each other, after years of being alone and we know our Captain has health issues but Ellen has heard your message in her heart and in her mind and we pray Lord, that there is no problem that cannot be corrected through faith and trust in you. Lord, I thank you for this precious woman you have given to be my wife and I ask you to watch over her and our children and Lord, to touch our friends with your love and comfort and peace that comes only from you. It is in your gracious Holy name, we ask. Amen.

The next morning Ellen dropped Ruthie off at Bitty's and drove on to Tiny World infant Day care to leave the twins. Bitty had offered to keep the twins but after considerable prayer Daniel and Ellen agreed the task was too daunting for newlywed Bitty who would have it no other way except Ruthie continue to stay with her. "She starts Kindergarten and we won't have our time together. You have to let us go on as we have these years. Why our hearts would break if you separated us now."

Ellen called in to work, saying she would be late. She had asked a friend to fill in until she arrived and was granted her request. Turning in at the Police Station, she noticed Chester's official vehicle was parked to one side of the building. She entered and asked to see the Captain.

Chief of Police, Chester Mayfield, was examining a map of the county and glanced up as the door opened. "Why, Ellen is something wrong?" Alarmed, he rose to his feet, extending a hand and motioning for her to sit in the chair in front of his desk. "Can I help you?"

Heaving a sigh, Ellen began, "Chester, I don't know where to begin. Do you remember God giving Ruthie a message for little Andy when he was in coma after the hit and run accident?" Chester nodded. "Well, I have that same gift. And when the Lord gives me a message, I have to deliver it. And it isn't easy, because the recipient may laugh or protest that the message is not for them, when truly it is."

Chester was feeling a bit uneasy. "Who, exactly, is this message for, Ellen?"

"How are you feeling, Chester?" Ellen leaned forward, her eyes holding with his. "The Lord told me to tell you, go to your doctor and let him run tests. As quickly as you can see him, Chester."

The slump of Chester's body was a direct acknowledgement; they both knew God's message was correct. "You think something is bad wrong, Ellen?"

"I'm only a nurse, Chester, and in this instance merely a messenger. But you do have grayness to your countenance and I very much hope you will make that appointment. It may be necessary to keep your health issues controlled."

"I'll do it, Ellen." For a moment, Chester allowed his head to fold into his hands as his elbows were propped on the edge of his desk. "I haven't felt well the last few weeks and I've been loath to tell Bitty. She is so happy and you know it is my utmost desire to make that woman happy. I like to never convince her to marry me...and now this."

"It may be a simple warning, Chester." Ellen arose to leave. "But if God thought it serious enough to send you a messenger, then follow through. Daniel knows. We prayed about this last night. I needed serious back up." She grinned, reaching up to hug him. "We love you, friend."

He was drawn to remember their wedding day, all the friends gathered in their honor. Harriet and Marigold had outdone themselves. He'd wondered about the huge tent installed in the back yard, but that was where Harriet's artistic bent took hold, all china and crystal, a splashing fountain and the beauty of his bride outshining the wonder of it all. Ruthie had dropped rose petals and Bitty's pride in her was quite evident. Even though his own daughter had not come, the day would hold forever in his memory, but what had he done now? He had known for days something in his health was off- key but he'd promised Bitty a life of good, for better or worse in sickness and health, whatever it took, he must keep his promise.

Chester made the call. His appointment was at two in the afternoon. The doctor had been advised by his nurse and actually had taken time to speak to him. "Don't forget the appointment," he said.

"I want you to go over to the hospital and have a few test run and if I'm not mistaken I can tell you tomorrow what I think is going on. It all depends on how quickly they can do your blood work."

It chafed Chester's spirit, not to tell Bitty. What would she think? Truth of the matter resounded in his head, those months of trying to persuade Bitty they could have a better life together and now this? He would wait until the blood work was completed. Then, he would tell her.

CHAPTER NINE

"WE KNEW YOU HAD PROSTATE cancer, Chester. When I sent you to that specialist he was supposed to take care of the matter and the medicine seemed to be working according to the records he sent to me but now your PSA is completely out of bounds. Have you changed your life style in any manner? You know once I put you in his hands I haven't seen you in a while."

"You know I'm married, again."

The doctor stopped short, from moving the stool he normally sit on. "That should make a man happy, not sick." He pat Chester on the shoulder. "Well, we will just look a bit further into this matter."

Chester was at an all-time low. He had pursued Bitty until she had given in, married him, in spite of fear. She had buried one husband, and she didn't want to go through the illness of a second. Once inside the Police car, he slumped with his head on the steering wheel trying to think. They were happy, but could he pull this off, not telling her when there was the possibility things were ready to go wrong. During the time Bitty refused talk of marriage and for the length of time they'd agreed not to see each other, he had taken the doctor's advice. There were three alternatives. He chose the one he felt most to his advantage. What went wrong? It was supposed to stop the cancer from spreading in his body.

Hadn't the Oncologist warned him? He could hear him now. "Cancer is like a seed in a river, except we are speaking of your blood stream. It can wash up wherever it chooses. Our literature, in spite of research reminds us, within ten years of treatment, cancer might return. Let us rest our case on the word, *might*."

What was the pastor's scripture, the one about the bird? Back at headquarters Chester searched for the small Bible, kept in the side drawer of his desk. He knew the scripture was in Matthew, thumbing through the chapters he found it; now he read from chapter six, "Look at the birds of the air; they do not sow or reap or store away in barns, and yet your heavenly Father feeds them. Are you not much more valuable than they? Can anyone of you by worrying add a single hour to your life?" He read on through the scripture, searching for hope. His heart pounding heavily, Chester read the last verse of the passage; *therefore do not worry about tomorrow, for tomorrow will worry about itself. Each day has enough trouble of its own.*" Laying the Bible back into the drawer and closing it, he shook his head. That was certainly right. He was no closer to knowing what to do than when he started.

Then, speaking directly to him, one of the scriptures stood out in his mind, "Oh you of little faith?"

"Cullens?" he called to the outer office, "do I have anything important scheduled the next hour?" Heaving a huge sigh, Chester rose up from the chair. There was just enough time to tell Bitty.

"WHY ARE YOU LOCKED IN the basement?" Marigold wagged a finger Matt's direction. "I know you. You are painting something you don't want me to see. Come clean." She finished sitting the bowls on the table. "Why don't we eat now, while Pumpkin is sleeping and I'll feed him later?"

Matt pulled her into his arms. "Have I told you lately how much I love you?" He felt her body tremble, before the giggle came. "Why is it, I think you will swoon and fall into my arms, instead you giggle, Tinker Bell?"

She smacked a loose kiss on his lips. "Because, Farm boy, I'm different, not so easily swayed by your charms." She looked up into his eyes. "Remember, that got me in trouble and your parents, well your Mother hasn't forgotten. I'll never be invited to family dinners."

"So we married secretly. She has to get over it. Worse things could have happened."

"Do you long to return to farm with your Dad?"

"Maybe someday but not right now." Matt slid into the chair. "Shall we say grace?"

She was always blessed by Matt's asking the Lord, after he had thanked Him for so many things, to take care of his little tinker bell wife and their son. "Give them long days of life," Matt would pray, "And if it is your will, Lord, allow me to be with them to protect and care for them."

Gripping his hand, silently Marigold thanked God for a good husband. "So what are you painting?"

"Curious, aren't we?" Matt grinned. "When I'm finished I will show you, first."

"Hmm. So it isn't for me." She thought a moment. "Is it for Bitty?"

"As you know, artsy girl, oil requires drying time. It is drying and while it does, I'm working on that man behind the plow we talked about." He grinned. "You can fairly smell the dirt." His eyes drew a thoughtful expression, "Isn't it funny that Bitty is filling her big old Antebellum home with turn of the century type paintings."

"But they fit," Marigold agreed. "She has made that big old three story a beautiful home."

A week later, Matt brought the paintings up from the basement. "If you hadn't set up all that good system to resemble daylight, I'd feel concerned over these," he said as he placed them against the wall, "but you did a good job, Art girl. I could have been on the beach in Florida."

"Hmm," she murmured. "It's all in the light bulb. Let me see your tan." She was watching as he stripped away the muslin covers from the paintings. "Oh, Matt." Her heart fluttered at the amount of talent in her husband. "They are divine. I feel the energy...and the sweat in the horses and the man behind the plow just like you mentioned last week." She pouted, "but you wouldn't let me see them."

"Now you see them. Call Bitty and ask if we can come over. I've had to be so patient in waiting through the drying time, now I want her to have them." He was turning the smaller oil to face the larger, for transport. "Can you carry our Pumpkin? We will have to take the truck, since the plowboy is large."

<hr>

"THE PORTRAIT IS STANDARD SIZE, Bitty," Matt explained, "Sixteen by twenty, plus the frame."

"Oh, my goodness." Bitty's eyes filled with tears. "Look at our Captain; Chief of Police Chester Mayfield in person, in uniform. And this one Matt, you have done a wonderful job; those horses, leaning, as they pull the old plow with the farmer behind them. I can see the dirt rising up behind their hoofs."

"You really do feel it, don't you, Bitty?" Marigold clapped her hands. "Where are you hanging them? I'll help you. That's what I do you know."

"First, Matt, let me pay you for the frames, which are picture perfect. I love them." She reached to hug him, her arms around him and Pumpkin, too. Thank you." Bitty, whose whole life had been spent hiding emotion, found her heart full to bursting. "I'm overwhelmed that you would do this for me…and Chester's picture, in uniform, I can't say enough."

"These are our gift to you, Bitty." He was beaming. "Frames, too. I know an art dealer at a Gallery."

Overwhelmed, Bitty sit down at the table as a fresh burst of tears ran down her cheeks. "Sit down, you two, I've something to tell you. Ellen and Dan already know, but you all and Anne and Harriet don't." She sought to wipe away the tears as her eyes filled again. "Chester came home yesterday morning, left work, in fact, to tell me his cancer is back and the doctor is searching for new treatment."

"Aw, Bitty." Marigold rose to wrap her arms around their friend. "I'm so sorry."

Matt sit in the nearest chair, clutching Pumpkin to his chest, the weight of Bitty's words hitting hard. He had forgotten to tell Marigold; Harper had put him in charge of the men that day saying he had to visit his friend who was dying of cancer. "And it started with cancer of the prostate," Harper explained. "Moved to his colon, then his lungs and he's only fifty eight years old. It's doubtful he'll go home."

"Where is Chester, still at work?" And without thinking, he asked, "What age is Chester, fiftyish?"

Nodding, Bitty replied, "There's something stirring at work but he didn't go into it." She sighed heavily. "I guess he thought this was enough news for me for one day." Turning at the sound of a vehicle outside, Bitty saw Dan's Escalade pulling up to the sidewalk. "Look whose here, and no kids, now where could they have left our babies?" She met them at the door. "Where are the kids?"

"Ellen's Mom and Dad drove in and they're playing and you can bet they will sleep well tonight after a few hours with all three." Acknowledging Matt and Marigold, Dan ask, "What's going on with you two and look at Baby Matt. Swollen gums forgotten for the moment, the baby slept sound on Matt's shoulder. "How do you get a baby to sleep?" He shook his head as if it were the question of the century. "At our house, if one stirs the other answers." He laughed. "I don't know what we'd do without Ruthie."

"I could use Ruthie, sometimes, but then I have Harriet. I'm surprised she isn't here." Matt grinned.

"She will be," Bitty replied. "When you called to say you were bringing the paintings over I called her and as soon as Anne and Andrew return from wherever they were going, she said they would be over for a viewing of Matt's work."

"Bitty, why do I sense this is more than a viewing of Matt's paintings?" Marigold asked. "I already feel alarmed and concerned over how Chester must be feeling but what about you?" The group agreed with various comments. "What can we do to help, Bitty?"

Bitty twist the folds of the apron she was wearing, glancing around at her friends. "You all know I like to never have given in to marrying Chester." She took a deep breath. "I think I knew I loved him from the beginning but I watched Larry, my first husband, die and I just didn't want to take on anything else because I might not be able to handle it." She paused, staring momentarily at the floor. "Little could either of us know Chester would have cancer of the prostate? But before he arrives I just want to tell you all, it isn't the care giving situation that scares me. Should this situation turn bad, I will be right by his side but I truly have learned prayer changes things and I'm asking you for your prayers and yes, contrary to my usual self where I do everything alone, I will listen to your counsel and maybe even your opinions." Her laugh came between a sob and an attempt at levity. "It has been more than we considered and I think we are both shocked this is happening."

"Then it is all right if Chester wants to talk about it; he will not care for us knowing." Marigold reached across to pull Bitty to her side. "You know we love you, don't you, Miss Itty Bitty?"

"Who told you that?" Bitty thought a minute. "You spend a lot of time with my Ruthie, don't you?"

CHESTER ARRIVED TO FIND SEVERAL cars parked in the drive and the sound of a hammer and drill inside the house. Daniel was sitting opposite the love seat that held a sleeping baby Matt. The two men shook hands as Chester asked, "Where's everyone? And can you imagine sleeping through the noise?"

"From experience, what I'm wondering is, if he will sleep tonight or if Marigold and Matt won't."

"What are they doing?"

"Go look. I think you will enjoy what you find. I know I have a solid admiration for Matt's talent."

"Guess you've heard my news?" Chester lingered as Daniel nodded. "Not what I wanted."

"It sucks. I'm truly sorry." Daniel reached out a hand, and Chester gripped it hard. "Sit a minute and tell me what you're thinking?"

"I don't know what to think." Chester settled into his brown leather chair. "One minute life is good, then you hear the big C again and life becomes an emotional whirlwind, not to mention the way your faith does a wobble here and there. One minute you're optimistic, the next a doubting Thomas."

Agreeing, Daniel seemed to be gathering his thoughts. "If you need me for anything, to listen, to do some odd job for you, just call me and I'll do my best but Chester, first find out your options. There's new ways of treatment. Who knows what there is out there."

After an hour of hugs and words of caring, everyone left. "Let's go for a drive," Marigold suggested. "I don't know about you but I feel blue. It's like if we fear the worst and we really don't have all the info." They rode in silence, even baby Matt in his seat strapped in the back watched as the landscape filed past.

"How's the new girl working out?"

"She's learning." Marigold turned to face him. "What do you think about your boss, since he's her father? Has he ever spoken about what happened that she had to go to prison?"

"He doesn't say much, but Andrew lived in their house for a while when Harper took him in to keep him from going to prison." He heard her quick intake of breath. "Yeah, that's right. It seems he got roped in with that guy that killed the police officer, PR man or something and nearly got sent away."

"I knew from Anne there were problems but I thought he was going to prison for lack of child support. He lied and got their son, the first time and it was really hard on Anne. You mean there's more?"

"He used to be on drugs or sold them, something of that order, and got caught when he stole Walden's car, then the Judge allowed him into Harper Gipson's, let's say for lack of a better word, custody. Anyway, Andrew says you won't find better people than the Gipson's, but they've suffered sadness in losing their only son, then there's your assistant who got in trouble and was sent off."

"Stop. Stop, the truck." Agitated, Marigold was looking at a building alongside the road. "How far is this from our house? Two miles, or so?" She was motioning for him to turn into the drive. "I've got to walk around this building, Matt. Did you see that For Sale sign?"

"No, Babe, I didn't." Stopping the truck, as she was already climbing out, he shook his head. He could only sit there with the baby while his wife trekked around the building, peered in windows and caused him to fear the police would arrive any minute if she set off the alarm. "I guess it's o.k., bud," he said as Baby Matt awoke fussing in the back seat. "We do know the chief of Police, don't we?"

"Is this perfect, or what?" His son's mother climbed back into the front seat, glancing at her Pumpkin with a big smile on her face. "Push the button, Matt, let's see how far it is home. You think a mile or two?" She was excited. "This close to home and I've not noticed it for sale. Didn't we used to see cars parked around here? That's all I remember. Cars."

"As far as I know it was a used car dealership which explains the cars."

"Well, if the Insurance Company sends the check through that they promised, I think if I had to lose Mom and Dad in that accident, they would approve of this to be the beginning of my launch into the business world. This location is great. Traffic both ways, and think of the tourist that will stop."

"Have you actually narrowed it down?" Matt glanced her way after checking traffic to pull back onto the road. "I mean, you know what you plan to sell?" He considered the location, on the main highway that led up town, with no other route of entrance, privy to Main Street and River drive used by tourist and sight-seeing groups. He could only wonder why the car dealership had vacated the lot.

"Why narrow it down? Why not have several venues, that way if one doesn't work the other will?" She grinned. "I plan to give Jonathan Hunter a run for his money if you can hold out to do more paintings."

Matt groaned, "You would pit me against my adversary, artist of the year, J. Hunter?"

"How many painting do you have stored in your basement studio, Farm Boy?" She was dialing Ellen's number. "Ellen, I need your prayers. I think we've found the building for my business." She paused. "I know, Ellen. I can pray but I might not get it covered so I'm asking you and Daniel to help us."

CHAPTER TEN

"WHAT DO YOU MEAN?" HARRIET was trying to catch up. Marigold talked so fast, she wasn't certain she understood the gist of the message. "You've found a building, you haven't seen the realtor, and on one walk around the premises you have decided?" Concern raised its nosey head. "You aren't moving, are you?" Feeling sudden relief when her daughter said, no, they weren't moving, she wondered that Marigold called her at all and was more than happy she did. Maybe they were beginning to think a permanent relationship was a good thing; after all she loved Pumpkin with all her heart. No. Quickly she corrected her own thoughts; she had vowed to call her grandson by his name even if there were confusing times in the presence of his father. Matthew the father, baby Matthew, the son, for now, but what would they do when baby Matt was six years old? She would think on that later. For now, Marigolds assurance they would not move relieved her anxiety. She continued to listen to her daughter.

"Of course, if I can help in any way, I will be glad too." Marigold's laughter sounded in her ear. "Yes, yes, Hattie and I will continue to keep little Matt while you work. We love him." She couldn't refrain from asking, "How does Matt feel about this?" Her own laughter was spontaneous when Marigold said she had Matt in the basement doing an oil painting and might not let him out for several weeks.

On Monday, Marigold met with the Gallery owner to discuss leaving. Mr. Garrett was an elderly man whose wife was in the first stage of Alzheimer disease. "We have no children to carry on our work, Marigold. Perhaps it is time, to close shop and take care of

Miriam. Who knows, with the medication perhaps her disease will halt for a time and we could travel a bit." With that thought his sad eyes brightened. "It's a terrible disease. I've friends going through the same, and one tells me his wife no longer recognizes him, in fact she chooses others over him when he goes to visit. Sad. Very sad."

"I'm sorry, Mr. Garrett. You deserve to travel. Sometimes life doesn't seem fair. I'm truly sorry."

"No. You mustn't be sorry. It's the season of our lives, not yours. You must find your own niche and go with it." He smiled, "You've been a great help. Before you, we considered closing shop and now we must. Unless, you would consider carrying on, we could arrange for you to rent this building."

"I would love to continue the Art Gallery, Mr. Garrett, but I think it's time to move to a new location and that is my next step. I have an appointment. After that, I'll let you know; if you are sure you can keep the Gallery open with Haley at the helm, because this is a bit sudden."

"We've been considering for three years, now," he replied. "Go to your appointment with my blessing."

Within the hour she was touring the building she and Matt had found on the Main Street entrance. "Why did the previous owner leave this property?"

"It seems he was involved with money laundering."

"Money laundering? How does that work?" She was astonished, was this bad news? She hoped not.

The realtor stopped walking and stood staring at her with a curious expression. "I really don't think you or I want to know. It's illegal and from what I'm seeing with the former occupant of this place… it doesn't sound like his future looks too bright."

"What about the property. Is there a stigma attached to it, due to the circumstance?"

"You mean, is the law going to confiscate the property?" He shook his head. "No, this property is owned by one of our judges. Can you imagine that? This fellow with the car dealership thought he could pull off money laundering due to who owned the property and right under the Judges nose. I know the Judge and since the problem evolved, he said he should have been suspicious when not one car left the lot, the fellow just moved them around. The judge had to recuse himself from the case."

"On what grounds? I need assurance there will be no legal issues if I purchase this property."

"The Judge could recuse because he had personal financial interest in this property and only rented it to the car dealership. Let us say he did not want anyone questioning his impartiality to rule fairly. If the jurors thought he had made up his mind about the dealer being a bad person, that's one thing but if the judge has already formed an opinion whether the person is guilty or not, wouldn't that go against the grain? Our Judges are presumed to be fair in the law and impartial to all who enter the court."

"Aren't they both the same?" She questioned.

"Not really. We can each realize the character of a person, but that doesn't make him guilty of a crime until he is proven guilty. Maybe he's bad but he was twenty miles away when the crime happened.

Marigold's mind was in a spin. Matt would be cautious. Who would know the legal aspects of this situation? A second opinion, maybe even a third were needed. Lord, help me, she was silently pleading as the realtor walked with her through the building, explaining the oil on the floor in one area was probably spilt there to make the area and the business appear credible. Harriet and Andrew came to her mind. Really? She questioned the Lord. There they stood, in her mind, staring back at her. All right she agreed.

She thought about the realtor's statement as she drove home, her mind flitting to Matt's mother, who would not bend and seemed incapable of allowing her own grandchild's mother a place in the family. For all she had been through with Matt's father nearly dying, Marigold thought she would see the folly of grudges kept and at least make an effort to know her son's wife, but she wouldn't. Rejection stung and words were a two edged sword that continued to hurt. "She has no place in our lives," Matt's mother had said. "The girl down the road fits your lifestyle; this one will take you to your grave." Harsh. How could anyone be so cruel that loved their son? Sweet precious son of her own, Marigold loved Pumpkin. He was everything she longed for in a child, sweet temperament, loving and smart. Now, Harriet was adamant she call him another name before he started Kindergarten. While that was a long way off, she wondered could they call him M. J., the initials of his name, Matthew John?

Haley would be wondering if she were returning to the Gallery. Today, she wasn't. If Harriet had the time, she needed advice. It would be good, if she timed her visit to Harriet's when Andrew was most likely to show. For the remainder of afternoon, she would park her car out of view and go downstairs and pick up a paint brush and see if she still had one iota of talent in her hands. Street scenes were in. Marigold began a sketch of South Park where the geese swam year round. She would paint it in medium shades and let the brush marks define.

It was five fifteen when she emerged to peer across the lots to Harriet's and see the old clunker Andrew was driving these days as he worked with the poor of the city; according to the Judges jurisdiction; Andrew must work with the poor who could not afford an attorney, therefore, he would give back to the city in order to keep from going to prison. She imagined they appreciated his old car.

Tripping along, with stain on her fingers from holding the artist brush, she wondered that she was seeking advice from a woman she once thought a miserable cold hearted winch and Andrew, a conniving ex-husband to her friend. She remembered Anne often upset by his shenanigans in regard to little Andy, their son. Maybe a leopard could change its spots, wasn't that one of Harriet's old sayings? A grin covered her face, now as she was reminded she and Harriet had dealt each other some pretty cold blows, too.

She knocked twice and walked in. "Oh, my, is something wrong?" Harriet rose out of her chair, "Our baby is still in his nap." Marigold motioned for her to sit back down.

"Nothing's wrong. I need advice. Where's Andrew?" She saw Harriet's puzzled frown. "Really, nothing's wrong. I went through the building I was telling you about but I want to be sure there is no problem."

"He and Anne have Andy in the garden. They are watering his flower. You know the one we planted." Harriet always felt she had to go slow with Marigold, fearing she would run away. "Tell me about the building."

"It's a strand building, metal siding that looks like wood and the lot around it presently is all gravel, but that could change. I tell you where it is, down where Main Street leads off to River Drive, once a car dealership."

"I haven't a clue."

Andrew came into the room, followed by Anne and their son. "What about the car dealership. I hear rumors."

Marigold explained the situation, "Do you think there could be legal problems for me if I buy the property? I understand the previous occupant used it for illegal purposes."

"Let me look into it and I'll get back to you. I truly doubt too many have jumped on to it, yet, because of what you have just told me. But," he sighed, a deep heavy relieving sigh, "If it means anything to you, the Judge mentioned is the one who set me on the right track, otherwise I'd be wearing regulation clothes, looking out a barred window and wondering why I ever did wrong?"

"And why did you?" Anne poked him in the ribs. "You put me through the grinder."

"You mean I put you through the fire, right?" Andrew grinned, leaning over to buss a kiss on her cheek.

"Can you trust him, Anne?" Marigold eyed Andrew through squinted eyes. "That's a lot of water under the bridge. You better watch it buster, you got the whole group to contend with if you hurt her again."

Andrew was laughing. "Don't I know it? I've had a warning from every *one* of you. You're like a pack of animals guarding your own."

"And don't you forget it." Marigold glanced at Anne. "Give him a while longer to see if he holds."

On Saturday, Marigold called Harriet. "Matt's agreed to keep Pumpkin, if you want to ride down to the place with me. We might figure out what to do with the landscape, so it doesn't look like a car dealer's."

Delighted, Harriet was waiting outside when Marigold pulled in. "Thank you, for asking me."

"Who else?" Grinning, Marigold added, "they're all tied up. No, honestly, I thought of you first."

"Well, that's certainly the way we used to go at it. I'm relieved that's over." Harriet studied her daughter's profile, wondering if she had resembled the girl at that age. "So, have you bought it? Andrew said he saw no future problems, didn't he?"

"It is in Sale Pending stage, Andrew is checking previous owners, making certain there are no liens against it, the usual, but yeah, I think so. Sadly, I'm using money that comes to me from Mom and Dad dying, but they would be happy knowing it will be a blessing to their daughter's livelihood."

"What if Matt decided to return to the farm to help his father?"

"He says that's not likely with his mother's state of mind that I'm not suitable for their son."

"That's pretty harsh." Harriet felt the blow to her own system. "I'm sorry for them, happy for me."

Minutes later, Harriet gave the building her best report. "At least its sound. You should never have to replace that roof. The colors are a bit disturbing on the outside but once you add a few facades, hang a few plants and grow a patch of grass around the front, it will warm up to business."

"You mean like Cracker Barrell. No one would ever make the comparison. This looks more like a two story with the Old Chapparel bent, don't you think?" She eyed the color. "What if we painted it?"

"You don't like the outside color, either?"

"I hate it."

"Me, too." Harriet's grin matched Marigolds. "First time we ever solely agreed," they said together. "The floors good. I'm surprised they have the wood look, wide plank is in. A few hanging lights, you know, on chains."

"Vintage bordering on Victorian," Marigold nodded. "We're on track. When can we get started?"

"Do you trust Hattie with Matthew John?"

"Matthew John, huh?" That sultry look, Marigold saved for enlightening moments, covered her face. "Sounds a bit large for a little boy, doesn't it? Matthew John. I guess my Pumpkin will grow to it."

"You sure you have the funds to start this business? I can help you."

"Harriet, the lives of my parents were worth more than the price of this building. I can renovate within reason and fill the place with stock. Now, if I can just keep Matt in that basement. Should he break an arm on construction work, I'll have to kill him."

"Are his paintings really going to be a huge part of this enterprise?"

"You tell me, what did you think of Bitty's Plow Boy?"

"Outstanding. I could smell the dirt." The two laughed. It was a beginning of cohort consortia.

CHAPTER ELEVEN

D R. ANTHONY WAS STUDYING CHESTER'S records. "Amelia," he called to the outer room. "Get Dr. Franklin on the phone, please. Seems there's been a mistake in what I'm seeing in his report and in what our new patient has told us." The conversation was lengthy and Dr. Anthony, as he placed the phone was as confused as when he first saw the report. He glanced at the clock. Mr. Mayfield would arrive shortly.

The niceties were covered. Dr. Anthony understood Chester Mayfield was the chief of Police in the nearby Cape. The lady with him was his wife. He had undergone a surgical procedure, two years prior, which was to remove the prostate. Recently, a PSA test revealed a higher than usual level of protein, thus an appointment was made.

"Mr. Mayfield, your urologist has referred you to me because your PSA reading reached 14.0. You already understand a prostate-specific antigen of that amount often signifies cancer of the prostate, and Dr. Field ruled out a urinary infection as the cause although your record states you have urinary inconsistencies during the night. You are up often. Is that correct?" His patient nodded.

"We need to discuss what is listed in your records. What is your understanding of the surgery pertaining to your problem?"

"Dr. Fields sent me to an elderly oncologist who recommended I do nothing that all men will sooner or later have a problem with the prostate but if it does occur it is a slow process before becoming a serious matter. But I asked him to pursue the matter farther than his own opinion and he did."

"I am puzzled that there are no records from the oncologist, only what your primary care physician has sent me." He glanced at the paper. "Dr. Fields."

"Yes, sir, as I understand, Dr. Franklin has since died and there was no locating the records of his patients."

"That must have seemed very strange to you, but I suppose stranger things have happened." Dr. Fields rose to sit on the edge of his desk, peering into Chester's face. "Now, it is your understanding you had a prostatectomy. Meaning, the removal of the culprit that was causing your PSA levels to rise in the first place. But, before that you were administered a Lupron shot which was given to slow down the process of the cancer and give you time to consider which treatment you would receive and in time a second and third Lupron shot was administered by your urologist, keeping the PSA levels intact. Until now."

"Yes sir." Chester was beginning an uneasy feeling that more was wrong than he imagined.

"Well, sir. From what I glean from these papers, you had a biopsy where a sample of tissue was removed and the cells inspected by a pathologist. Your biopsy determined the cancer began near the site of the biopsy and had not spread further according to both a CT scan and a bone scan the doctor ordered thereafter." Dr. Fields arose to walk around the desk, to point to a chart on the wall. "This is what the ordinary healthy prostate looks like and that's what we want. Unfortunately, when cancer cells present, we see pictures similar to this scale."

"We have good news and bad news." He sighed heavily. "I've learned through inquiry, your oncologist, Dr. Franklin has indeed died and not many of his patients were aware Alzeheimers was claiming him in the last years of his practice and becoming fearful he would lead his patients down the wrong path, Dr. Franklin gave up his practice with the intent to retire but unfortunately, he died soon after and what happened to his records, no one knows. Such is the path Alzeheimers takes, it is savage. Now, that may be your good news, the part that the cancer was contained near the biopsy sight."

"However, you did not have a prostactectomy. Evidently, the Lupron shots controlled the testosterone which would have fed the cancer. Then, you failed to return to Dr. Franklin when his staff no longer answered the phone and you thinking everything was in control reverted back to your primary doctor, Dr. Fields. Am I correct? And he hooked you up with an urologist in case there was further need of Lupron?"

"Yes sir," Chester was squirming inside. He had so many issues to deal with he had let his own health slide, all the while trying to coerce Bitty into marrying him. The signs were there all along and now he had to deal with them, but what if treatment was too late?"

"I believe, Mr. Mayfield, we will sit you up for both bone and CT scan, next week. Today, I want lab work and an EKG. I'll expect to see you back here the day after the tests are done and we will go from there."

Bitty's head was in a spin. She hadn't said a word, only listened. There were no questions left unasked in her way of thinking. Maybe because of her Chester had failed to recognize the signs of his body. She felt she had contributed greatly to his problem. She glanced down at the pamphlets the doctor's nurse handed them as they left, saying, "Take time to go through these pages, these are the newest treatments available."

"You are awfully quiet," Chester said as they were driving home. "What are you thinking?"

"I'm wondering how much to blame I am, why didn't I see something was wrong?"

"It could never be your fault, Bitty. If I couldn't see it, how could you?" He sighed, settling dejectedly into the seat. "Tonight, after I check on everyone at the station, will you help me go through those pamphlets? I guess we have to decide on which treatment, if there's reason to go through with it."

"Oh, Chester," Bitty's eyes filled with tears. She reached for his hand. "You can't make it sound so fatal. We haven't come this far, to lose each other."

Pulling his hand free, he reached across to pull her closer to the center console. "I didn't mean to upset you. I guess I'm just upset inside, myself, and I should keep it from you."

"Don't ever do that. I couldn't stand it."

"I'm glad I have you, Bitty. Life's pretty tough going it alone."

"AUNT HARRIET," RUTHIE STOOD BEFORE her. Andy was asleep and Matthew John was being rocked by Hattie. "I know it's almost time for Bitty and Uncle Chester, but I don't know why I stayed with you today, instead of going with them. They always take me."

"Sweetheart," Harriet drew the child into the chair beside her. "Sometimes adults have business they must take care of and it would be boring to you. Is it so hard to stay here with Andy and Matthew John?"

"No, ma'am." She watched as Harriet pulled a book from beneath a stack of papers. "I know that story, it's about a little girl and seven dwarfs. They do everything. Just because they are little, doesn't mean a thing."

"You are so right," Harriet agreed. "Have you seen what Marigold is doing at the new business?"

Ruthie giggled. "She's painting things in different places on the walls. The first time you saw her feathered van you didn't like it."

"No, not in the beginning," Harriet agreed. "Because I didn't understand and not understanding I didn't see the faces in the feathers like you did, Ruthie. Let's see, there were several; Mercy, Hope, and Goodness."

"There were more," Ruthie yawned, as her eyes closed and she joined the other children in naptime.

Bitty found them sitting together in the big chair. Harriet's glasses were pushed up on her nose and her arm was around Ruthie, holding her close. In the room across the hall, Bitty saw Andrew asleep on his bed and beneath the curtained top crib, Matthew John lay on his stomach with his behind pushed up in the air. Bitty smiled for the first time that day as she reached out to waken Harriet. She could hear Hattie stirring in the kitchen. "Harriet," she whispered, "Can you lay Ruthie down and come out into the garden so we can talk? I know Hattie will listen for the boys to wake up."

Yawning, Harriet followed. "Is something wrong? Well, I know it is but I mean is there more?"

"Chester had blood work and an EKG. It seems his heart is pumping strong. But we found out today, the minor surgery Chester had was only a biopsy, not a prostatectomy." She saw Harriet's frown. "I know. It's a long story." She explained the circumstance of Chester's medical records and added, "He will have to make up his mind as to which treatment he wants, by this time next week."

CHAPTER TWELVE

"I DON'T WANT TO WEAR the purple dress," Ruthie whined. "I want to wear the white one with the sash Daniel gave me."

"Sweetums, why are you being so grumpy? It's not like you. I was hoping you would wear the purple because we will all be coordinated, not looking like we came out of a cramped barrel."

"Now why would you say that," angrily, Ruthie stomped her foot, then slumped down onto her bed, tears rushing to her eyes as she said, remorsefully, "I'm sorry Mommy. I do feel grumpy and I don't know why."

"Shall we stay home from church? This is not like you, Sweetums. I know you. I think we should stay".

"No, I want to go. I will be nicer. I'll wear the purple dress and the pink sash. Go on and get the twins ready."

Ruthie eyed the dress with a wicked eye. She was always nice but today she felt mean. No, that's not nice, maybe she felt sad. No, she didn't feel nice at all. Her head hurt and her throat. She felt of her head, it was cool, no fever. She sighed. Maybe she just wasn't ever nice at all.

They drove to church in silence. She couldn't figure out why they seemed worried; Aunt Harriet, Anne and Andrew, Marigold and Matt and even Mommy and Daniel. Something was wrong with everyone. Lulled by the cars movement and the sound of the motor, the twins were asleep. She closed her eyes, it might be enough time to pray and ask God what was wrong with everyone and her, too.

Brother Joe met them at the door. That too, was strange, usually he was milling around up front but today it was as if he were waiting on someone, then she saw Uncle Chester and Bitty entering the sanctuary. Brother Joe hurried to meet them taking Uncle Chester and Daniel away, as he searched for Matt and motioned for him to follow. She wondered where they disappeared to as Marigold came hurrying from leaving baby Matthew John in the Nursery workers capable hands. Even behind their smiles, Ruthie sensed unrest. When Harriet and Anne arrived with Andrew and little Andy behind them, she began to settle down. Everyone was here, in attendance at Christ Church. The organ sounded and the music became a calming force as Ruthie read the words from the screen on the Podium.

"Please stand for the reading of God's word as we turn to Jeremiah Chapter one, verses four through seven. The word of the Lord came to me; before I formed you in the womb I knew you, before you were born I dedicated you, a prophet to the nations I appointed you. Ah, Lord, God, I said. I do not know how to speak, I am too young. But the Lord answered me, Do not say, I am too young. To whomever I send you, you shall go; whatever I command you, you shall speak."

Brother Joe began, "This scripture explains the calling of Jeremiah to be a prophet; his preparation for a life's work. This is God's sit down with a young prophet, telling him, I knew you before you were born, long before you were conceived, I've worked with the people behind you for generations, your parents and their parents. I've given you God loving parents that have taught you the way of salvation and righteous living. Had I not, how could you explain such to a world in need?"

"This is your gift, Jeremiah, my preparation of you, spawned through generations of believing people. Don't tell me you are too young. I am with you. That's the difference; you have me to rely on. You will go where I send you and speak the message I give you to deliver."

"How young are we when the Lord speaks to our heart and we make a commitment to live for Him?"

"How often do we go against the grain, questioning what we are facing? Is it human nature to question? We say, here I am Lord, trusting you and now look at what is happening to me? Is this something you want me to go through, and tell me Lord, what purpose does it serve?"

"Remember the verse, "Before you were born, I dedicated you." Brother Joe's voice softened. "I knew you. I loved you. I considered who your parents would be. It was important you have parents dedicated to me. That they love you, as I have loved you."

"Do we realize, whatever we are going through, our Heavenly Father is there? We are never too young to know this. No matter the age, if we face difficult situations, decisions, if you please, He is there. He knows every move you are going to make in life."

"I knew a couple, on up in the years of life, considering a move from a rural area to be near a hospital. Due to health issues and so as not to burden their children with having to leave jobs to drive them, their thoughts were we will be closer to whatever it takes to fill our needs within a driving distance we can make ourselves. But the husband was fretting, we are leaving our children behind, he said. I cannot bear it. The wife replied, but if we stay here and you continue to work the many hours you do, our children won't have a father and you thought it best we move while we could be independent and not have to call on them. They made the move. But the husband continued to fret until finally the wife in frustration asked, 'do you not think, God knows every move we make in life? Surely He has a plan to watch over us, doesn't he?' Pastor Joe smiled, leaning toward his people, "Within two years, both of their children moved down the road from the parents, and the wife asked the husband, 'Now, where would we be, had we not prayed about it and felt God's prompt to move?'

"Today, are you trusting in the Lord? Are you sharing the burdens of your heart with your Heavenly Father? The scripture reminds us, before we were born, God set up a plan for us, which included his great love. If he created us special, unique and dedicated, then would he not entertain our staying in touch? No, He does not abandon us. He is there, for the asking, to help us in the purpose of our lives."

"We are never too young or too old to put our lives in the hands of the Lord. Can you hear him calling? Can you hear him saying, "Why I knew you before you were born, I laid out a plan for your life but I also gave you freedom of choice to make your life what you want it to be. No, you are not too young to come to me, nor too old. I've been waiting. Have you made the move?"

◆

LISTENING, MARIGOLD COMPARED THE WORDS of the sermon to the huge decision in her life. She was spending an enormous amount of money she received from the accidental death of her parents. She had prayed, the contract was being prepared for signing. Yes, she believed God had given her an opportunity. Had she fret? Yes. But she prayed and God gave her the answer.

Ruthie's heart was pounding beneath the light fold of fabric of her dress. "You are never too young." Brother Joe's words went around in her head. She traced her finger in swirls on her bible, listening. She believed in Jesus. She knew he died on the cross for the sins of the world. She had not done terrible wrongs but she sometimes found herself not pleasing to others and God saw everything. God had given her a gift. Then, she decided. If God cared enough about her to give her a gift, she must give back to Him. What did she have to give? She doubted God wanted her toys, He was creator. She would give him herself. It was what was wrong with her. She had thought about it long enough. She had to do it.

Chester with Bitty on his right and Daniel on the left felt unsettled; no one knew what the other was thinking as they listened to Brother Joe. Salvation was the root of the sermon. If you had not made the choice, it was time. God knew every twist and turn in your life. So what were you going to do with your life? *He knows your decisions, the choices you must make.* Bitty reached for his hand and gave it a squeeze. It was as if she knew his thoughts. He breathed a sigh of thanksgiving. He had to do it. Jesus was calling.

The altar call was under way when Ruthie stood before her mother. "Momma, I need to go, up there, to the front."

Glancing down, Ellen wondered but asked anyway. "Why, do you need to go to the front, Sweetums?"

"Brother Joe said I am not too young. Jesus has spoken to my heart. I am supposed to go."

"Do you know why, Sweetums?" Ellen was sitting now, peering into her daughter's serious eyes.

"I need to be saved. I've asked Jesus into my heart. I asked him to forgive me of my sins. God is my heavenly father and he knows my heart. Brother Joe, said he knew me before I was born. God did."

"Ruthie," Chief of Police, Chester Mayfield, leaned across Daniel and asked, "Would you like to walk to the front with me? I believe Jesus expects something from me, today?"

Smiling, Ruthie took the Captain's hand and stepped out of the pew. Ellen and Bitty followed. It was an exceptional day of rejoicing in the lives of the group that worshiped together at Christ Church. Ruthie sighed with relief. She hadn't quite figured out why she was so grumpy that morning, except she had dreamed a most unusual dream during the night and she knew being five wasn't too young, as the people in her dream had reminded her. No, she listened and she knew when Jesus called you were supposed to answer. The people in the dream had made her grumpy. If she were older, perhaps she wouldn't have gone to church but she was young and the scripture said you were never too young and Uncle Chester said you were never too old to accept salvation.

"Are you sorry for your sins?" Ruthie was asked. "Do you believe Jesus died for your sins?" Uncle Chester also replied, "Yes," to both questions. She was glad they walked the aisle together. She had a feeling the devil knew she was ready to receive salvation. He probably planted those people in her dream. The grumpiness was gone. She felt as happy inside as Uncle Chester looked.

CHAPTER THIRTEEN

T HERE WAS A LOT OF laughter coming from the kitchen. Hattie had prepared a great meal for Harriet's guest and then left to spend the day with her family. Harriet had told her not to come, but she came anyway. There was fried chicken, mashed potato and gravy, green beans, fresh corn and a salad that looked absolutely appetizing, by the women's standards. "Let's see what all she has in this creation," Marigold was saying as Anne stepped into the room where Ruthie sat with a book. Harriet had invited the Gipson family and the daughter was sitting quietly with Ruthie. She didn't look up when Anne entered. The twins, Matthew John and Andy had tired from playing with the children at church and were now asleep in Harriet's room.

"How do you feel, Ruthie?" Anne planted a kiss on Ruthie's cheek.

"Good." Ruthie smiled at Anne. "How do you feel?"

"I want to be baptized when you are, Ruthie." Anne waited for Haley Gipson to raise her head but she didn't. There was something about the young woman she didn't understand. She was different.

"Why didn't you go up with me and Uncle Chester?"

"I didn't want to take away from your special commitment to the Lord."

"Oh, Anne, He has room for all of our commitsments."

"Yes, I know. The word is commitment, Sweetheart. It means we promise something; in this case we give our self to the Lord. Did Brother Joe explain, baptism doesn't save you, it's our way of showing the world we have changed and we are walking a new path, following Jesus."

Ruthie nodded, "Momma said you already gave your heart to the Lord, why didn't you get baptized?" Her somber eyes rest on Anne. Now she wanted everyone to receive the Lord.

"I'm going to talk to Brother Joe this week, Ruthie. It's past time. I intended to do it earlier."

Ruthie appeared to be in thought, her eyes on Haley. Harriet was calling everyone to be seated for lunch. If Haley knew Jesus she seemed to have forgotten him and she needed him. A lot.

"Oh, you sit a beautiful table, Harriet." Dorothy Gipson's delight was in her face, wreathed in smile.

"Nothing do our Harriet, but use the china, the silver and the crystal," Marigold piped up, her own laughter filling the room. "Once I used paper plates and orange cups and I heard she thought I was doing Halloween instead of Thanksgiving. Maybe it was the black tights Ruthie and I wore, I dunno."

"Who told you?" An indignant Harriet asked. "I don't remember saying any of that out loud."

"No, but you thought it." Marigold hung an arm around Harriet. "I know you did."

"Matt, would you bless the food, please, and make retribution for your terrible wife."

"Now that, I can't do." Matt grinned. "Let's bow our heads. "Heavenly Father, creator of the Universe, we bow before you, now, asking your blessing on the food Harriet provides even as we thank you for the blessing of friend and family, and the precious Word we have heard in this morning's service. We ask Lord, that we have ample time to put your word to use in our lives that we may be a witness to others of your love, your grace and mercy. Thank you for Ruthie and the Captain receiving salvation and for all the good you give into our lives. In Your gracious name. Amen."

"Marigold will delegate seating," Harriet said. "I'll bring in the hot rolls and all will be ready." She smiled. "I'm excited to have you as guests in my home. I pray we will continue this time of sharing."

Grateful she was seated by the little girl and not too closely situated to the adults, especially Anne or Andrew, Haley served herself as the food was passed around and for the most part she remained quiet. On the other hand, her father's voice boomed through the table conversation, as always enjoying people, food and conversation, while her mother's soft voice comforted Haley's anxiousness. Ruthie smiled sweetly and answered appropriately when asked a question, but Haley could tell her mind was on other matters. Strange, she thought, in one so young. And her mind returned to the pastor's message. 'Why worry and fret when you were created according to a master plan, even before the womb, designated and loved by your heavenly father? *Why' indeed and where was he, her heavenly father, when she was sent to prison? Soul sick, Haley turned the matter away from her heart and listened to the idle conversation.*

Harriet's delicious lemon ice box pie had been served on chilled glass plates, a sprig of parsley to accept the color. The table settings, the food, could have been on a page in a ladies' magazine, and now the pie.

Ruthie noticed Haley staring at the parsley. "It's a bitter," she said, meeting Haley's puzzled expression. "Aunt Harriet told me and Andy, it's a bitter, but it's a sweet bitter, which means when you tastes it after the lemon pie it will kind of take away the heaviness of the lemon pie."

"I always wondered why those little green sprigs were on plates."

"Now you know." Ruthie grinned. "She said if your stomach is hurting, the parsley helps with that, too."

"I think I should try it, then." Haley couldn't keep from smiling back. "How old are you, anyway?"

"I'm five but I feel six because I read more than most kids my age."

"We have a lot in common, I like to read. Is the book you were reading earlier a good one?"

"It is. It's about a secret garden, and it's printed in words for kids. When we finish, would you like to see Harriet's garden?" Ruthie leaned to whisper to Haley, "See the man sitting by Aunt Harriet? He used to be a doctor, now he is a gardener."

"I'd love to hear that story, Ruthie."

They walked through the garden. Haley offered to help clear the table but a robust girl of color had swept through the door, coming from Mrs. Becker's kitchen. She was fully dressed in a maid's black uniform, her black hair in a roll at the back of her neck and a smile that would melt the heart of a witch.

"Why Latana Mae, what are you doing here, and in uniform?"

"My grandmamma, Hattie, sent me and I don' ask her if I could wear her uniform. I never had a nice uniform like this. Where I work at the hotel, they tell us a pair of black slacks, a nice blouse will do."

"And you being the night time manager wish for other?" Harriet arose to hug Latana Mae. "What exactly did you have planned, or I should say did Hattie tell you to do?"

"Why, I'm to buss the table after you and your guests retire from it, stack the silverware, because you don't want it in the dish washer, nor the fine crystal or the china. Is that right, Miz Harriet?"

"You may put the glasses and the dishes in the dishwasher, but since the silverware has hollow handles I will do those later, myself." She hugged the girl again. "This one is a college graduate. I've known her since she came into the world and Hattie brought her when there was need to, and we'd not accomplish a lot on those days because this baby was so cute and full of antics."

Latana Mae smiled, her arm coming around Harriet in a hug. "This one," she replied, smiling, "funded my college education. Now I'm studying for my Master and that is why I work nights as a hotel manager." She glanced around at the empty plates. "Now, when you finish that pie, scoot on into Miz Harriet's great room and I'll see to everything else."

Shortly, Ruthie led Haley through the garden. "I thought Latana Mae was pretty in her uniform, did you?" Haley nodded, as Ruthie asked, "Have you ever worn a uniform? I haven't."

"Unfortunately, Ruthie, I have." They stood staring into the goldfish pond, the stream of water making a soft gurgling sound. "This is a peaceful garden. My Mother has a garden behind our house. She enjoys working in it at the end of the day."

"What does she do during the day? I stay with Bitty and we garden, too. She lives next door, then there's Marigold and Matt and Pumpkin who live in the third house. Do you like working with Marigold?"

"I do." Haley had wondered where Marigold and her family lived, but she tried not to ask questions. If she didn't, then perhaps no one would ask questions and expect replies concerning her life.

"Had you rather not talk, Haley?" Ruthie's perception was on guard. "I have the gift of discernment. Do you know what your gift is?"

"You mean, gifts, as in scripture, from the Bible?" Ruthie nodded. "No, Ruthie, I don't know. Maybe, there's one on getting in trouble?" She grinned and Ruthie did too. "Just kidding, tell me what your gift does for you."

"I feel things. Momma says that means I'm sensitive to other people's feelings. I know you were sad, is that the word, or confused with the sermon this morning. I felt it and then at the table you were very quiet, even if everyone is new to you, you are older and they wouldn't care if you talked."

"I don't want to talk, Ruthie," Haley confessed. "Once, something happened to me and I'm still mulling it around in my head trying to figure it out."

"Why don't you let Jesus have your problem?" Haley stared at this child. "It's not that easy."

"Why? All you have to do is talk to him."

"I talked to Him for months and nothing happened." Haley confessed, wondering why she was having this discussion with a five year old kid. "So I know about talking to Him, it doesn't work." Bitterness engulfed her soul, swarmed around her and carried her through the void of yesterday when nothing happened into today when she listened to the sermon and wondered about the pastor's words.

"You are here," Ruthie whispered. "What if it is all part of God's plan just like Brother Joe said?" Ruthie's eyes were luminous. "What if the best part of your life is just beginning?" She was standing peering up into Haley's eyes, her own holding an ancient truth, wisdom beyond her age. She reached for Haley's hand, "Come on, there's more to see down at the end of the garden by the fence."

For a moment, Haley hesitated, allowing the goose bumps to clear her system. "How old did you say you are?" She heard the giggle, felt the tightening of the little girl's hand as she replied, *five but I feel like six.'* Giggling herself, Haley said, "You know, Ruthie, this is the best part of the day, being with you.

"WERE YOU UNCOMFORTABLE, HALEY?" HER mother's question brought her back from the inner workings of her mind, as they rode home from Mrs. Becker's. "You were so quiet, I wondered if you wanted to leave, even before the lunch began."

"I did at first," Haley admitted, "But the little girl, Ruthie, showed me the garden, we talked and for some reason I began to feel at ease. You know, they are a very strange group of people."

"Peculiar people," Harper boomed. "The Bible says his people will be called a peculiar people, and these seem to be genuine Christians."

"Does that mean they never make a mistake, Dad?" She hadn't intended her words to be edged with sarcasm but they were. "I mean, if they knew my history, are they so nice they would shut me out, maybe keep me away from the little girl as a bad influence?"

"No," Dorothy's voice, soft and loving, replied. "I think they would draw you near and help you through your time of uncertainty, when you feel things are difficult."

"I don't want to talk about it." Haley withdrew to her shell of protection. "I'm fine." But silently Haley remembered the peace that had come into her in the garden as Ruthie held her hand.

Though the Gipson's left early, the others lingered, finally to gather in Harriet's garden to view the newest blooming plants. Ruthie led the way down the path holding Andy's hand. Marigold swapped the diaper bag she was carrying for Matthew John, whose teething problem had reared its ugly head.

"Ma's garden is beautiful," Matt whispered, knowing someway Marigold would poke him in the ribs.

"Look, Farm boy, you may pray a pretty prayer for one so young, but you don't get away with foolery. I'm on to you. I know your shortcomings."

"Me?" He grinned. "I'm not the one put the baby bottle nipples in the lower tray of the dishwasher and melted them."

"Those are not shortcomings, those are accidents."

"Well thought, I guess, but *it was I* who got up at two in the morning and went to the nearest *all nighter* and bought new ones."

"What am I hearing about dishwashers?" Ellen and Dan were bringing up the rear, a child in each arm.

"You don't want to know." Marigold said, laughing. "Another one of those *baby* stories."

"We're having more than a few of those." Dan and Ellen exchanged glances. "But now, our oldest," Dan said proudly, "seemed to hit it off with the Gipson's daughter, who may have felt a bit out of her element with us old married folks."

Harriet had been silent to this point, "I've been in situations where I was a bit uncertain, maybe our united front is a bit intimidating. We do talk easily among ourselves."

"I wonder if it is our speaking about God's love that troubles her." Ellen offered. "She almost withdraws. I felt it and reminded myself in the days to come to pray for her."

Marigold was fully aware of the reason Haley was quiet, but it was not hers to reveal. "Why don't you pray for her now, Ellen, and we can each add her name to our daily prayer list."

As every head bowed, Ellen realized, as a whole, they had felt the girls need. She began, "Father, we seek you now, asking in your name for this young lady, that whatever matters of the heart are troubling, whatever her need; you know already and we are asking as a loving body of believers that you touch Haley with your mercy and give her comfort and peace; the comfort and peace we experience when we come to your throne of grace, seeking the answer to our own problems. We thank you for a day of blessing through worship and fellowship and we ask you to go with us through another week of life. Help us to realize you are ever present in our lives, forgive us of our sins and keep us safe beneath the wings of your care. Amen.

"What did you and Haley talk about?" Ellen asked as they were riding home.

In the back seat, between the two sleeping babies, Ruthie replied. "We talked about Jesus. I told her to let Jesus have her problem." She closed her eyes and was asleep, there was nothing more to say.

CHAPTER FOURTEEN

"WE DID A LOT OF praying, today," Bitty said as she and Chester prepared for bed, "First at church, then lunch and for the new girl. Did anyone take you aside, secretly and pray with you?"

Chester grinned, turning out the light and settling into the bed. By the moonlight streaming through the window he could see Bitty as he reached across to pull her closer. "You know they did. Matt and Daniel and I stepped into Brother Joe's office before services began. Brother Joe pulled a few deacons in and they agreed in prayer. Even laid hands on me and I felt God's power through those men."

"I thought so."

"As Ellen says, God works in mysterious ways because by Brother Joe having special prayer for me, it made it easier for me to walk the aisle and give my heart to Jesus."

"I thought you did that as a kid."

"I thought so too, but I hadn't stayed faithful in attendance, I strayed away. It seems only fitting I re-commit myself to the Lord, don't you think and be baptized?"

"Baptism doesn't save you, does it?" She moved into the hollow of Chester's body, yawning. "I remember Ellen saying it's more of a person showing the world they are a follower, that if one is not ashamed to be named as one of the Lord's people, then he won't be ashamed to call us His own." Her yawning was creating an ebbing to her words. "I can't quote scripture like Ellen does, but I'm beginning to understand it. You know," her voice waned, "You have to make up your mind about treatment."

"I know." Chester's voice held a troubled tone. "Here I am, wanting to walk in the ways of the Lord, trust him, look to him daily for wisdom in whatever I do, and I can't come to terms with this treatment thing." His arm tightened around Bitty. "I've got to know the side effects, Bitty. Will it embarrass you if I ask some really deep questions?" He heard her sigh. "You know what's bothering me. We just got married not too long ago, and now I'm told they will remove my prostate one way or the other and all those old wives tales floating around out there; If they do remove it, I'll pee my pants or wear a diaper in old age, intimacy is threatened, it just goes on and on. I've heard the horror stories."

"Chester, go to sleep. We'll face this tomorrow. Surely, God is greater than all these problems, or we don't need Him."

"That's pretty harsh, Bitty. That may even border on blasphemy." Chester chuckled. "Are you awake?"

"What'd I say?" Bitty tried to rise out of the warmth of the bed, all snuggled up to Chester's body but she felt heavy and her eyelids wouldn't open. "Did I say something wrong?" She tried to rise. "I'll ask forgiveness right now. Oh, mercy."

"It's all right," Chester's laughter came full bloom. "I didn't know I was talking to myself. But, maybe you got a bit of it. Turn out the light, Bitty. You're right; our God is bigger than all our problems." While Bitty slipped back into the warmth of sleep, Chester lay there another hour with a busy mind and open eyes wondering what the doctor would say in tomorrow's visit as he held Bitty closer in his arms wondering if the outcome of his surgery would make a difference in their lives.

THE NURSE CALLED CHESTER'S NAME and led them to Dr. Anthony's office and told them to be seated. Chester's file lay on the desk but they dare not touch it. The appointment was supposed to be at ten o'clock but the doctor was running late.

"Why do doctors put temptation in the way?" Bitty whispered, staring at the file on the desk. "But then, there's not supposed to be anything in that file that you don't already know." She huffed a little frustrated sound. "My blood pressures spikes when I'm sitting in a doctor's office."

"And you talk more," Chester chuckled. "Weren't you the one last night saying we must trust in the Lord?"

"Well, yes," indignantly, Bitty heaved a huge sigh, "But it is hard waiting."

Dr. Anthony chose that moment to appear, shaking hands with them and sitting on the edge of his desk as he picked up the file. "Your PSA level has risen significantly higher, Mr. Mayfield, which denotes going ahead with treatment as quickly as possible. There are a few pros and cons for each treatment but we can discuss that further unless you can tell me today which treatment you are leaning toward."

"I understand Robotic treatment takes fewer days recovery than the open surgery for prostate removal while open prostatectomy lessens reoccurrence but has life changing side effects to consider."

"True. But your goal is more than the time required to heal, Mr. Mayfield. There's a much larger incision with open prostate removal. Data tells us a positive margin of success is twenty three per cent with open Prostatectomy, nineteen percent with laparoscopic and I believe robotic gets a bad rap with only a twelve per cent margin. Now, understand I'm speaking concerning the surgical margin whether any cancer was left or possibly returns. That's not to say the side effects over time are different."

"I noticed you finished the test I ask you to undergo, and on the reports your physical being shows you are in good shape for surgery. Prostatectomy has more of a risk of damage due to the nerves that surround the prostate and rectum which could result in erectile dysfunction and in any surgery to this area there can be potential damage to the urinary tract. That happens because the prostate sits just below the bladder in close proximity to the urethra which responds to many surgeries in strange ways. Now, being newly married, you might want to know, with the right procedure, there shouldn't be danger to those cavernous nerves deep within the penis that warrant preservation of sexual potency after surgery. Same is to be said of the urinary tract and incontinence in the long run of life. In the surgeries I've participated in; the majorities who have chosen open prostatectomy are now experiencing urinary incontinence, meaning frequent trips to the bathroom through the night and more UTI's."

"Each treatment has benefit and each treatment has down fall." He placed the file on top of a stack on his desk and arose. "Do you want me to have my nurse schedule your surgery, or do you need more time?"

They stared at the doctor a moment before Chester replied. "Dr. Anthony, I believe we have chosen the Robotic method. Go ahead and schedule surgery." He knew Bitty was squirming with embarrassment. The doctors words had to be said but Bitty had rather read them than hear them.

ANDREW CLOSED THE DOOR ON the Jet Stream, his favorite name for the old clunker he was able to purchase from of all people, his friend who had sold him the BMW. He remembered their conversation. "Man, you've hit the bottom of the barrel," Jack said, shaking his head wearing a rueful expression. "Never thought I'd see Andrew Graves in anything like this."

"Where'd you get the old girl, anyway?"

"Some ya-hoo traded it in. Can you imagine? It's a wonder they didn't park it on the back lot."

Patting the hood, he hurried on in to Matt's wife's intended purchase. Jack hadn't had to worry over the old car for several months now and it ran like a dream, just looked like a nightmare. He found Marigold, bending over a map of sorts, and she looked up as he approached. "Morning."

"Thank goodness you are on time. The Judge called to say his session ran over, but I wanted to hear from you, are there any legal complications; If I buy this place, the previous people have no holds on it."

"It's clear." Andrew laid his brief case on the wooden barrel, opened it and brought out a sheaf of papers. I ran it all the way back to being built; there are no liens, no legal matters to alter your deal with the Judge. He wouldn't want that either. So, I guess, when he arrives you both sign on the dotted line and we get the process of making it legal started."

"Do we dare begin renovating or must I wait?"

"Normally, I'd say wait, but if it's only cleaning you will be doing," he smiled, "I checked and rechecked. It is clear and with Judge Northcutt, it will go through just fine."

"All right!" Marigold's enthusiasm returned. "High-five." She and Andrew slapped hands together. "I have another call to make and this metal roof hinders clarity, so I'll leave you here with Haley and step out back. You remember Haley, Mr. Gipson's daughter, from Harriet's luncheon?"

Haley turned her back and stared out the window.

After what seemed minutes passed by, being ignored. "You don't like me, do you?" Andrew asked.

"I don't know you."

"I'm clean. I'm serving citizen hood like any normal person," Andrew tried teasing, realizing it wasn't working. Haley had moved toward the door. "I think it was an affront to you, knowing your parents had stashed me in your brother's room. I'm sorry about that, maybe it would've been more interesting if they had moved me into yours." He sighed. "All that girly stuff. Yeah, more interesting."

Haley did an about face. "You had no right to be in my brother's room." Tears smarted behind her lids and her fists were clenched.

"Hey, I meant no har…"

Smack. Right across his face, interrupting his ridiculous attempt to apologize when he didn't mean it at all, Haley was dead center on target.

"Whoa." Marigold returned in time to see Andrew's stunned expression. "Haley. What are you doing?" Astonished, she glanced from one to the other. "He didn't make a pass at you, did he?" She stared at Andrew, "No, he wouldn't. I've seen him look at his ex-wife with those moon-struck eyes." Hands on hips, she glared at the two of them. "It's a good thing my party wasn't available, otherwise I guess you two would have declared war. Now," She demanded. "What is the meaning of this?"

"Let *him* tell you." Haley's voice was surly and rebellious. "I'm sure *he* will make it interesting."

"I, ah, I," Andrew paused to think, now that sense was returning to his mind. "I think I insulted her, not just now but the day I met her at her parent's home, too."

"What did you say?"

"You wouldn't understand."

"Then, Haley, you tell me what happened or why did you slap Andrew."

"You can fire me, if you wish. I'm going home. Mr. Wonderful, here, can help you. I doubt if he has ever got his hands dirty."

"Wait just a minute," Andrew fumed. "I worked with your dad, I bet you wouldn't say that about him, little spoiled rich girl." She was heading toward the door. "You're really a piece of cake, babe."

"Don't call me that. I'm no body's babe and especially not yours."

"And I can certainly see why." Andrew straightened his shirt sleeves, touched his tie. Today he was dressed in his lawyer clothes; tomorrow, if Harper didn't get wind of the run in he had with his daughter, he would be working construction. He couldn't figure out why he had resorted back to his old ways.

They heard the sound of her car starting up, then the crunch of tires on gravel. "Well, I guess I'll be cleaning this big old place all by myself," Marigold said, "Thanks to you." She glanced through the window seeing Haley disappear down the road. "She is supposed to check in with her camp psychologist later this afternoon, I'm betting after this she runs and not to the session."

"I was only teasing her. She's strung as tight as a kite. Does she never bend?" Andrew's frustration sounded in his voice. "Honest, Marigold, I didn't say anything to create or disturb her." Andrew blew out a breath. "I seem to have a strange effect on that young woman."

"You know her history, don't you? After all, you lived in the same house with her parents."

"Yeah, I got bits and pieces of it, but I didn't know the girl and I'm not sure I want too."

"Then get used to seeing her. It seems her parents are switching churches and Harriet has taken a liking to them. I have a feeling we will see her and her family quite often, and at church by the way." She rolled her eyes as if to say, *church, buddy, where people refrain from slapping faces and teasing women.*

"What did you mean by those *moon struck* eyes?"

"Why in the name of good aren't you two remarried?"

"She won't have me back until she's sure I've changed."

"Anne won't have you back until she is sure you've changed?" Marigold repeated. "You must have been a really bad boy." She shrugged, "Not my problem. I guess we'll all wait with Anne."

"Boy," Andrew wiped his forehead. "You all are one mean pack of women."

The Judge was coming up the sidewalk. "Straighten your tie," she said, "and let's get this show on the road."

An hour later the papers were signed. There was a matter of the legal work, which Andrew would handle. Marigold and the Judge shook hands, as he said, "If you ever need anything, Mrs. Langley, feel free to call on me."

When the door closed behind him, Marigold shrugged her shoulders together as she gave a sigh of relief, "I must say it's a bit intimidating doing business with a Judge, but he wasn't a bad sort."

"Now what?" Andrew surveyed the open building. "I've got three hours until I play lawyer again. Tell me what needs doing, and I'll help you."

"Not in those duds. Huh uh, mister. Just trot on down to wherever you go to tackle the paper work and I'll be happy. I want to see everything legal. Cleaning is one thing but for renovation I need security."

The Marigold project, as Harriet called it, began. The building underwent professional painting. "The paints supposed to last twenty years," She told Harriet. An excavator arrived on lot, scraping away the gravel that lay up to the building foundation. Once the gravel was moved back, a local sod service moved in to lay the sod in six foot wide strips. "It looks like ribbons. Oh, my I'll have to water it, until the roots take hold." Next, supplies began to arrive through the back entrance. "Boy these double wide garage doors, do make it easier. Those garden room sets are huge." The hanging baskets appeared outside, dropping from ceiling height chains as the last chandelier was hung inside. The atmosphere bordered between a French boutique and country charm. "It's been done before," Marigold said, feeling proud. "We did this one together, though. I think it smarts, what do you think, Harriet, encouraging the community to bring in the work of their talents will pay off. It's a business of the people offered to the people. Huh?"

"But you must watch what you select, even if it is people from the community. Only quality work."

"I know. I know." She sank wearily into a patio chair wide enough for two. "Just in time for Summer," She replied, "and very comfy. I could take a nap." Closing her eyes, she thought of Matt's way of teasing Harriet. "How about you, Ma?"

"I'm just too tired to rise to your banter," Harriet replied. "Scoot over; I need to get off my feet for a moment." And there they sat, for the entire world to see, coming to grips with mother and daughter-hood, after twenty some years of estrangement. "Ah, this feels wonderful, what if we do go to sleep?"

"WHAT'S THE WORD ON CHESTER'S surgery, have you heard from Bitty?" Daniel sit his briefcase on the floor and crossed over to where Ellen was dicing vegetables at the sink. "Umm, you smell good," he nuzzled her neck, "I don't believe I've experienced a woman smelling this good, before."

"Silly." Ellen laid the knife to the back of the sink. "That's the onions. I hope I never smell like that." She turned into his arms, as he lay a kiss on her lips. "The surgery is day after tomorrow; the doctor worked them into his schedule. Don't ask me how?"

"Why not?"

"Because his scheduled patient died."

"That doesn't sound good." Daniel was snacking from a stalk of celery. "I hope it didn't have anything to do with prostate cancer and if it did, that Chester doesn't hear about his demise."

"Newspapers don't print the cause of death if it's medically related. And if your wifey wasn't a nurse, you wouldn't know why either. Which means you haven't heard this story."

"I still don't know why the man died but it is sounding mysterious. So, tell me." He picked her up and sit her on the counter. "I'm assuming the twins are asleep, otherwise you'd appear frazzled and crying for other reason than dicing an onion." He grinned. "So the patient had prostate cancer and died, but why?"

"It's the age old story, the man failed to seek medical care in time and the infection in his body took over."

"I don't get it. What does Prostate cancer have to do with this case, and where was the infection and what was the doctor supposed to do for the patient. Just tell me."

"Some ten years ago, the man developed cancer of the prostate, had brachytherapy, in order to take out the cancer. That's radiation seed implanted in the prostate, remember? It was described on one of the pamphlets we studied over with Chester and Bitty. Anyway, the cancer returned, by way of the cancer spreading into the lungs along with a terrible infection that required surgery to empty a buildup of fluid but the patient had lingered too long before seeking medical attention and while the lab was running cultures of his blood to know which antibiotic would wipe out the infection, the man died."

"Lord, help us, if Chester and Bitty get wind of this, he won't go through with the surgery, then what?"

"I cannot divulge the information and neither can you. I'm just saying, even if there are treatments for any medical need, there's always the chance of infection, or hemorrhage, who knows what?" She sighed. "Not as much chance of hemorrhage with Robotic methods as with the knife, but Bitty will be worrying over Chester being put to sleep and a million other things. Just wait and see."

"It makes me sweat, just thinking what the man's going to go through."

"There's surgery every day. Statistics are with the patient, actually."

"Are we going to sit in the surgical waiting room?" Daniel asked.

"I don't think so; Bitty said Chester is too easily embarrassed. They'll go it alone."

"Then what?"

"Home to recuperate. What are you thinking?"

"I'm thinking, while Chester is on medical leave healing, it would be a good time for the honeymoon trip they put off." Pulling her down from the counter, his arms went around her, "But then, maybe not."

Ellen grinned. "I did hear something about a delayed trip but knowing Bitty, I wonder if it will happen."

CHAPTER FIFTEEN

"MY TEETH ARE CHATTERING," BITTY pulled the light jacket closer around her body. "I don't know about our plans, Chester. Maybe we should back out on the cruise. I'm perfectly content to stay home."

"I made the arrangements, Bitty. We promised ourselves a honeymoon and we are going to have one."

"Well, you promised. I don't know what a honeymoon's going to do for us. Besides, we've been married long enough now, it don't matter." Bitty shivered, wondering if her body temperature was more from concern than the thermometer reading on the wall. "You all right, Chester? I'm freezing."

"I'm fine, Bitty." He grinned. "Same as I was five minutes ago, when you asked, and the five before that." He pat the sheet, "Come over here, they will be coming for me in a few, and I need to see your face, not just hear your voice. You sitting all huddled down there, worries me a bit." There was a knock on the door as Bitty arose. "Come in," Chester said, and the door opened to Daniel and Brother Joe.

"We came for prayer," the pastor said. "And you have a whole troupe agreeing with us out in the waiting room." Taking Chester's hand, he saw the look pass between husband and wife. "You two just as well know, from what I've figured out about these people you call friends, nothings private where surgery is concerned, they show up, pray, leave, return, and work it according to what they consider the purpose of God's love."

"Oh, my goodness. Whose out there?" Bitty's eyes filled with tears which she hurriedly wiped away.

"I LEFT HATTIE IN CHARGE of Andy and Ruthie," Harriet said as she sat with Bitty. "Marigold took Matthew John to the new place with her and the others had to return to work. Of course, Hattie called Latana, in case she needed back up but she won't. Ruthie and Andy are busy building a bridge with those building blocks we purchased on-line."

"You know how to order now?"

Harriet nodded. "Times have changed. Anne taught me enough; I'm dangerous but courageous on the computer." She noticed Bitty watching the clock. Reaching across she took her friends hand. "The doctor said it won't take long, Bitty and when Chester's back in his room I'll leave you two alone." She sighed. "Did I tell you, I've decided, I'm buying a car. Andrew's teaching me how to drive, after all these years and that old clunker he drives makes me wonder when it's going to take its last spin. Imagine, Bitty, we met him in a hospital sitting about like this, when we were watching over Anne after the wreck."

"We didn't trust him, either. We worried when we left and he was still in her room."

"Things have changed. Who knew, one day the barrier would lift and we'd become friends." Harriet settled to one side of her chair, peering intently at her friend. "It's all because of God's love, isn't it? He takes our cold hearts and warms us up to set aside our own problem and understand someone else's."

"God has certainly done a work on our group," Bitty admitted. "I had my own reservations, and all the while I thought my life was fine. I was doing the best I could, but with Ellen guiding me through scripture, which she did gently; she never gave up on me." Bitty sighed. "Well, in time I began to see the peace God gave Ellen could be mine as well. I hadn't realized there was more to life."

Harriet chuckled. "We weren't hardened criminals, nothing like that, just a hard case."

The door opened. "Mrs. Mayfield, we have your husband back in his room. You may go in now."

"Is everything all right?" Bitty reached for Harriet's hand, heading toward Chester's room.

"The doctor is waiting for you, Mrs. Mayfield."

"I'll talk to you later, Bitty. Call me if you need me." Harriet gave her hand a squeeze. "You hear?"

Within the hour, Harriet had taken a cab home, checked on the children and called Marigold.

"How did you get home? I told you I would come for you."

"You have enough to do without bothering with me." But Harriet smiled. That this long lost child she had found would offer, made her feel good. "Just thought I'd let you know, I'm home. I'm going to look for a car this afternoon."

"Harriet, you can't tool around town in a cab, looking for a car. Why don't you do what I suggested? Better still, why didn't you call the guy from your company to run you around town?"

She heard the exasperation in her daughter's voice. "I didn't want them to know I was looking for a car. By what you suggested you mean I should call the Lonzo's." Harriet thought for a minute. "It's my business, Marigold and I don't want everyone's opinion about my starting to drive at my age."

<hr>

"I CAN'T BELIEVE THAT MOTHER of mine?" Frustration reigned in Marigold's voice as she turned to where Haley was cleaning the windows of a display case while Matthew John slept cozy in his carrier by her helper's side. "The Lonzo's have a practically new car sitting in their drive, which they need to move before they back into it and they insist Harriet can buy it for a very reasonable price and she won't bend or even go see it."

"Why don't you take the car to her?"

"I hadn't thought of that. Would you help me?"

"Sure. It's all part of my job." She smiled, "but this is the sweetest part." She pointed to Matthew John. "But, Marigold, always lock everything up when you leave. I think someone has been in the building."

"The guy who has done the renovating has a key. I'm sure he stops by to check on things."

"I'm not sure about that, it's just that I find things I straightened the day previous day, disheveled the next." She noticed Marigold wasn't listening as she rummaged around trying to find her cell. And maybe it was just a coincidence she kept thinking someone was pilfering the shop. She would probably be paranoid the rest of her life, trying to walk a straight line, so as not to go back to prison.

"I'll call Anne and see if she can arrange for us to do the car thing this afternoon." Marigold stepped away to make the call, returning to Haley, shortly. "We're on. Anne called Mrs. Lonzo and she will be home and would love to go with me to Harriet's house to see what she thinks of her SRX."

It was quite an entourage' in Harriet's drive that afternoon. Hattie and the children were in the kitchen making cookies while Miz Becker prepared to go car shopping. She answered the door bell to find Marigold holding Matthew John in her arms, a diaper bag and her purse hanging from one shoulder, Haley and Dr. Lonzo's wife behind her, standing there smiling. "Where's Harriet?" Marigold asked, beckoning the others to follow her. "Don't tell me she's left, already? That's why we came as quickly as we could." Hattie was reaching for Matthew John ready to find his grandmother.

Harriet had heard voices; arriving from the hall adjacent to her bedroom. "Why Marigold, what a pleasure, Mrs. Lonzo and Haley." Her voice tinged with surprise. "To what do I owe this honor?"

"Come see our SRX," Mrs. Lonzo said, beaming. "Marigold believes it fit you perfectly. Doctor and myself have too many fat friends to fit nicely in car, but you, Harriet, will fit very well. Come. I show you." Ushering Harriet through the door, "We take a ride," she said. "You will like SRX."

"Well, that certainly went well." Heaving a pent up breath of air, Marigold let herself down into the nearest chair. "All our effort, and Mrs. Lonzo takes charge, just like that."

Haley giggled. "If your mother takes the car, does it matter who gets the glory?"

"Not at all. I've just saved my inexperienced mother from a very vulnerable experience and at the same time a few thousand dollars. Don't they say once a car exits the lot, the value drops?" A new thought popped into Marigold's mind. "While we're speaking of cars, what is that you are driving?"

"One of Dad's refurbishing projects. It doesn't look like much but runs like a top. Not that I can go that fast, I'm still under probation of sorts and Bowie would just love for me to mess up."

"I would've thought you had a shiny little toy of a car."

"I do," Haley admitted, "But with Bowie, my check in guy who is a Federal Marshal at the camp, I try to keep a low profile, you know, don't play up the spoiled little rich girl thing."

"This has worn me out." Marigold shrugged the diaper bag and purse off her shoulder. "I didn't know having a second mother could be so stressful." She laughed. "She probably doesn't either."

Hesitating, Haley said, "Tell me your story. I've only heard bits and pieces."

"Seems we have nothing else to do while we wait for our charges. I'll tell you mine and then it's your turn. Agreed? But do remind me to tell Harriet, Andrew will help with the papers if she takes the car."

In an hours' time, Haley and Marigold bared their life history, a car was purchased and a relieved Marigold was ready to return Mrs. Lonzo to her home, this time leaving *our baby* as Hattie was prone to call Matthew John, before she and Haley tackled once more the unwrapping and placing of many items in *the new place*. "I've got to come up with a name. We can't keep calling this *the new place*.

"Why not Marigold's, that's catchy." Haley let the name roll off her tongue slowly, "*Marigolds*." Hesitant, she lay a hand on Marigold's arm. "I'm sorry your husband's parents won't allow you into the family. I've been through something similar and it hurts."

"WELL, HARRIET," ANDREW DID A funny gesture with his lips together and his eyebrows up, weighing in on Harriet's purchase. "You made a good deal. Are you ready to take the test, so you can spin around town in your new car?"

"I think I have the book down pat, but the driving concerns me a little, do you think I'll have to Parallel Park?"

"You think you have the symbols memorized, the rules of the road, all that?" An amused smile lit Andrew's face. "Not questioning your intelligence but those symbols can mess you up."

"Come with me," Harriet motioned he should follow as she led him to her office, just off the main hall, tucked away from the busyness of the house, quiet, and as he would see the essence of Harriet Becker. She brought him to a cherry fronted cabinet that ran floor to ceiling and opened the doors. There, on felt lined panels were numerous certificates and interesting documents, pinned to the liner.

Peering intently, Andrew began to read the titled documents. "Why, Harriet Becker. You've finished enough classes and have enough hours to be a lawyer." He was amazed. "When did you do all this?"

"I was alone for a number of years, Andrew. What was there to prevent me from a college degree, from a business education? My husband left me in charge of a vast operation. It was my duty to understand the workings of such."

"But you never drove a car, Harriet. Why?"

"I did not involve myself in the workings of society, Andrew. I arrived at each class, listened and went away as an unknown. It satisfied me. It was my plan but I did not become involved with others. Besides, there was always someone from the business at my beck and call to take me wherever I chose."

Andrew whistled. "But you missed out on a lot. The communication or interaction with people."

"Yes. I did."

Suddenly a smile wreathed Andrew's face. "But you know what, Harriet? You are a grand old girl."

"I'm not *that* old." She replied, pleased. "So, shall we take a little drive and you tell me if I'm ready."

"I can hardly believe the great Harriet Becker never owned a car."

"No one said I didn't own one." Harriet chuckled. "Had you been around or shall I say *behaving* at one time, when we gave Marigold a birthday party, I remember telling Mr. Silverman to take my car for supplies and he replied, 'Harriet we need a truck, but when he returned in that nineteen ninety Lincoln, his words were, 'It may be as long as a hearse and have the room inside of a truck, but Harriet, you won't believe how the people stared at me in that Lincoln.'

Andrew stared at Harriet Becker. "You never cease to amaze me."

THE GRAND OPENING OF MARIGOLD'S was scheduled. First, everyone would attend Christ Church, gather for lunch at Matthew and Marigold's home and then discuss the big event, planned four days away.

Worship in song set the stage and brother Joe's sister sang a song of praise she had composed from Bible scripture. "If I lift up my eyes unto the hills from where my help comes, I will see the eternity God has put in man's heart, from beginning to end, His glory shines through, in the healing from sin, I will glorify Him, He who neither slumbers nor sleeps, I will glorify Him."

"It is so simple," Lauren Hill, said. "Sing along with me. Let your hearts worship and glorify our Heavenly Father. We won't worry about the second and third verse; today we will praise him with the first." The congregation sang out, as Lauren Hill led and Pastor Joe smiled ready to lead in scripture.

"Let us remain standing for the reading of God's word, followed by a prayer of thanksgiving. Our scripture today prepares hearts for new beginnings and following worship service we have three baptisms ready to do business as soldiers for Christ. Today's scripture is found in Isaiah. Let us begin Isaiah chapter forty three, verses eighteen and nineteen. Remember ye not the former things, neither consider the things of old. Behold, I will do a new thing; now it shall spring forth; shall ye not know it? I will even make a way in the wilderness, and rivers in the desert."

Looking back; Isaiah 42:16, God said, "I will bring the blessed by a way they know not, I will lead them in paths they have not known. I will make darkness light before them and crooked straight. These things will I do unto them and not forsake them." He paused. "I will not forsake them. This is the prophecy of the coming of Christ and the pleasure our creator feels with those who believe in Him. When Jesus comes into your life, He makes darkness light as He becomes your guide through the underbrush of life; if you are weak He makes you strong. The minds of men and women can become wise through Him."

"Perhaps, you are not new to the life of a follower. Still, there are new happenings in your life. A new job, a different career, something is opening up that you need the best start you can possibly have. You are already a Christian, saved by the grace of God. But let us think about this; If man does something new, on his own, how long does it last? What about the new Christian? You've accepted the Lord as Savior. Your old life is over. You are a new person inside where no one can see. How will they know the difference? This is where the shackles of the past fall away, you are new in Christ. Now you represent him. Mercy and grace spring up; streams of mercy appear in your life as did the streams in the dessert where God made a way in the wilderness."

Brother Joe's face took on a glow of awareness given to him by the Lord; his countenance became the look of inner peace, of knowledge he wanted each one in the congregation to have. His voice grew bold, his eyes held the mystery God was revealing to him at that very moment. Ruthie leaned forward, listening. Haley's heart did a skip was it possible to put all things behind her, would people forget the stigma of her going to prison? Marigold wondered if Brother Joe considered her business endeavor a new beginning, because it was. The lives of her parents were embedded in the very foundation when the doors opened in four days. Ellen, considered God's love, twice blessed in the twins, with an eternity of love tied up in Daniel and

Ruthie. God's love, she sighed, content as Daniel twined their fingers together. Bitty's thoughts were wrapped around the miracle of medicine. No longer was the healing touch of Jesus evident on the earth, and yet it was, in the work of the medical society. Chester seemed to be healing, as he confided he had arranged the honeymoon that meant so much to him, delayed due to unforeseeable circumstance, in those first days of marriage. Hoping to please Bitty he had booked a passage on a cruise. She was apprehensive and didn't know why. Each person searched their own soul. Anne was serene in life, perhaps for the first time, since Andrew's change appeared valid. He had asked her to marry him again and she was giving serious thought to the matter. Listening, one by one, they were drawn into the beauty of God's promise. Even now as Brother Joe brought the sermon to a close, they found *truly it is good to be in the house of the Lord.*

"If there's a new beginning how are you going to handle it? Are you dedicating yourself to the one who saved you? Have you cut ties with the past? It's simple, will you trust in the one who saved you?"

A HAPPY RUTHIE HUMMED IN the back seat, wedged between the twin's car seats. Her hair had not dried completely because she was baptized along with Anne and Uncle Chester.

"What are you singing, Sweetums?" Ellen had been listening to Ruthie's humming which had put the twins to sleep, otherwise there would be a clamor of excitement as they had Ruthie locked in and all to themselves.

"It's that new Lauren Hill song, Momma. Don't you like the words?" She began to sing. "If I lift up my eyes...unto the hill from where my help comes, I will see the eternity God has put in man's heart...from beginning to end, His glory shines through...in the healing from sin I will glorify Him. He who never slumbers or sleeps...I will glorify Him."

"That was beautiful, Ruthie." Ellen clapped her hands, softly, lest she waken the twins. "Maybe, some day you will sing before the congregation as Lauren Hill did today."

"I don't have to sing like Lauren Hill, Momma, God wants us all to glorify His name."

"How do you remember the words, Sweetums?" Ellen realized she only remembered glorify His name.

"They just come. Momma, did you know Uncle Chester is going to get sick again?" Ruthie's voice had changed from glorifying her Heavenly Father in a mystified way to a serious forewarning of things to come. "God hasn't told me whether to tell him, yet. I don't want Uncle Chester to worry."

"Oh, no, Sweetums, Uncle Chester is recovering nicely from his surgery. Where did this information come from anyway?"

"I dreamed it."

Ellen relaxed. "It was probably just a dream, Sweetheart."

"I don't think so, Momma, but God hasn't told me yet."

Daniel, listening, reached for Ellen's hand, giving her a reassuring glance, as if to say, *leave it alone. Time will tell.*

Ellen sighed. For years she had struggled with this gift, which prompted her to tell people a word from God. She was only the messenger, but messengers were often concerned how a message delivered was accepted… or not.

Daniel parked the Escalade in the garage. "Go on in, Hon. I'll get the twins and Ruthie can carry the diaper bag. Everyone will be here, so that means you have to get the show on the road and you don't have Hattie to back you up."

It was true. Ellen had yawned through worship service, due to the fact she had stayed up late last night preparing for today's dinner with the group. Was it worth it? Yes, she thought, but having the twins warranted a need for rest. Starting Monday she would work only three days a week but it would be twelve hour shifts. She wondered what that would do to her family, but then they would have more of her the other four. It was worth a try. Silently, as she made mental notes of what needed doing towards dinner, Ellen thanked God that she had Daniel and Bitty. *Bitty, wonderful Bitty, a second grandparent to her children, loving them and wanting them near. God bless Bitty.*

"I DON'T KNOW HOW YOU do it," Dorothy Gipson was helping clear the table. Daniel was showing their guests his last addition to the back yard garden, allowing Ellen time to pull the room together after lunch. "You have served a delicious dinner. Your home is marvelously meticulously clean and straightened and you work."

"I'm cutting down, starting this week." Ellen shrugged. "Daniel helps, a lot, then there's Bitty. She can't seem to forget she used to do everything and her hands are full with Chester's surgery and keeping Ruthie." Sliding the plates into the dishwasher slots, she said, "There is one problem, if Bitty and Chester do go on the cruise I have to find someone to keep Ruthie those days I'm working."

"Can I help? I work from our home office. I could have Ruthie." Dorothy brought the last load of dessert dishes in from the adjoining dining area. "I would enjoy having Ruthie."

"That's sweet, Dorothy, are you sure?" She placed the dishes into the remaining space, closed the door and pressed a button on the dishwasher. "I'm not one to push my child off on someone."

By the time everyone was leaving, still discussing the sermon and Marigold's grand opening, it was settled, if Bitty and Chester continued plans for the cruise; Ruthie would stay with Dorothy.

"MARIGOLD?" HALEY'S VOICE SOUNDED DISTRESSED. "Marigold." She heard the clacking of Marigold's strap sandals on the wood floor. "I hate to bother you, but do you seriously think your previous owner would do this?" Haley felt the niggle of fear, again, seeing the merchandise strewn on the floor.

Staring at the scramble of clothing on the floor, Marigold glanced to an open window. "We had that wind, Haley, it could have knocked those scarves onto the floor, they are pretty light weight."

"It looks like someone dashed by in a hurry to exit to me and knocked them off."

"The doors were closed, Haley, locked; with the key in my pocket." The firmness in Marigold's voice was enough to waylay further comment. She turned to see to a thousand things in those last fifteen minutes before the crowd arrived. "I know you worry and fret, Haley, but I'm not seeing anyone trying to do us harm."

Wishing she could go home, Haley set the items on the stands back onto the display shelf. Words from the Bible, above the shelf, made her feel uneasy and ashamed that she wasn't trusting as were the rest of the group, but she really wasn't one of them. What Time I'm Afraid I Will Think On Thee. She sighed.

Would the signs be accepted, who would buy them? One of Matt's paintings was displayed on the upper high angle of the ceiling and above it, the words; 'They shall rise up as on wings of Eagles.' The grandeur of the painting was evident; a mountain scene with an eagle flying across the horizon. Perhaps her favorite was Marigolds own painting of a cottage by a bubbling brook. A post lamp bid welcome to those who passed by. Husband and wife's paintings evolved on a different scale, nothing comparable except excellence in style. Haley longed for a place of her own, free from the shackles time in prison left imprinted on her life. If only things were different, if Race had not died, if there were someone to call her own; there wasn't. Her thoughts flit to the tall Southerner who befriended her *and kissed her* and last of all to the unknown face of the Southern belle he was to have married last Christmas.

Starting toward the counter where she was designated to hold to when the doors opened, Haley glanced down and found a man's money clip. It wasn't empty. She knew it was not Marigold's and Daniel wore a wallet. Someone, a man, had been in the building and lost the clip. She could not tell Marigold, lest Marigold disdain her suspicions. She suspected she was getting on Marigold's nerves.

The doors opened promptly at ten o'clock. A rush of well-heeled ladies entered, to immediately settle and make note of the items the shop presented. Crockery, jeweled items, faux jewelry, candles, a few flower arrangements Marigold made and the paintings, displayed above heads, making use of the tall ceilings, Matthew's paintings spoke to hearts. Haley glanced around, Harriet was behind the counter that overhead held the oil of a steam engine coming around the bend, steam pouring out as the engine burped and belched a fume of dark smoke in its race against time. The sign read; *A time to get, and a time to lose, a time to keep and a time to cast away.* And there was the one, she understood; painted by great demand because it was first seen in Bitty and the Captains' home, Man in the field, a farmer with his hand on the plow behind a team of magnificent horses, tilling the soil, the colors so vibrant you could feel the dirt and see the sweat on the man's brow. *Who knoweth the spirit of the man.* Yes, Haley pondered, who truly knows anyone?

She slipped the money clip into her pocket. She would be watchful. She would be careful. *'Better is one hand filled with quietness, than two filled with travail,'* the sign by her station read. Haley pondered the sign; it made no sense at all. She would mention that to Marigold.

"GRAND OPENING ON MAIN STREET tops list of downtown shoppers," Marigold read from the newspaper. "So we made front page," She ran her hands beneath the heavy strands of her hair and brought them up off her neck. "I'm not sure my body will slow down and my feet hurt." She wailed, "I am so tired."

"But it was a good day," Harriet replied.

"Ma, how can you look so put together. It's the end of the day and we have been trampled, pounded and in general abused."

Wagging a finger her direction, Harriet eyed Marigold with a fateful warning, "Don't call me Ma, and it was your idea to open a shop. So here you are. You made good money and you're wailing?" Yawning, Harriet reminded, "Tomorrow you are on your own. Hattie has a doctor appointment. I will see to *our babies.*"

"Have you lined anyone up to take your place?" Marigold's words seemed to fade out as she yawned.

"As a matter of fact, yes I did. She will report to work tomorrow morning thirty minutes before opening."

"Ma, you didn't even let me interview your person. What if I don't like her? It's my store."

"Get over it. No need for that, I know she will be a hard worker and bring a new element to your shop. Her name's Caroline Hawkins. Her husband died last year and we've stayed in touch."

"What's the new element?"

"You'll see. People are drawn to her." Harriet picked up her purse. "I'm out of here. Good night."

Marigold watched her drive away. "Haley, let's lock the doors and see if we can find our way home." As she drove she wondered if Caroline Hawkins would show up the next morning.

CHAPTER SIXTEEN

"OH, CHESTER, I JUST DON'T know. Something about the whole thing worries me."

"Would you worry less if I told you the money is spent. We are going while I'm on sick leave. We'll come back all tanned and healthy looking and be the envy of all."

"Can you get your money back?"

"No." Chester chuckled. "Shall I pack the bags for two weeks from now? Or do you want to?"

"Two weeks?" Bitty groaned. "You mean I have two weeks to think about being out on the water in a ship? She shuddered. "I don't know about this, Chester Mayfield. Traveling a highway is one thing, but the ocean? I don't know." She was sitting the suitcase out of storage in the downstairs closet.

"It will be here before you can shake a stick," Chester said. "Good thing we got our passports before the wedding." He carried the larger case. "You know there's a limit on weight?" He sighed, "We'll find out when the time comes, I suppose. But then, you or I can weigh ourself, then with the suitcase."

Chester was right, the two weeks passed quickly. Meanwhile, Bitty and Dorothy Gipson became acquainted as she had volunteered to keep Ruthie, rather than finding a day care for five year olds that normally required at least a year's apply in advance. Harriet was beside herself that Ruthie wouldn't be staying with her and Hattie, but Mrs. Gipson had offered first. Ellen's words were *if Bitty is pleased with Mrs. Gipson, that's all the verification we need.* The group gave them a rousing sendoff and they left to drive to Memphis to spend the night in a hotel near the airport that would deliver them the next morning.

Chester had encouraged Bitty to change cars and they would be leaving it in the hotel's VIP area the length of the trip. "It will be fine," Chester said. "It's only a car." Now it was morning and people were loading on to the bus that would take them to the airport. He saw Bitty glance at her car on the lot and felt her apprehension. "Don't worry, hon, everything will be all right. If we could've left St. Louis airport it would've been the same, but they didn't have a straight flight to Seattle."

"It wouldn't matter where we start from," Bitty whispered, lest those around her could hear. "I've traveled the highways, but not the skies. It's all new to me."

Chester studied her between hooded lids. This little woman who had stolen his heart was a profound study of mixed emotions. Since the surgery, Bitty seemed to question eternity's hold on him. She had lived through her first husband's illness and hadn't planned to experience the same again, now she was doing her best to see to his needs. The doctor said the prostatectomy went well. He sighed. Perhaps this vacation away would allow a semblance of normal to return to their lives.

The airport was bustling with the usual activity of hundreds of people streaming the hall ways. Luggage was checked; they went through the line of personal inspection and came at last to the Stewardess who welcomed them. Chester was as happy as a school boy, taking her hand. "We're movin' on up."

They boarded the plane, stored their carryon's overhead and prepared for the flight. But it wasn't Bitty into the flight, who felt nausea, it was Chester. "It's got a hold on me," he admitted after the fifth trip to the small rest room. "I feel green as a lizard around the ears."

Once more buckled into seat belts, the nausea began; Chester's forehead was damp with sweat, a heavy feeling in his stomach. "They had these patches," he showed them to Bitty, "at one of the vendors in the airport. The guy said it would reduce my nausea, what do you think should I put them on and see?"

"If you think it will help." Bitty read the package. "Hmmm." Then, she asked, "Chester, you don't think these things happening to you, the nausea and such, are related to your surgery, do you?"

It troubled Chester that she held such concern over his present state of discomfort. Here he had promised her she would see none of the angst and grievous ways of ill health in him she had seen in her Larry and now for some curious reason every way he turned, he, who had always been the picture of health, was undergoing a series of small health problems. "No, I asked the doctor, Bitty. He said the surgery was successful and it must have been, since we left the hospital twenty four hours after my having it done and we're almost a month away…" She seemed to accept his answer.

Smiling, she pat his hand, "I needed to hear your thoughts on the matter. From this point on, I'll do my best not to fret. I didn't come to this conclusion on my own either. She pointed to a young woman trying to find something out of her carry on. She wore a yellow T, and was completely unaware of Bitty and Chester reading the words on the back of her shirt. "After you have suffered a little while, the God of all grace, who has called you to his eternal glory in Christ, will himself restore, confirm, strengthen and establish you."

"There's a name of a church in smaller letters, can you read them?" Chester was squinting, but the words were small. "Something, something, street." He began to laugh. "Well, where ever the church is located, that's good advertisement. You never know when a person might need the message." They heard the roar of the airplane's motor rev up, as he leaned to kiss her lightly on the lips. "Let's have a good trip."

They were served the usual fare, given soda and peanuts or crackers twice through the trip and for the most part enjoyed seeing the fluffy clouds outside the window as the plane went through. "When we land, the hotel will have someone waiting for us, and if nothing goes wrong we have time for one excursion before dinner tonight and departure on the ship tomorrow."

"How did you arrange that?"

Chester squeezed her hand. "I had help, a certain person who understands computers much better than I, did this for us." His face wreathed in smile. "I believe the patches are going to work, thank the Lord, I cannot imagine coming this far to be under the weather the whole time."

———◆———

"DID BITTY HAVE ANY QUALMS about flying?" Daniel checked his watch. "They should be leaving Memphis about now." He glanced Ellen's way. One twin was sitting in a high chair, while she dressed the other. "What do you want me to do?" She pointed to Sammy as he laid the paper aside. "Here we go, Sam," slipping one arm behind the boy's body, he brought him up onto his shoulder. "Aren't they a bit young to be sitting in the high chair?" A big burp sounded as Sam wiggled against his dad. "Well, this one should feel better." Daniel yawned. "How many hours did you get last night?"

"Five, I think." Ellen brought Daniel's name sake up from the counter, and placed him in his father's arms next to his brother. "Now, to answer your questions. I'm sure Bitty had qualms about flying, but she will be all right, I can't help if your son's scootch down in their chairs, they're plenty old and big enough to sit in them, what else will we do? They have to learn to feed themselves."

"Well, number one here, could give his brother a little help. "You got to watch out for your brother," he peered down into the faces of his sons. "Who would've ever thought we'd have two at a time. Do twins run in your family?" Not waiting for her answer, he continued on, "Not in mine. They did good to get me."

Passing by, with her arms full of dirty baby laundry, Ellen stopped to peck a kiss on his lips, "and I'm so glad they did, Mr. Gates. Otherwise, I'd still be counting shoes at the shoe store, going every day to the hospital instead of staying here two out of five and changing diapers, washing clothes and burping two strapping boyos. And to your first question, No, I don't think twins run in our family."

"You think that's right, Number Two?" Daniel settled back into the rocking chair Ellen had moved into the kitchen. "You know, that doesn't sound bad. They could go through life as Number one and

Number two." He grinned as the boys, reached for his face, then clasp their hands together, forgetting him. "What do you think?"

"You know the problem with naming sons after their father? You call one; the other doesn't know when to answer. Although your plan is brilliant, meaning number one and number two, we probably should stick to calling our boys by their names, Sammy and Danny." She came to put her arms around his neck, standing behind him, as she looked down on their boys. "You, big daddy will always be Dan or Daniel. None of that Pumpkin stuff, Marigold has gone through."

"Yeah, Harriet solved that one didn't she? Now, Pumpkin is Matthew John. A big name for a little boy, but he's growing into it." Groaning, he knew he had to go to work. "Can I stay home today, Momma and play with Daniel, number one and Samuel, number two?"

Ellen pulled the play pen closer to the sink where she was loading dishes into the dishwasher. "Fraid not, pappy. Boys have to have food and diapers and wipes and shoes and let's face it, they just keep growing, so you got to go to work, Big Daddy and provide for their welfare. There's college and vehicles and girlfriends for them, the list just goes on and on..."

"I got it." He was rising, with difficulty, one boy in each arm. "Help me, Momma."

They settled the squirming boys into the playpen. Daniel turned to Ellen before leaving. "You are the dream of my life. I don't think there's a happier man under God's sun."

She came into his arms, her own around his neck, head against his chest listening to the beat of his heart." I love you, Daniel. Every day I thank God for our life together and for our children." She felt his arms tighten around her as Ruthie returned dressed, hair combed and ready for the day.

"Am I your children, Daniel?"

He stooped to stare into her eyes, a smile leaving little indentions around his own. "You bet your boots, Ruthie Elizabeth Anderson. You are mine."

"Then why is my name different?" She slid closer to Daniel. "I want to be Ruth Elizabeth Gates, like Danny and Sammy's last name."

Daniel and Ellen stared at each other.

"I told Miss Dorothy and she said my name has a Biblical meaning like my brothers, but I don't know what that means."

"You and Miss Dorothy discussed your name?" Ellen let the information sink in, Ruthie saved important things for Bitty. "How long has this been bothering you, Sweetums?"

"Since Danny and Sammy got here. I thought you would do something about it." Her solemn eyes were pinned on Ellen and Daniel. "Can't you?"

"I'll look into it," Daniel replied. "Now, I have to hit the road. Will you help your mother with the boys?"

"I will," Ruthie's smile returned. If Daniel said he would do something, he would. "I'll read to them."

The phone rang as Daniel was leaving. It was Marigold. "I don't suppose you have plans for my little apprentice, today?"

"She plans to read to the twins."

"Don't suppose you'd turn her loose to come with me to the store?" Marigold's voice was wistful.

"Do you need someone to read to you?" Ellen asked, mischievously.

"As a matter of fact, I'm thinking of a new line of books and she could be my co-pilot on the project."

"Ruthie, come talk to Marigold. She has a favor to ask of you."

"WHAT'S NEW, RUTHIE?" HALEY MET the five year old with a hug. "I've been wondering when I'd see you again."

"I wonder about you, too, Haley. Are you having better days?"

"I'm trying." She grew quiet for a moment. "Ruthie, how does your gift work? You told me you can tell about people's feelings. You said it was the gift of discernment. Does your gift only involve people or can you tell about things?"

Ruthie stared hard at Haley, trying to decide what to say. "Gifts God give you are never to be used to bring glory to yourself. I think that means I can't be proud of what God reveals to me. Is that the word? Reveal?" She had grown suddenly very serious. "I know you are worried that someone is coming into the building, but Marigold said it's the carpenter man."

Cold chills ran down Haley's spine, and if she could touch it she was certain her hair was standing on end. "You heard us talking about that?"

"No. I think I just knew it."

"Was it the carpenter man, Ruthie?"

"I don't know, Haley. I'm only five years old and I don't know if God wants me to talk about this." Tears were building in Ruthie. "I'll have to ask my Momma."

"Oh, Ruthie, I didn't mean to upset you. It's just that I'm afraid something will happen to Marigold."

"Then God wouldn't want anyone to hurt Marigold. God wants good for us. I know that."

Seeing Ruthie was trembling, Haley moved on to another subject. "Marigold wants us to go through these books the salesman left and see which ones we think will appeal to little children."

"Am I a little child?"

Ruffling Ruthie's hair, Haley grinned as she said, "I'm not really sure. You seem to know a lot for your age."

"That's why I feel like I'm six instead of five."

The serious moment passed and soon a pile of discards filled the box, while those selected lay on the table. "I really like this book," Ruthie said. "It makes me think of my brothers. They can't talk yet, but they sure can cry."

Haley had to laugh. "That's an old one, Ruthie. The Sky Is Falling has been around a long time."

"I like it."

Nothing more was said of their conversation until Marigold was locking the door. Haley was helping Ruthie with the seat belt in the back when Ruthie said, "It wasn't the carpenter."

HALEY REALIZED SHE HAD TO investigate. Dinner dishes were cleared and time was on her hands. "I'll be back in an hour." She said. "I may go to a friend's house." She didn't want them to worry. It was a white lie, but she *was* going to an old friend, Marigold's. She parked down the street and waited. An hour passed. Lights along the street dimmed, one by one and she knew it was time to return to her parents, when she saw the Suburban pass, turn around to drive by Marigold's shop again. Parking adjacent to where she was sitting, the man got out of the vehicle and walked to the back of the building. It wasn't long until the glow of a light could be seen moving around. Someone was in there, with a flashlight, and she intended to see who it was.

Reason told her to call Marigold, her parents or even the police but what if it was the Carpenter? It was going well, she made it alongside the building, found the back door unlocked and stepped inside. Reaching for the nearest wall, she thought she knew her way around, but when a hand grasps hers the last thing she heard was a scream. Hers.

She wasn't certain where she was being taken, only that strands of raffia were tied around her wrist and feet and she was sitting upright belted into the back seat of the suburban with her mouth taped. She tried to talk but the tape across her lips was stuck tight.

"Just hold it together, girlie," a male voice called back. "I mean you no harm, I just came to get what belongs to someone else and I have no earthly idea why a girl like you was wandering around in the dark." He gave a sort of snorting laugh. "You want to tell me? Oh, I forgot, your lips are sealed."

She realized they had left city limits and were headed down a dirt road. But where? Corn fields lined each side of the road and there were ruts in the road. It seemed they were at the end of the world, other than the head lights it was pitch dark, until they came to a house. She could barely make out the defining edge of the yard but she saw the silhouette of a barn to one side and a grove of trees on the other. The driver stopped the Suburban, came around to her side to open the door and unfasten the seat belt. "Get out. Walk ahead of me and if you try to run I'll knock some sense into your head with this flashlight."

I will make the darkness light, the crooked straight. Now where had that come from? Haley walked toward the house, dim with a light seeping from beneath a shade at one window and only a trace of moonlight shining on the path. It was from the pastor's sermon. She was certain of that. Words from the various signs in Marigold's shop began to pass through her memory and words she and Ruthie discussed. "Why are you taking me away from town? Why am I here?" She asked. A strange calm had come over her when she silently repeated Ruthie's verse, *what time I'm afraid I will think on thee.*

She hadn't had a good look at this man. "Let me go, I don't know you, and there will be no charges pressed against you." He was jerking the tape away from her face, and then pushing her through the door.

His laugh was not happy. "Just tell me this; did the carpenters bother with the floor?"

"The floor?" She thought about the renovation. "No, they were satisfied with the floor. Why?"

"Missy," his words softened. "Just stay inside while I make a call and maybe you won't get hurt."

At least he hadn't called her girlie, maybe that was a good sign but she couldn't relax just yet. She hobbled to the door; he had loosened but not removed the raffia. In the dark, hands out to guide herself, she listened. He was mumbling about the floor boards and a secret compartment.

"This is Earl. I couldn't find what you wanted, but I got something else, instead. What do you mean drop it in the river, you want no evidence?" Earl swore. "Man, I can't do that. No, it's not important to me. Man…No, I didn't find it. You're sure? You want me to go back and give it one last look?" Now, there were words being said that got his attention. He listened.

"Man." Earl stuck the phone in his shirt pocket and rubbed his hands together. "Go back to the business and give it one last going over and then dump whatever I got that he don't want, and bring him what he does." A huge sigh issued from his belly up, he hadn't dared tell the past owner of the car dealership he had a woman, no, a young girl on his hands. How was he to know someone was there? Why was she there, anyway? Dump her in the river? Why she was just a kid, like his own granddaughter. How'd he get in this mess? Makin' a fast buck, just because he needed it and Jackson was an old buddy. Jackson with his own tale in the crack. Buying them both a second phone so there would be no taping of conversation, Jackson in a different state hiding out in his town house. Well, Earl Simpson lived in the Cape and he couldn't leave. He fumbled in the other pocket of his shirt, bringing out a crumpled pack; he'd have a cigarette and think this thing through. If he kept her from seeing his face, maybe there'd be no need to dump her. Jackson hadn't asked what he had that he didn't want, now had he?

Haley hobbled away from the door, sweat had broken on her brow, and she tried to wipe it away with her banded hands. The raffia was strong and cutting into the flesh but she'd known worse. Now she wondered what her fate was. In the glow of a night light she saw a sparsely furnished house, rooms beyond, maybe a bachelor abode, not much amiss and nothing to brag over.

The door knob turned, her captor entered and headed toward a back room to return with an old sheet. Tearing strips from one end, he came then to stand behind her. "I gotta tie you up, girlie. This one goes over your eyes and the next your mouth, and once you are back in the Suburban, I'll secure your feet and hands. I can't have you runnin' away. Now you cooperate. My friend says throw you in the river, but if you do what I say, maybe I won't have to."

Haley shuddered, wondering what was said on the other end of the line. "Get in," he was saying. "Lay down and don't make a noise. We got business to attend to. It's going to be a long night."

She knew they traveled back over the ruts, through the corn field and recognized the sound of the tires on pavement once they hit the highway. Through the strips of sheet covering her eyes, she thought there were ripples of light and dark, maybe street lamps, she wasn't sure. There was the stop when he was gone for a long time, then the satisfied grunt as he lifted something into the back seat of the truck. The engine turned, he eased out of the parking spot and headed away from wherever he had been. She lost count of time, allowing her body to relax and alleviate the tension as she fought trying to slide into sleep and then as the hour passed and they were still driving she had no charge over her own body. Haley slept. Once she thought she heard the hollow sound of tires on metal, maybe space below.

She awakened, disoriented, completely confused to her surroundings. She had slept. It was a bad dream, no it was a night mare and it was real. She tried to recount the evening. She left home, supposedly going to meet a friend, but went to Marigold's. No, she sat in her car on the street, until she saw someone going inside and followed. From there, everything went hazy. She was tired, her hands and feet were tied and she was gagging from her mouth dry and unable to breathe. Settle. Settle. Calm down, you're panicking; she formed each thought, wondering at the dark she was experiencing. Where was he, the man who cautioned her? Had he abandoned her and the vehicle? She listened.

No one came through an ordeal like this. Cold fear surged through her veins. She had to get out. How? She drew one foot up, trying to push against the strips wound around her legs. Futile. No, she couldn't give up. With her hand she pushed at the ties around her mouth. Tears were wetting the strips around her eyes, she sobbed, the sound muffled through the cloth, keep pushing, push. Push. Little by little the material was giving, the cloth fell around her neck, she bent her head. If she could bite into the strip around her wrist. *Oh, God, help me, she cried out silently, her soul bared, her fears escalating. Help me, I'll do whatever you want, just help me. Please help me. What time I'm afraid. What time I'm afraid. What time I'm afraid,* she said the words over and over in her mind while she chewed at the material binding her hands. Time was passing. She hit raffia, it tore her lips, they were bleeding, she knew but she could do nothing about that, she kept trying, her hair falling around her face, the strips around her forehead that blocked her from seeing felt tighter, how could that be? Then she realized, he had looped the strips because they were long, allowing one section to connect to the next. He had not torn them apart, when the strip over her mouth fell to her neck it tightened the one around her eyes. She had to get her hands free. Her gums hurt. She spit the bits of straw from the raffia, tried to gain saliva, but her mouth was dry.

She heard a noise, a door slamming. Listened. She was parked on a side street. People were living life within calling distance. Weren't they? What if she called out and it was her captor who heard her? One arm fell free, the second was easier now, but the raffia tied in knots. She left it, working on the band of material over her eyes, pushing, pushing. Pushing until it came free. Where was the street lamp. She could surely loosen the strips around her feet if she could just see, but it was dark. Was she in a garage or on a street? It was an alley, no street lamps. Hurry. Hurry. What time I'm afraid, what time I'm afraid.

A moment's elation, followed by caution as the bands fell from around her ankles and she lifted her feet, now on her knees, peering out the back window. She had to climb across the seats to find the door handle. Her feet weren't responding to the command. Work. Work. Move. Help me. Second row doors were locked. She climbed over the console to the front, prayed her numb legs would hold her up as she slipped from the vehicle to the ground, hurrying to close the door and the light from within the vehicle. Her legs buckled. She couldn't feel her feet. She crawled a distance, feeling the roughness of concrete and dirt mixed. Then she commanded her feet to respond, up on one knee, the other, foot on the ground, slowly slowly one step then another, go down the street, keep going, find a place to hide. Bushes. Bushes. Yes. Yes. She searched for her pants pocket. She had lost her phone and her car keys but the small liner to her wallet was there and the money clip she had found on the floor in Marigold's shop. *Help me*, her busy mind kept pleading to the God she feared was not listening.

CHAPTER SEVENTEEN

BITTY WAS ENTHRALLED WITH THE woodwork of the ship. Chester shook his head. He would never understand women. The grandeur of the ocean mesmerized him, volatile, unleashed power, dangerous only steps away and she thought of the woodwork. He had to smile. The waves sometimes higher than the deck, sprayed droplets where they sit and the stewards brought warm blankets, for all around there were huddled groups of people, sometimes only couples, out on the deck in the midst of the turbulence.

"This is the life, Bitty, no one saying so and so called, no pressing matters to take care of." She nodded. Renovation of the old house and bringing Ellen's home back to the antebellum of its day had opened an awareness in Bitty, an appreciation so to speak of the fine skill men possessed in doing so. Even now, she was studying the obvious upkeep of the ship, freshly painted floors holding up to the ocean mist.

"The wood in the ship is cherry, isn't it, or would you say walnut?" Bitty sighed, content at last. "I wasn't sure I'd like this, Chester. Nothing but water beneath us and sky above, but you were right, it is grandeur. If I hadn't seen the movie, I would be bowled over by the opulence of the ships décor, but in a way it prepared me."

"The Titanic?" He raised his head to stare at Bitty from the warmth of the blanket. "It was pretty lavish." He reached for her hand. "I love you Bitty Mayfield." He sighed, "Guess I should call you by your given name, now that you're mine and I have the papers to prove it." He pat her hand, "my beloved."

"Don't you dare," she blushed. His endearments washed over her like warm water in the shower. He loved her, she felt it, it was in her soul, fresh and lasting Chester Mayfield was happy as a duck in water. "I love you too," she said. There, it was getting easier to say because she did love him and had for a long time. The concerns of his health were fading away, those demons that had kept her from marrying him, plagued by the anguish of losing her first love in a battle of health issues. She settled back to enjoy Chester's gift, his love and the cruise that seemed important to him; their delayed honey moon.

They walked on the deck at midnight, stared at the mystery of God's creation as clouds floated past the moon silvering their surroundings, spoke in whispered words about their future and held hands as lovers are prone to do, finally to settle warm and blessed into the comfort of a bed where someone had shaped the cabin towels into an octopus, a rose, or whatever humorous phenomenal creature they chose. It was good, their hearts and minds were sated. They were one with a future.

The third night, Chester groaned, slipping from the bed, padding into the bathroom. Smiling, in spite of his pain; he glanced to where his bride lay sleeping. He wouldn't waken her, not until morning. For the first time, since leaving home, he uncapped the bottle of pills Bitty insisted they bring, *just in case*, and took a pain pill. Returning to bed, he pulled her into the hollow of his body, let the medicine work, in the morning they would face the problem.

Bitty wakened, her eyes on the cherry wood clock on the dresser. Five a.m., a blanket of darkness. Chester had turned off the light she left on. *We don't have our surroundings memorized, no need bumping into things as we move around, she'd said.* She found the switch, made her way into the bathroom, padded back to the bedside. She glanced at Chester, leaning over to study his face. A pallor, she felt his brow, pasty; and she remembered the nausea, the explanation of being air sick and the prevention of being sea sick by using the little patch behind the ear, which apparently wasn't working.

Climbing back into bed, in his sleep Chester reached for her and she settled once more, spooned warm and comforting to his big body and yawning fell asleep with a fleeting wonder; he needed to change the patch for a new one and the fact that he was sleeping through the effects must mean not to worry.

THE BUSHES WERE SCRATCHY, BUT Haley feared moving. Earl had returned to his truck, backed out of the alley and headed the direction she supposed they arrived from. She wondered how far he would travel before realizing she was not tied up in the back. The fear of retaliation sent adrenalin coursing through her veins. Move, she commanded her tired limbs, find a safer place. The difficulty of legs performing after hours of restraints, when they felt like blocks of wood was almost impossible but after staggering attempts they remembered the function she had always taken for granted. It seemed an eternity until she found a building with an alcove and a trash retainer of sorts to hide behind.

From that position, she heard rather than saw a vehicle pass by, continue on, return to shine lights on the building; a door opened, she heard a curse and knew it was Earl. He stepped within feet of the trash bin, talking to himself in an agitated voice, searching, cursing, and finally retracing his steps back to the Surburban. She noted the advance of the vehicle, the open and shut of the door, the muffled voice of Earl, demanding, beseeching as his curses mounted in the night and then there was quiet.

She waited. She thought an hour passed. A police car cruised by. The last avenue for safety, not knowing if they picked her up what they'd believe and whether they'd send her back, home or to prison she dare not seek their attention? Would they believe she had nothing to do with the midnight journey? And was this Tennessee? She recalled the words she'd seen on the container when lights shined on it. Shane's Garbage Service, *you make it, we take it.* Memphis, Tennessee.

Daylight would come and where did that leave her? Dishelvedged, her lips torn from chewing the raffia, not to mention the state of disrepair to her clothes, she was a mess. She blew out a breath, no one would consider her, other than a person they would want to ignore, she was certain. She searched her mind; did her family know anyone in Memphis? Surely her father with all his business associates had at some time mentioned a name. Did she know anyone?

She found herself in the midst of steel girders, a new building going up, with a sign touting the builder's name. Southern Bros. Construction. Southern. The name whispered in her memory. Southern. A smile flit around her torn lips, *the kiss*, the Neanderthal, his last name was Southern. *Jeremy Southern. Thank you Jesus.* Here she was, in probably the worst state of shabbiness; remembering a kiss. The hit on the head must have done more than knock her unconscious. But he had said his father's business was actually located on the outskirts of Memphis, heading South, into Mississippi and a new one planned for Marion. Marion would mean in Arkansas. Would that business project have gone through?

Disappointed she sagged against the first panels of the building. What else had he told her? Think, Haley, think. Fingers in her hair, she flinched as she examined the knot on the side of her head around to the temple where a second blow must have landed. And her head hurt. She wanted to cry, just sit down on the dirty ground and bawl her head off, but she had to think. The new business would be North, across the bridge, wouldn't it?

She was so tired. She crept to the back, where a stack of lumber rose up probably four feet high and there was a box with its lid missing, the pressed wood showing its splinters but most importantly to Haley, turned on its side the box had the glorious appearance of a haven in the storm, laying on one side, its lid missing, a shelter where she could rest for a while. It smelled used but she doubted that.

Grateful, she lay; full length, her back to the box bottom, the other side a roof over her head. Closing her eyes, she dare not sleep. She went back, deep into the recess of her mind to relive her escape into Memphis, before Camp Cup Cake, not knowing if it were the drug cartel or the feds following her, where she met Jeremy Southern. Arkansas was mentioned in the conversation. "Do you know where Marion, Arkansas is?" From his height, he had peered down on her. "Before you crossed the bridge, north of here?" He could not understand she was in great plight, fearing for her life, not knowing who was stalking her and for what reason and she did not explain. She nodded. "You seem concerned over my future," a bit smug, she thought, but then she had just met him, "There's a dealership my dad is considering purchasing, I would be in charge of that business." Leaning down, with that solemn expression, he said, "Maybe you will drop in and see me in a few years."

"I doubt your little southern belle would be pleased with my appearance. Didn't you tell me you will be married this Christmas?" His eyes held hers. Surprisingly to both, he kissed her.

Here she lay, in a wooden box, rehashing in her mind a conversation nearly three years past. It had to be the hit on the head. Then she remembered, she was trying to make connection with someone who might help her. And Jeremy would. There had been an attraction between them, call it what you want, one kiss was not the end of Jeremy Southern's sweet nature, and she found that disconcerting, he had a fiancée. The question was, how was she to get back across the bridge, into Arkansas and locate what was at that time only in thinking order. The Southerns' may not have purchased the dealership. Her head hurt, she didn't know if she were hot or cold and she could not fall asleep, nor could she stumble around in the dark. Daylight was coming.

She felt hands on her body, someone trying to turn her over. She came awake, sitting up to hit her head on the side of the box. A boy was grappling with her, she clasp one hand around his wrist and jerked hard, his head hit the side of the box as he lost footing and she rolled from the box, her body against his legs. He fell across her. She lost hold of his wrist. They struggled, she came up victorious over him, one knee in the center of his belly, her hands pushing his arms behind his head. "What are you doing?" She had fallen asleep and now there was enough light to see him.

To her surprise he laughed. A boy, about fifteen, wiry, his clothing not in a lot better shape than her own but his face was clean. "What are you doing?" He smirked. "You ain't no lady, out here on a constructions site. These men wouldn't touch you. You're as dirty as a pig."

"Will you not run if I turn you loose?" Her arms were beginning to buckle; she was surprised she had him down. "What were you trying to do?"

"Well, I sure wasn't going to hurt you physically but you got that money clip hanging out your pocket and I could use money for breakfast."

"And where would that be?"

"Your pocket, dope."

Her eyes tightened. "I meant, is there a restaurant, nearby?"

"They wouldn't let you in." He grimaced. "No, I won't run. Just let me up. This is embarrassing."

"Here's the deal. I need to make a call. I need someone to drive me to a certain location across the bridge. You want breakfast. I'm hungry, too. Can you help me?"

"Maybe. Show me the money."

"Turn your back."

"Why?"

"You want breakfast money?" He turned, waiting. She examined the money clip. "How does ten dollars sound? You go buy breakfast, find someone to drive me across and there's another ten for you."

"Are you crazy?" He faced her. "Ain't nobody going to drive you across the bridge for nothing."

"Will a twenty take care of *that* person?" They locked stares, each daring the other to make a move.

"Maybe. Gimme the ten and I'll see about breakfast first but you gotta move on down, the guys will be on the site and turn you in."

"Just where do you suggest I go?" Now she smirked. "What are you doing out here on the streets?"

"None of your business." He punctuated his words with a curse and dared her with a stare to correct him. "Go on down, about two blocks, there's a building that has a broken window, crawl in there and wait 'til I come back. It'll take a while, the place don't open til seven."

The rest was history. The kid needed the ten pretty bad. He returned with two egg sausage biscuits, and two drinks, handing hers over. "I kept the change. Now where's my ten?"

"Where's my driver?"

He groaned. "Got no driver, got someone who will let you make a call. Rufus will be along. Had to go steal his Momma's phone."

Great. Now she was hob-knobbing with a thief. She sat on the floor eating the biscuit, happy to have it. By the time they'd finished eating, a black boy came sauntering by the broken window. "You got money?" He smiled, white teeth flashing behind his full lips. "My Momma find out I took her phone, she whup my butt. So hurry up, make your call and give me the money. Twenty dollars."

"Whoa. Not twenty for one call. Five."

Rufus pulled back on handing her the phone. "Ten."

"You're lucky there are small bills." She pulled out a ten.

"You're lucky my Momma got a phone. Don't use up all the minutes."

She pressed Safari, googled green and yellow dealerships, John Deere, Marion Arkansas; it shone in the rectangular box. Southern Equipment. She pressed the call button. A man answered. "May I speak with Jeremy Southern, please?" She heard the man call to someone, *is the boss here, yet*. Minutes passed, with Rufus glaring at her. "Hello, may I help you, this is Jeremy Southern." She could have cried. "This is Haley Gipson, I met you at the Farm and Gin Show a few years back, do you remember me? I need help."

His gentlemanly southern accent came across the miles, "Lady, I don't recall meeting anyone named Haley Gipson, could you enlighten me?"

Then she remembered. "How about Laurie Stokes, do you remember her?"

A laugh sounded. "Is that you, Laurie? You still playing cops and robbers?"

That smarted. "Jeremy Southern, I'm in real need of a gentleman. Can you help me if your wife won't mind."

The laughter ceased. "She won't mind at all. Where are you?"

With Rufus help she gave him instructions. "What's your name?" She asked the breakfast boy. 'Glenn,' he said with his hand out. "Huh, uh. Neither of you get any money until my ride arrives." She shoved the clip back into her pocket.

A truck pulled into the lot and when she was certain it was Jeremy, tall and lanky stepping out of the pick-up she handed across Rufus money. Jeremy whistled. "Honey, you are a sight for sore eyes."

"Ain't she?" The boys said together as Rufus ran away, 'before my momma miss her phone,' he called over his shoulder but Glenn stayed, taking it all in. "She was asleep in that big old box back there," he explained importantly. "I brought her breakfast."

Haley gave him the eagle eye, showed him a ten and an extra twenty. The meaning was you shut your mouth and you will come out ahead. Grinning, Glenn reached for the money. "I got it," he says.

"How old are you and where are you staying?" Jeremy asked, waiting for an answer, his eyes pinned on Glenn.

"Here. Builders." Sarcastic, Glenn added, "What's it to you? I'm seventeen until tomorrow."

"Come with us, I'll find you a job and I know where there's a camping trailer needs an occupant." He glanced at Haley. "I think our lady, here, Miss Laurie, could do with a bit of sprucing up, too, don't you?" they all climbed into the cab of the truck.

"Sorry, it's a bit snug, the three of us in here, but I came as quickly as I could. This truck was parked right outside the building and the keys were in it. It's used when one of the men has to go out on call, so we need to get on back."

"No body ever come this quick for me," Glenn said. He pat Haley's knee. "You must be special."

"Yeah, our Laurie is special." Jeremy grinned. He was glancing at her as if he liked her.

She recognized the sounds, the tires on the bridge, reaching solid road, it was vivid in memory. Finally her body eased, her head drooped. She felt safe. She could...*She tried to shake her head, clear the fuzziness of her mind, as Yolanda and Elise paraded around a room, Bowie, no his name was Bodie telling them to settle down, and then there was this kid, Glenn, he said was his name. She felt so alone, where were her people? Race was gone, his parents deserted her, where was Mom and Dad? Then the tall guy stepped into the circle, he reached out a hand to her, he was smiling and he kissed her.* If she was dreaming, she liked her dream. She heard the sounds of traffic but she could not…

"She's asleep. I had to sleep on the ground. She had my box."

Jeremy glanced Glenn's way. "Son, you are not seventeen years old. Now, how old are you, really, and where are your parents?" They drove about a mile, until Jeremy glanced his way, again. "Question still stands. You might as well tell me, I'm offering you a way to better yourself, but I can't get caught up in the legal system. Tell me your story; I have friends I believe can help you, so right now help yourself."

"My daddy died, my Mom remarried so she'd have help with the girls. I have three sisters, Carrie Ann, Sophie and Bethany." Glenn paused. "He likes them but he don't like me, says I'm rebellious and need discipline." Glenn's voice sounded defiant. "My Daddy wouldn't abide his slappin' me around."

"So you ran? How long you been on the road?" Jeremy was listening to the thick accent. *Louisiana.*

"Since the weather turned warm. Problem is, I got no money, lost my clothes and I'm tired dodging the police."

"How old did you say you are?"

Glenn recognized the set of the mouth; the pinpointed eyes on him. "Just turned thirteen."

"Which state?"

"I aint' sayin."

They arrived. Jeremy drove around the sprawling building with its showcase windows, out to the edge of the property where the family's hunting camper set. "Get out, and help me with this lady."

Glenn grunted. "I'll help but the mess she's in, I ain't sure she's a lady."

Haley wakened when she felt a hand on her arm, shaking her, while a voice as liquid as syrup said, "Laurie, come on in to our home away from home. See what you can do about fixing yourself up. You hear?" *You hear*, that heavy Southern accent, the one she remembered and whispered trying to imitate some nights as she lay in bed wondering what happened to Jeremy Southern. *Was he happy with his little southern belle? Did he remember her? She remembered him. Race was becoming a memory.*

She came awake, crawled out on the driver's side to stand there taking in the home away from home. "I thought you said a camper." What she was seeing was a fifth wheel Mobil, large enough to house a family. "So what do you use this for, clandestine meetings?" They were walking toward it.

"That is definitely a thought," he rubbed his chin briefly, opening the door to help her up the steps. "My family loves hunting. Through the years, we've graduated from a tent that froze our ears off, to a one room camper. Well," he grinned, "Let's just say we enjoy this one, tremendously."

She wanted to sink onto the nearest chair, but he seemed to have other plans. "Come with me," he said. "No, not you Glenn, you're next. There's a shower." He stopped in the middle of a hallway, turned to study her a minute and then proceeded to a closed off bedroom, pointing to the small fully equipped bath. "I think my sister may have left a change or two of clothing, feel free to go through them and use whatever you need."

"Shoot, you got anything that'll fit me?" Glenn was standing in the doorway. "I could live in this joint."

"If you come clean, you might wrangle a night or two, with supervision, since you're not eighteen."

Haley's scream interrupted Glenn's second interrogation. "What *is wrong* with her? She makes me nervous."

"I have an idea we're going to know what's wrong pretty quick."

A distraught woman stood staring at them. "Why didn't you tell me I looked this bad?" Indignant, with hands on her hips, she did indeed look deranged. "To think I could've been picked up, if I tried to cross that bridge on foot."

Glenn was smirking. "They don't allow pedestrians crossing. I saw the sign."

CHAPTER EIGHTEEN

ARRIVING AT WORK, MARIGOLD WONDERED why Haley's car was parked on the street and the door to the shop was still locked, although she had given Haley a key in case the day arrived she needed her to open. Haley had come with an attitude Marigold could not process. There seemed to be a bit of sadness, but she hid it well and in the period of time they'd spent together stocking the store, not once had she allowed herself to give away any information. There might be hidden secrets she was keeping to herself.

They all, in the group, surmised Haley had taken the rap for an erstwhile boyfriend, who was dead or as community whispers canted, whisked away to another country, *maybe* living life while Haley did prison time. She remained stoic. Marigold probably knew more than the rest but five year old Ruthie had become Haley's trusted friend. Smiling, Marigold loved her little apprentice and wondered how it was going, Ruthie spending two days a week with Haley's mother until Bitty and Chester's return from the cruise. A smile tipped her lips; she wondered how the cruise was going. Good, she hoped.

BITTY AWAKENED, THINKING SHE HEARD Chester groan. Easing from the hollow of his body, she edged off the bed to glance at him, startled immediately as she laid a hand on Chester's forehead. "Chester. Chester, wake up." He opened his eyes, letting them slide back shut. "No, you can't sleep. You've got fever. Why, you're burning up." She was fumbling at bottles on the bedside table. "Didn't you take an aspirin, last night?" He was turning over, pulling the sheet up around his neck. "Huh, uh. You've got to take something to make the fever go down." She stepped around the end of the bed, into the small space between bed and wall and shook his shoulders. "I know what we do when Ruthie has a fever. Get up," she pulled him from the bed. "Get in the shower. Here, take this pill, too."

For some reason she noticed the thrum of the ship motor and then a bell's ringing. In reality the bell signified breakfast being served, this ships own personal prompt for passengers. It reminded her of bad news and the poem "For Whom the Bell Tolls," and she shook herself for such morbid thoughts. *It was his surgery, a delayed reaction; he'd been too busy the last few days, preparing for the cruise, pulling odd ends together.*

"If this fever hasn't left you, by ten o'clock, you'll have to see the ship's doctor."

Chester was coming awake. Groggy, but now his eyes were open and the natural morning needs were kicking in. He stumbled into the bathroom. Stood in front of the toilet, a very long time, before he called out, "Bitty, I can't pee."

Breakfast held no further thought, at a quarter 'til ten they were sitting in the ship's infirmary. Only one person was ahead of Chester's appointment. Within the hour, the lady doctor, then her assistant had examined Chester and decided to cath him in order to drain his bladder which by now was causing great pain due to its full capacity but they were having difficulty doing so.

"I can't imagine this," Doctor Brown said. "We will be nearing Victoria soon and I believe it is best that you leave the ship for medical attention we are not equipped to give you on this ship." She was looking behind Chester's ears. "Ah, ha," she said. Removing the small transdermal pads supposed to keep one from experiencing sea sickness, she held them for Chester to see, "Sometimes, it has been suggested wearing these patches messes with the bladder's function in men." Observing his disbelief, "However, that being said, she continued, "you still need medical attention."

"I'm not going to a hospital in Canada," Chester's words were adamant. "I'll go home, first."

"Mr. Mayfield, we are out in the middle of the ocean and the next stop can be Victoria. I strongly advise you to take my advice."

"No, ma'am. I'm heading back to the states as soon as I can get off this ship and hop a plane."

"You'll have to sign a paper releasing the ship's responsibility, Mr. Mayfield." The doctor's lips were compressed in a straight line, and her eyes were cold slits.

Chester slid off the table, "I'll need to get out of this gown, now where do I go?"

She motioned toward a small room that contained a stool and a sink. It was then Chester glanced down. "I'm bleeding," he said, as his eyes sought out Bitty, looking as grim as he felt.

The next hours would be relived over and over as first Chester, then Bitty, called airline after airline seeking means to return home. "No, ma'am, your previous reservation of return will not work, we have to find an opening for now and yes ma'am it will cost you double on such short notice. That's not a factor, yes ma'am. Your plane will touch down at three forty five in Memphis. We will have a wheelchair available and someone on standby to see to your husband's needs."

Though she had never handled such, Bitty was direct and efficient. She secured seating, though they would be separated. She called Ellen for advice on the best way to transport Chester from Airport to the nearest hospital and thanked her profusely, for the first time wishing she could give in to the tears building and the need to wail and beat her fists upon the wall that her man was suffering and by the blood she was almost certain it was something the doctor and her assistant had caused, but in all fairness she kept her suspicions to herself.

Before departing the boat, the doctor appeared one last time, papers of dismissal in hand. "I implore you, Mr. Mayfield, reconsider this folly. Your kidneys could shut down and kidney failure on an airplane that has its own destination can create severe repercussions."

Chester was drawn into a frenzy of pain and couldn't answer. Bitty drew herself up to all sixty inches. "Thank you, Dr. Brown. We are on our way home. Our biggest problem has been gaining passage and your ability to empty his bladder again before we begin our journey."

"That's the problem, Mrs. Mayfield. There will be no one on board to continue the process."

"We have no stops, Dr. Brown. It's my husband's decision and though I may not agree," Bitty took a deep breath. "It's his decision and I'll do whatever I can to get him to Memphis and into a hospital."

Chester was seated in First Class, Bitty took her seat on fifth row by a ritzy dame that made it immediately clear, *the window seat was hers, she didn't want to talk and please don't disturb me.* Bitty's natural independence returned. "I have larger problems than you, Miss," she said, gripping her purse tightly in her hands as she listened to the revving up of the plane's engine while praying a safe trip to Memphis. It was going to be a struggle. They promised a car would be waiting to whisk them through evening traffic North to South to the hospital and a Urologist that would take care of her husband's need. He hadn't drunk any fluids, surely his bladder would hold, besides the group was praying.

It seemed an eternity. The stewardess gave her regular reports on Chester. "He does have a low grade temperature, but those pills the doctor prescribed seem to help. Yes, he is sleeping, why don't you try to get some rest?" But Bitty couldn't sleep. She sought comfort in reliving Ellen's words to her before they disconnected the phones. "Bitty, God honors prayers. The scripture reminds us where two are gathered together, in His name, He is there in their midst. Find it in Matthew chapter eighteen, eighteen through twenty, if you have your bible. God is saying, when we pray he honors our prayer, He listens and the Holy Spirit quickens and guides us." She had realized Ellen was hesitating. "Bitty, this may be one of life's largest hurdles, just don't lose faith. If his eye is on a sparrow and we are all praying then I know, God's eye is on that plane. Let the Lord, lead, Bitty." Bitty dug into her purse to find her Bible.

She slipped the small New Testament back into her purse. "So you are one of them?" The woman by the window had observed Bitty's reading and putting away the Bible.

"Yes, I am." And God prompted her heart to do something Bitty had never done before. "May I tell you my experience and why I am a believer?" Making eye contact, she said, "It didn't happen overnight."

ELLEN CALLED DAN AND THEN Harriet. By noon, she had called everyone in the group a second time to relay the message; Bitty and Chester were on the plane, headed for Memphis. Ellen and Dan's children were in Harriet and Hattie's care, the Escalade was ready. With that, they left in order to arrive on time. The plane touched down, the ramp was installed for disembarking, as the Stewardess wheeled a chair into Chester's presence, seated him and pushed him down the ramp with Bitty following. Bitty was clutching her purse in one hand and pulling a large suitcase behind. Her new friend was in charge of the carry-on. "You have all that medical paraphernalia," she said. "I don't mind at all. I still don't understand how they could pull your luggage, in order to send you on your way. No carousel for you. I'll have to wait until they unload everything."

The woman clutched Bitty in a tight life gripping hug as they were parting. "I'll be calling you and as promised I will keep our conversation in mind. Thanks for sharing." She was gone, tripping through the terminal, a fashion plate in disguise, for beneath the materialistic layers, heartache had betrayed her need and she had listened to Bitty's witness and testimony that even an encrusted heart can change. If she had sensed Bitty's own desperation of the hour, perhaps God would use that too.

The Stewardess eyed Bitty, hesitant, thinking this small woman could not possibly man the wheelchair with its occupant, pull the heavy suitcase and walk the mile required to the front entrance of the terminal. So occupied in trying to manage their business, even now she was unaware someone was calling to her from the roped off area. "Bitty." Finally, the stewardess asked, "Ma'am, are you Bitty?"

"Yes." Bitty glanced up, for the first time questioning her ability to see this situation through. One look at Chester's face told her he wasn't faring well, either. "You wanted something?"

The Stewardess only pointed. "I believe those people are trying to gain your attention."

Bitty's face wreathed with smile. "I'll be right back," she said to Chester as she grabbed the handle of the big suitcase tighter and practically ran toward Ellen and Daniel. "Oh, thank the Lord," she said, more a sob of thanksgiving, "I don't know why you're here but I'm so happy to see you."

"But your're not speechless," Daniel teased, grinning. "Ellen said we must come and here we are."

Across the rope, Bitty hugged them both. "Let me go get Chester."

"Just roll him this far and I'll take over," Daniel was transferring the suitcase to Ellen as he spoke. "Can you manage pulling this and I'll push the wheel chair." Bitty was back with Chester, who tried to smile but the effort was a bland attempt. "All right, Buddy, let's get you to the hospital." They were stepping it up now. "Bitty, why didn't you request help?"

"I did, but I was told they are over-extended and it would be awhile, so seeing you, it doesn't matter."

"I've text Dr. Pinkstaff to see if he knows a urologist he'd recommend and he gave me this name and hospital. What do you think, Chester? Bitty?"

Chester groaned as Bitty said, "I hope he's there today." They were loading him into the front seat, reclining it until he was comfortable, while the two women climbed into the back and they were on the way. Within an hour, Chester was in a side room of ER, the urologist had arrived and relief was expected. "Oh," Bitty pressed her hands to her face. "I didn't have time to consider everything. You know, when you're working with it, your mind is busy, but now," She sighed. "I feel like falling apart and crying with relief."

The Urologist came to speak with Bitty. "I was able to get a catheter into the urethra, and I can see why the ship physician couldn't. What they did was puncture his bladder, trying to run the catheter through, but the catheter entered the wrong area. No doubt bacteria managed to get in and his body is trying to fight off an infection.

"We have him on an IV for the antibiotic and we need to keep him over night. Then, tomorrow he will go home with a catheter."

"How long will he need to be on the catheter?" Ellen asked.

"We were able to empty the bladder but there's a lot of swelling due to the puncture." The Urologist scrubbed at his chin, thinking. "I was told you are from Missouri. There are questions I must ask. Are you going to find your own doctor, or return here? How long since Mr. Mayfield had the prostatectomy? That leaves a bit of swelling in some men." He listened as Bitty relayed the information, then turning to leave, he said, "I tell you what, think it over, if you don't find a Urologist you feel comfortable with, come back here, otherwise call and tell my receptionist your plans." They thanked him and he was gone.

Approximately twenty four hours later, they arrived at the hotel where Bitty's car was parked.

"I'll ride with you, Bitty, how does that sound, Daniel? Chester will probably sleep all the way."

Bitty was out the door, walking around her car, the strangest of expressions on her face. "Look." She shook her head, astounded. Someone had knocked the driver's side window completely out. Inside the glove compartment was gaping, the cover hanging by one hinge and it was obvious, whoever crawled inside the car was further from caring than he was in hunting for something of worth. Chester sat in the Escalade; the whole scene made his head hurt. He closed his eyes, too weak to help Bitty.

After an hour of questioning the hotel staff, they realized they had reached a dead end. There was nothing more to do but drive the car back to Missouri, have it repaired and the glass replaced. Ellen and Bitty took the floor mat in the trunk, threaded it over the empty space where the window had been and slammed the door shut. "Let me drive, Bitty. This is enough to make a strong woman weak."

Handing over the keys, Bitty asked, "Did you say weak or weep? They both fit." Ellen exited the hotel property behind Daniel and Chester. "You know, Ellen, it's almost a test to see what it takes to break."

"And you're still standing, Bitty." Ellen gave her a quick one arm hug. "I'm so proud of you."

"Ellen, what's going to happen to Chester?" Amidst the noise from the flapping of the mat in the window, she had to ask. She had a terrible feeling in the pit of her stomach.

"WHAT A STRANGE COINCIDENCE," HARRIET mused. "Bitty and Chester are coming in today, and we don't know what's happened to your co-worker. Haley's car is still parked out on the street. Does that mean anything in particular?"

Heaving a deep breath, Marigold was still trying to add the *coincidence* Harriet mentioned to the one she had found when she opened yesterday morning. First she had checked the windows, finding not one open, therefore a breeze had not blown any of the items onto the floor and strangest of all one of the large tables had been moved. Examining the floor beneath, she had seen a loose board and assumed Haley had thought to cover it until nailed, and no one would trip over it. On closer inspection, she found the board easily removed, revealed a hidden compartment. Obviously, it was used to conceal something of importance. What? Her own scoffing had kept Haley from discussing the find with her.

Why hadn't Haley called? Not wanting to create a situation she chose not to call Haley's mother, then nearing closing time, Mrs. Gipson called. "Marigold, I'm afraid Haley ran into a bit of bad luck, this morning. She asked me to call you and apologize that she didn't come into work today."

Something about the woman's voice, lent no allowance to ask further questions. Quietly, Marigold accepted the conversation, saving her own queries for Haley. Throughout the day, she and Harriet waited on customers, opened boxes of new stock and tended to business. Ruthie was in the next room, having arrived with Harriet rather than stay with Hattie who was watching over the twins.

"Ruthie's quiet, don't you think?" Marigold asked Harriet and Harriet nodded. "Maybe worried over Haley." Pausing, Harriet heard the muffled sound of the television Marigold thought would entertain the child. "You know she's reading. You can turn that off. "Ruthie's been reading since she was three years old." Hearing her name, Ruthie came into the room.

"Are you worried about Haley?" Marigold asked.

"I was," Ruthie replied, solemnly, "but now she's all right. Whatever Haley tells you is true."

"How do you know?" Marigold stopped folding T's to stare at Ruthie. "Who told you?"

"I just know. I feel it right here." Bowing her head Ruthie lay her right hand across her heart, her left on her forehead. "I can't explain it. Sometimes Jesus tells me things." Her voice was soft, as she raised her head, her eyes were gentle. "Does Jesus speak to you?" She smiled. "You have to listen to hear him."

"OH, MY GOODNESS," HALEY STEPPED out of the shower, glancing into the mirror over the tiny dresser. There were bruises along her body, she guessed from being cramped and tied up. Her lips were swollen nearly twice their size but at least her hair was clean. The warmth of the water had taken away some of the stiffness. Now if she could find suitable clothing in the closet Jeremy had mentioned.

There were three outfits hanging on the rod. She checked the labels for size and saw they bore very good brands and possibly one would fit better than the other two size threes. She donned the medium size blouse which was loose, and the size five trousers that fit better than expected. Olive green trousers and a swirl of colors, green, gold, muted orange in the top, were good enough for her. She was relieved, more than any word would ever describe, insanely spontaneously happy to be found and especially by Jeremy Southern. Now, she wondered how he would explain her to the little wife.

"I'll drive you back to Missouri," he had said, leaving her to bathe and taking Glenn with him. "Let me know when you're ready." She finished by applying a bit of borrowed cosmetics from the drawer.

"You can leave, just like that?" That's when she remembered she must call home. She heard him say, he was the boss, but she was already using the phone he offered. He had an uncanny way of knowing her need, before she asked. His smile of encouragement warmed her heart.

"Mom?" She almost cried, hearing her mother's voice. "Mom. Something has happened. I'm all right." Her own voice sounded quiet in her ears, almost pleading. "Mom, please, can you trust me? Don't say anything to anyone about this. I'll be home soon and we'll talk." Her voice cleared. "And Mom, there will be someone with me, a good friend."

DOROTHY SUDDENLY WISHED HARPER WAS home from work. There would be only the two for dinner but she prepared for four, anyway, trying to concentrate on cooking, but the rice ran over and she nearly burned the pork chops. Finished with the salad, she placed the left over products in the drawer of the frig and stepped to the window for the hundredth time. It would have been better had she baked them together, pouring a can of celery soup over them, but her train of thought was on Haley and where she was the last thirty six hours. Surely she had not left the state that was detrimental to her freedom. Her mind was flitting here and there, remembering the day of court and Haley being dragged from the Judge's chambers, Haley pleading, "Daddy, please, Daddy." All the while both parents stood in full view of everyone with tears streaming down their faces. "You promised," her cries had been heard down the halls. It was the Feds promised, on Friday, that Haley was in the clear and would not go to prison, but on Monday she was sentenced.

Coming home, transition had not been easy, but Haley had not complained. Almost numb, Dorothy considered her daughter, agreeing too easily, careful with answers; Haley had done nothing to rock the boat, so to speak, no act that might send her back to prison. So what happened the night before? Where was she now and who was the friend? *Rumors kept circulating that Race was not dead, surely not Race.*

A path was worn in the carpet, from the front windows to the dining room and then to the kitchen stove. She heard tires on the drive and hurried outside. Harper was just getting out of the truck when he saw her expression and hurried to Dorothy. "Hon, what's wrong?"

"It's Haley." The tears ran down her cheeks, as she hastily scrubbed them away. "She will be here, soon but there's a problem." Dorothy leaned into Harper as he pulled her into his arms. "Oh, Harper, I've been so worried. What if it's something that takes her back to prison? She's just now beginning to settle in. What will we do? What will I do?"

Daylight was turning to dark, street lights were coming on, and then they were in full beam, a truck turned into the drive. Haley climbed down from the passenger side, and from behind the steering wheel, a door opened and long Khaki clad legs became visible. Tall, handsome and Dorothy prayed, courteous. She dared not move as the young man followed Haley through the door. It wasn't Race. Dorothy had fret the tales were true, that Race had not died but was living away and had now returned, his influence to further destroy her daughter. Vulnerable to his charm, she did not heed the warnings.

Dorothy later pondered; she reached for her child and Haley came into her arms, beaten, trembling like a scared little rabbit, and as she had many years previously, Dorothy soothed the hurt and fear as her love flowed through this grown up daughter clinging to her as though death were at the door. Harper's arms closed around them and they stood there, unmindful of the stranger looking on. At last, Dorothy asked for lack of another question, "Have you eaten? We had no appetite, but maybe now we have." Biding time, allowing her child to gather her thoughts, Dorothy was the mother Haley needed, the mother Haley had kept at arm's length since her return, the mother who would love her forever, hurting when hurt, holding on to the knowledge, as the Father in Heaven loves his children, she would love her child through the trials of life and wait for that love to be returned. Forever.

"I have to tell you what happened. It sounds unbelievable, but it's true."

"We can talk while we eat, if you wish, or if it will keep another hour, then you can tell us. You don't look as though you have eaten." Dorothy's child could pass for a poster of battered women.

"I'm starving." Haley gave a nervous giggle. "My last good meal was the night I was abducted."

"Abducted?"

CHAPTER NINETEEN

"WHO WOULD HAVE THOUGHT IT?" Harriet stood in the door way, watching Anne folding Andy's clothes. "I mean, it is the last thing you want to think of, a young woman abducted right there in Marigold's new shop. Doesn't it bring your own situation to mind? Garcia French mistakenly took you…and then Ruthie was kidnapped. You can't forget those times."

"I haven't forgotten, Harriet. I'm just relieved Haley is all right."

"Now, we have all been invited to the Gipson's home to discuss the matter, lest it happen again. I declare, I don't know if the business has been a good venture, or not."

"Marigold's?" Anne paused, a small pair of pants in her hands to stare at Harriet. "Why? What does that have to do with Haley's being abducted? Wasn't that just coincidental? Haley going there after hours, evidently got caught, in the way and the man panicked and took her with him?"

"No. The man was looking for hidden money. You heard the story. The previous owner laundered money for various businesses, taking it in, making it look legal," Harriet sighed. "You'll have to let Andrew explain the process to you. Anyway, I'm rattling on. I think what happened to Haley could've been Marigold and it makes me nervous. Can you imagine, the money was hidden in the floor?"

Anne was smiling.

"Is that smile for me, or is that Andy's picture of his daddy?" Harriet stepped near to study what was in Anne's hand. "Went through the wash, didn't it? He carries it in his pocket every day."

Anne sank onto the bed and reached for Harriet's hand. Harriet settled down beside her. "Now, what will you tell me?"

FRIDAY EVENING ARRIVED WITH DOROTHY scurrying about, a last minute errand to pick up the special dessert, giving a crowning touch to the dining room table and the small round white clothed tables she had set up for their guests. She had even invited the pastor, Brother Joe. She felt like the Biblical parent, her prodigal daughter had finally come home. True, she had been there months but not until experiencing the terrible fate of being taken from Marigold's shop had Haley allowed them to love her as the daughter they cherished and welcomed back into their lives.

She had to chuckle. What must the young man think of Haley's parents? It had taken a good while before he was even introduced along with the explanation they had met three years ago. Yes, he was the young man who had befriended Halley when she was on the run and ended up across State Line. It was Harper's idea, to gather their new friends and explain once and for all what had happened to Haley. "They're good people, Dorothy, and we want our girl blessed by their prayers, lest this happen again, all of us together will be on the watch for this man. And the Chief of Police is part of this group of friends."

"But he has just undergone some sort of surgery, Harper. What if it is too soon to discuss with him?"

Harper was not having it, "He's the Chief of Police, Dorothy. It's his job."

Fluffing the pillows on the sofa, Dorothy did a head count? Had she set enough places? She glanced around the room, happy and pleased that Haley had agreed on asking the group from church that had taken them in, to dinner. Their list of friends was greatly expanded when they were included; all because Haley was prone to think where they previously attended would not accept her back, they were now part of Christ Church. Harper was happy and Dorothy was happy when her family was.

Rushing through the door, Haley stopped to exclaim, "Oh, Mom, it looks marvelous." Then, she was in her room, the shower running, to return only minutes later, freshly attired her make up on and her hair in curls atop her head. "How do I look," she asked, doing a slow twirl, "Jeremy's coming."

"So that explains the glow you've worn the last few days and the happiness, I thought from being home?" Dorothy teased. "If I didn't know different, I'd say you look like a girl in love, but I'll just say, smitten. You've changed, Haley. Now you are attainable, not holding us at bay. You're ours now."

"Mom," Haley's eyes clouded. "I had to come to grips with my attitude. Race has finally left my thoughts. I felt resentful and terribly hurt that I had to take the brunt of not just my mistakes but his too. And his parents dismissed me from their lives as though it was all my fault, and it wasn't."

"I know." Dorothy soothed. "But now you realize your whole life is ahead of you."

"I don't want to go it alone, Mom. That's what hurt the most. I thought Race and I would be together. I had to grieve Race leaving my life, alone, in a women's prison where I cut grass and walked behind another person, and maybe now it has come to me, I learned something there, too, even if I was mean and hateful when I came home." She smiled, her eyes lighting up. "For almost three years I have remembered Jeremy helping me, that time when I was on the run and ended up in Memphis and I always had to remember he was engaged to marry his little southern belle that Christmas, but it didn't happen, Mom?" Her voice took on an excitement Dorothy hadn't seen in the months since Camp Cup Cake was behind her. "He said he remembered me, too, and no one else took her place because he was thinking of me but he couldn't find me because I had given him a different name." She saw her mother's frown. "I did. I didn't trust anyone so I told him I was Laurie somebody and that's who he kept searching for, but it wasn't me." Her laugh was filled with joy. "I think I love him, Mom"

"But you hardly know him."

"Really, Mom?" Haley reached to give her mom a hug that ended up with their hands together doing a turnaround in the middle of the room. "There are some people you know from the beginning, even if you've just met." Placing a kiss on her mother's brow, she said, "I think it's love at second sight, Mom."

"Second sight?"

"Yeah," Haley hugged her again. "We sparred a bit that first time, but then I met his family and I liked what I saw. But I tried not to think of Jeremy because he had this little fiancé' off on cruise with her Mother." Haley danced a jig. "That was the best cruise ever; she fell in love with some guy on ship."

Dorothy rolled her eyes. "Be careful, Haley."

"Oh, Mom, you know what he said, he remembered our kiss. So did I."

IT WAS A DELIGHTFUL EVENING. Their guests arrived; Harper welcomed each one, and asked Brother Joe to give the blessing before they settled down to Dorothy's good food. Hattie had volunteered to sit with the twins and Andy at Harriet's home leaving Ruthie the only child but staying with Miss Dorothy those days Bitty was away, a bond was formed and a special place had evolved on the sun porch where Haley's childhood doll house, *brought down from the attic,* was now Ruthie's enchantment with its tiny little people and furniture the size to fit a mouse.

"You like my doll house?" Haley slipped into the sunroom to find Ruthie.

"I love the little people. Your Momma made the prettiest little quilts and tablecloths, Haley. How did she do that?" They examined the rooms, set up as a normal house, with a mother at a sink, a baby in a bed and a daddy reading a paper as he sat in his chair.

"I wanted to thank you, Ruthie. I've heard through the grapevine you told Marigold I was all right. Did you know when I was in trouble?"

"I worried." Ruthie replied. "But you didn't want anyone to know. Please don't do that again, Haley. I don't know what to do. Momma says I will grow into knowing and that I must not fret and if I feel like fretting I am to pray."

"Did you pray for me?" Haley stooped low to peer straight into Ruthie's face.

"Lots." Ruthie sighed. "I was praying for you and for Uncle Chester too. I was busy praying."

Haley pulled her into her arms. "Your gift must be burdensome at times. I'm sorry I made you sad, but you are a blessing to me, Ruthie Anderson. I am beginning to understand God's love a little better because of you." Memory flit across her mind, *all you have to do is talk to Jesus*, Ruthie had told her.

"I may get a new name. Will you still like me?" Ruthie's expression changed to joy. "Ruthie Gates."

"Yay," Haley clapped her hands. "I'm going back inside; will you be all right out here, Ruthie?"

Listening to the captain, Haley wondered how he felt about her record and if it were wise to be discussing the man named Earl. Her father insisted, "if not the community, at least the group of friends, Haley, we don't know if this man is through with his search for money in Marigold's building even if it is your feeling he got all he was looking for. The building is Marigold's business. You are mine."

Daniel's hand tightened on Ellen's. She would be remembering Ruthie's kidnapping. Safe returns were not always the case as in Ruthie Anderson. The last name rolled through his mind. As promised, he was investigating her father's disappearance; if it were genuine the adoption would go smoothly. Heaven forbid, Jeffrey Anderson know his daughter had a special gift, he would use every opportunity for his own gain, to the point, Daniel suspected of setting her up as some well of knowledge and charging a fee for her services. He sighed, the burden heavy on his heart. Sometimes promises were not easy to keep.

Bitty listened to the story being presented. Marigold's helper had been taken, bound and unconscious by a man they suspected lived in the Cape and the only clue, his name was Earl, he was a grandfather and claimed he had agreed to find and deliver the money stored in Marigold's new place of business to the former owner. But no one knew a man named Earl. Her husband, Chief of Police, Chester Mayfield would run a search and scourer the town in search of the abductor.

Andrew sat to one side, studying the girl, her parents and the likelihood of this presentation being true. She smiled. That was different from the surly person he encountered first meeting in her parents' home and certainly not as acidic as the one who slapped his face, whose eyes were filled with anger and resentment. His escape from the hoods of the city had not ended, by the Judges decree he worked with them every day, seeing the despair of their lives and why they sought to differ but going about it at the expense of others, taking what was not theirs, their conscience bland and uncaring.

This Earl may have been caught up in doing wrong for need of money to help his family. Still, wrong was wrong and usually the stipend was high when the law was involved. He ran the files of his mind. He could not recall an Earl coming through. They might never find the man. With a silent breath of relief, Andrew Graves thanked God Harper Gipson saw something worth saving in him that Christmas. Now with Anne by his side he hoped soon she would marry him and their family would be whole again.

Matt mulled over the evidence. He liked Haley and knew she was telling the truth, what he didn't know was the likelihood of the people involved in their shady business returning. "What if we install cameras? Would that help? And Marigold does not go into the building alone, nor anyone else."

"Matt, that would be so unhandy. I have to run in and out as the vendors call on the shop."

Ruthie had edged to Marigold's side. She felt Marigold's resistance to Matt's last suggestion. She lay a hand on Marigold's arm. "You think I should do the Matt thing," Marigold asked, her irritation dissolving. "Well, for a while." A strange peace settled in her mind as she hugged Ruthie. "You little imp, you know something, don't you?" Oh, how she loved her little apprentice, "But you don't know what you know."

Across the room, Matt wasn't certain how he won that one from his stubborn wife. He sighed, if only his mother would come around to accepting Marigold. The pain around his heart increased as he considered Marigold's trying and his mother's continued rebuff of this Tinkerbelle person he loved to the point his heart ached, but there was nothing either of them could do to resolve the problem. He glanced to where Ellen was smiling at her child and the room dissolved of anxieties became the hub of caring people sharing what was going on in their lives. He had to leave his mother in God's hands.

Bitty's heart was full. Ruthie's gift came from God and she had to learn how to trust him to guard this little girl. There were evil people who would come to her, if they knew, people who would use her gift and throw her aside. She glanced around the room. Harriet, Anne, Marigold and Haley's eyes were locked on Ruthie as she went into her mother's arms. In a room full of people, these women made contact, the world would not know, God would use Ruthie and they would be her protectors. The bond had been set; it would not be broken.

Harriet called her people the next day. "If you find him, let me know. Do not hurt him."

Life continued among the group of believers who attended Christ Church. Brother Joe found himself lingering over the experience at the Gipson home. Something had happened, he wasn't certain exactly what but he came away thinking, these were a close knit group and God was alive in their midst. He saw encouragement and looking to the future, but he couldn't quite put his finger on what made them different. There was the fellow whose name had been in the newspaper, the girl who returned from prison and had recently been abducted and he had just learned Marigold was Harriet's birth child. Yes, they were a peculiar people and he prayed nothing else came along to disturb their friendship. It seemed they'd already encountered about every trial to test their faith.

TWO WEEKS PASSED AND IT was time for Chester to return to Memphis and the doctor there, or find a new one. "You know, Bitty,

I liked him, he explained things on a basis I could understand but I think I'll return to Dr. Anthony. He's closer and going back to work I don't need those long trips."

He was looking forward to the removal of the catheter. "It's uncomfortable, not to mention unnatural." Bitty, the new bride felt the warmth flush her face. She still blushed. Chester chuckled. "Now if we can just get my water works going again, I'll be a happy man." He enjoyed Bitty's naiveté. She was all he had wanted, pure and simple, kind and easy to love. "You will go with me, won't you?"

"But not in."

"What if there are words we need to hear together." His eyes held hers. She nodded. "Good." He said.

On the day of the appointment, Dr. Anthony listened to the story about the cruise, the flight back to Memphis and the punctured bladder. "I don't encourage leaving a catheter in longer than two weeks if there's a way not to, that's where the problem of infection occurs." The catheter was removed and the bag discarded. "Now, Mr. Mayfield, go home, drink a lot of water and keep the bladder and urethra flushed. That's crucial right now. We're having a CBC done to determine your blood count." He pat Chester's shoulder. "Do your best to flush your system."

They stopped for lunch and Chester began the water cleanse. Bitty was concerned. "What if you drink all that water and your bladder still doesn't work what then? Back to the catheter?"

Chester groaned. "I hope not. It feels like a knot in the wrong place. I tried not to complain but it is one of the most uncomfortable happenings in my life." Taking another sip of water, he said, "The doctor said drink lots, so I'm going to do the best I can." Arriving home, strangely tired, Chester sank into his chair. His joints were beginning to ache and he remembered the ache was similar to the time he had the flu.

The hours passed and Bitty kept thinking he would waken and go to the bathroom, surely his bladder was sending the message to empty. What did she know about these things? She could confide in Ellen, but it was such a personal matter. She tried to remember when Larry was sick and they did a CBC, wasn't that to determine if there were too many white blood cells? The only reason the doctor would order that would be in case of an infection, wouldn't it? Sighing heavily, Bitty tried to put Larry's death to the back of her mind. This was Chester, with a whole and sound body. But then, he wasn't, was he?

She wakened Chester from sleep. "It's six o'clock, Chester. I've sandwiches and chips with soup ready if you feel like eating." She wanted to say, and *you haven't been to the bathroom*, but she didn't. If she still undressed in the dark, he could certainly go to the bathroom without her prompt. She was very private. In the beginning it disturbed her that Chester would sit in his chair in the bathroom, mornings, watching as she combed her hair, applied the dab of make-up she wore and sprinted a bit of cologne on each side of her neck. "Why do you do this?" She asked. "I'm embarrassed. I know I'm a very plain person, Chester."

To which he would laugh. "I just like to watch you, Bitty. You've always amazed me and to me you are beautiful." She would blush and he would rise to leave while she dressed. "It's good to have someone," he would say, "But I'll leave you for the moment. Will you be in, soon?"

The pattern was set. Day after day, the ritual, until she joined him in the kitchen where he had coffee ready to pour and the toaster ready. Then, after she had made the choice of the day, Chester left for work. But for now, he was in his chair, his breathing heavy and she was worried. She shook him gently. "Chester, are you ready for a sandwich? Since we ate lunch out, I prepared a light meal."

Groaning, Chester rose up from the chair and they both recognized the effort required. "I don't know what's wrong with me," he said, "Sit here too long I guess." He headed toward the bathroom. "I'll just wash up." When he staggered, he hoped Bitty didn't notice; a feeling of nausea had come over him and his heart felt as though it would jump out of his chest it was beating so fast. "I'll just wash."

And pee, Bitty was thinking, but she didn't mention that normal function of the body.

Before he washed, leaning heavily on the sink, Chester felt the pressure, not knowing what to do; he moved to the toilet and stood there, contemplating, while his mind took on a hazy reality.

He shook himself, inwardly commanding his body to perform, but it wouldn't. "Bitty," he called. "I can't empty my bladder. It's full and I'm hurting. What should I do?"

Now, Bitty called Ellen. "I hate to bother you, but I don't know what to do. Go to ER?"

The catheter was back in, the bladder drained and the doctor on call decided the catheter must be left in until morning, "call your urologist, tell him what happened and I know he will want to see you."

"If this isn't the life." Chester apologized for the umpteenth time. "I'm sorry to put you through this, Bitty." The call to the clinic, next morning, had brought them back for an eleven o'clock appointment.

"HOW WAS YOUR NIGHT?" DR. Anthony leaned against the edge of the table, studying Chester as he was quieter than usual. "Your colors a bit off. According to lab reports on the CBC you do have an infection, which means you are back on the catheter for a while, let's say a week and then we'll try the water flush again and see what happens. Just keep emptying the bag. Take your antibiotic and go on back to work."

"This is supposed to be normal?" After closing the door for Bitty, Chester slid into the seat of the Police Car. "I try to remember we have young men who were soldiers fighting for our country that come back home with a trial such as this that's going to last the rest of their life. I'm ashamed, Bitty, that accepting this catheter is a hard task and too, it frightens me how quickly this thing has gotten out of control."

"Well," she sighed. "It's foreign to your body. I understand. Not completely, but I sympathize."

"I guess it's good I have to focus on what's going on in this town; otherwise I'd feel sorry for me." He tried to laugh but the bag on his leg felt uncomfortable and was a constant reminder. "I'll get the hang of this if it kills me."

CHAPTER TWENTY

THEY ATTENDED CHURCH ON SUNDAY and Brother Joe met Chester to welcome him back. "I designed this sermon around you, brother," he said, an arm around the chief's shoulder.

Chester groaned, "I hope not. Don't go telling my secrets." Brother Joe left, laughing.

Ruthie's voice rang out pure and praising; praising the Jesus she read about in her New Testament and the Heavenly Father of the Old Testament. When Jesus Father spoke to him when he was being baptized was one of her favorite passages. Now as the song ended, Ruthie's heart burst with love for the people of Christ Church, for her family and friends in the pew, and Sammy and Danny in the Nursery.

"Today," Brother Joe said, we are speaking on adverse times, when those trials you wished you had never heard of catch up with you and catch you off guard. May we stand for the reading of the word. James chapter one, verse two through four: "My brethren, count it all joy when ye fall into divers temptations; knowing this, that the trying of your faith worketh patience. But let patience have her perfect work, that ye may be perfect and entire, wanting noth-ing." May God bless the reading of the word and extend his blessing to you. You may be seated."

"Really, James," you may be asking. "Be happy and full of joy when hard times come, like if I especially want to learn patience and you are guaranteeing me I should want for nothing?" There was a wave of agreement through the congregation. "Verse thirteen of the same passage tells us," Let no man say when he is tempted, I am tempted of God; for God cannot be tempted with evil, neither tempteth he any man." Do we understand, God may allow the trial, but He will help us through it?

"Do you advance in your faith during the trials of life, or do you back slide, so to speak, which I mean you fall back to the times when you questioned everything, you don't question losing salvation, because who God holds in his hand cannot be taken away, but you question why me? What did I do to deserve this? Philippians 4:13, "I can do all things through Christ who strengtheneth me, and verse 19 My God shall supply all my needs according to his riches in glory by Christ Jesus." Now, with scripture promising we are taken care of, why do we fret and worry when trials come?" I think if we read the book of Philippians we glean the knowledge, God is near. He has not abandoned us. We may be going through the fire but we will come out as gold, refined, a better person for the ordeal we went through. It can be a health issue, the loss of a loved one, the horror of tragedy. Is there a worse tragedy than what we face daily seeing the news and the treatment of Christian's in other lands, the beheading of innocent children? How do we go through troublesome times?"

"We must learn to trust wholly in the Lord. What does Christ offer that nothing else can; no other religion? When you receive salvation, by the blood Jesus Christ shed on the cross at Calvary, you have eternal life in Christ, a gift you have done nothing to deserve, a gift that money cannot buy and the devil cannot take away. It is a gift of God, less any man should boast. You ask forgiveness, repent of your sins and allow Jesus to come into your heart. He will be there when you need Him, when times are hard."

"Can we persevere through the hard times. Will we put our trust in the Lord who died a death of agony on the cross for our sins, allowing Him to do a work for us, when our job is to hang on and trust Him?"

Chester hugged the pastor as they were leaving. "You had me going there; I sure didn't want my weaknesses revealed."

"Yeah," Brother Joe pat him soundly on the back. "You hang in there. God's not through with you."

BITTY WOULD REMEMBER THE PASTOR'S words a hundred times over in the following days. Chester tried to return to work, but weaknesses overcome his body. She found him often, sitting huddled beneath a blanket. "Are you cold?" She would sit at his feet on a small round foot stool, peering into his face.

"I'm so sorry, Bitty, that I have brought you to this."

"Shall I call Dr. Anthony?"

"We called him yesterday, and last week," Chester sighed. "I'm to continue the antibiotic."

"I don't think it's working."

Ellen dropped by after work. "Chester," she leaned down to hug him. "I'm praying for you. I could just cry to see you like this." She kissed his forehead.

"I could cry, too," he replied, sinking deeper into the blankets folds.

From that day on Ellen dropped by each afternoon; her shift ending early, gave her time to check on Chester and Bitty before picking up the twins and going on for Ruthie at Mrs. Gipson's.

"It's killing me, Ellen," Bitty said, tears in her eyes. "Not just seeing Chester suffers but I miss Ruthie and I know she mustn't be around this sadness. Is she all right with Mrs. Gipson?" She led Ellen to the bedroom where Chester rested, since yesterday, too weak to walk further.

"She's fine, Bitty." Ellen stood before Chester. "Chester, may I look at the bag? I want to see the color of your urine." When he nodded, Ellen raised the pajama material towards his knee and stud-ied the urine, cloudy with maybe a tinge of blood, but she made no statement other than, "thank you, Chester."

Bitty followed Ellen quietly to the door, stepping outside to close it firmly. "What did you see?"

"Bitty, an infection can take hold and roar through the body. I'm not happy with what I see. If you will give me the liberty of speaking with Dr. Anthony, there's something I think he must order. Otherwise, you may be calling Chester's daughter to come home to see her father." Ellen reached for Bitty, "I'm sorry, that sounds harsh but you are my friend and I've seen this happen on the floor. In a matter of days, an infection can kill the patient if it's not stopped."

"But he's been on antibiotics two weeks now. What else can we do?" Bitty felt the panic rising. "I knew, Ellen. I've watched him fading away. And when he is in bed, he curls up like a baby in fetal position. He's on antibiotics, Ellen."

"What if they aren't working?" Ellen's calm expression belied fear. "Ask Chester if you can put my name on his record to discuss this situation with the doctor, otherwise the law denies me that right."

Having done so, next Bitty called Harriet. "Harriet, I spoke with Dr. Anthony's receptionist. I need to add Ellen's name on my and Chester's medical record. She is going to fax the forms to you, if you will fax them back this evening after I sign." Harriet's soothing reply eased an anxious moment for Bitty but the kindness brought tears. "I don't know, Harriet, Ellen said it's bad and there's one more thing needing to be done."

Ellen drove to Dr. Anthony's office. She was there when the forms from Harriet's fax machine returned and asked to see the doctor. "Dr. Anthony, I'm Chester Mayfield's friend. Have you seen him in the last week?"

"No, but I can't discuss this with you, Mrs. Gates." He was reading the name tag she still wore, "Unless your friends have given you permission." His receptionist handed over the forms. "Well, Mrs. Gates, it seems the forms have mysteriously appeared. How can I help your friend, my patient, Mr. Mayfield?" He bent his head to listen. "This is done at the hospital but you think we can do this?" His eyes held hers. "You're sure we can keep a sterile field doing this in Mr. Mayfield's home?"

"He looks too sick to travel to the hospital, Dr. Anthony."

"We'll see what we can do," Dr. Anthony replied.

WHILE THEY DROVE TO BITTY'S house, Ellen called Daniel to pick up the children. Bitty met them at the door. Dr. Anthony was shone into Chester's room where he lay curled up under the blankets. "This man needs to be in the hospital," Dr. Anthony's voice relayed the shock he was feeling at the moment.

"Or home health," Ellen suggested. "In view of what we are presently experiencing at the hospital." Her own eyes unblinking, she met Dr. Anthony's stare. "He doesn't need any other problems at the moment. Remember there are a lot of patients with the flu." She realized, the doctor was processing what he was seeing in Chester and the truth in her words. Chester Mayfield could not risk further complications due to the state of his immune system. Years of experience and case after case, had to be passing through the doctor's mind and they would all know when he decided what must be done.

"Mr. Mayfield, we are going to draw blood for cultures." He turned to his patient's wife as he and Nurse Gates accepted what lay before them. Speaking almost as if to himself, he said, "Keeping sterile, we will draw Mr. Mayfield's blood, to be added with antibiotic. It will take three or four days for the culture to grow, but that's the only way to find the correct antibiotic for the infection. It's plain to see, the ones we've prescribed are definitely not working." Taking a deep breath he asked, "Are you ready Nurse Gates? Let's go over the instructions since you and I are the crew. First we keep the area sterile, our gloves sterile and in general know what we're doing so we don't contaminate Mr. Mayfield's blood. If you will, read it to me."

Ellen read. "Locate the vein, loosen the tourniquet and cleanse the site, swab with iodine moving in an outward circle, fan to dry." The good doctor seemed unaware he was voicing each step through the process. "Iodine is chlorhexidine-gluconate solution." Pausing he leaned back studying his patient.

"We let the iodine dry on the skin." Now Doctor Anthony was examining Chester's arm to find a vein. "This kit has a vacuum tube to draw the blood, Dr. Anthony, and the Vacutainer allows us to switch vials without changing needles as we evacuate the blood into the culture bottles."

"So we won't further contaminate the blood we've drawn," Dr. Anthony agreed as he inserted the needle. He watched as Ellen wiped each vial, removed the cap of safety needle and read, "Push and hold vacutainer on top of vial, monitoring so as not to overfill." All was quiet as the doctor moved one by one through the bottles until all were filled and Ellen marked the Bactec vial labels. "Now, pressure on the site as I remove the needle." His voice was almost reverent.

Though it was stressful, the two completed the drawing of blood, secure they had kept a sterile field. Dr. Anthony placed the bottles inside a special carrier for the lab where they would continue the process. He turned to Bitty. "I'll refer your husband to Home Health. Because he will continue receiving antibiotic through I V, a home health nurse will come twice daily to administer them. He's not only in need of the correct antibiotic but he's dehydrated Mrs. Mayfield, for a time they will relieve you. They will monitor output of fluids as well."

Ellen breathed a sigh of relief. "Thank you, Dr. Anthony."

"Not many nurses will cross the doctors or call them out, Nurse Gates. I should thank you."

Bitty showed the doctor to the door. Returning to find Ellen she was practically in shock, barely registering what was happening. "Ellen, I need to rehash this, whatever you call it, the doctor's instructions. Someone will be coming to take care of Chester. It's that serious?"

"Yes, it is, just as you feared." Ellen was hesitant to add, "Bitty you might want to at least speak with Chester's daughter in case she wants to come see her Daddy."

"Is he going to die, Ellen?" How could they have reached this point? Her mind was trying to grasp the situation. "I mean, just Sunday Chester was laughing and talking about our future, as soon as he gets the catheter deal taken care of. I mean I can't..." Words were nothing, Bitty sank into the nearest chair and brought the apron she wore up to cover her face. "There was no warning it would go this way..." Her shoulders shook, but there was no sound until finally she said, "Oh, Ellen, what has happened?"

"Maybe it will all go away. If they are able to find the correct antibiotic it will make all the difference in the world."

"You mean what they've been pouring into him hasn't worked? Then why continue?"

"I don't know, Bitty, but there's the dehydration, too." Ellen was shaking her head. "I've got to go home, Bitty, but if you need me, I will come after the twins and Ruthie are in bed. Just say the word."

"I'll see how it goes, Ellen, just hug Ruthie for me and tell her I love her."

Ellen kissed Bitty's cheek. "Go make the phone call to Chester's daughter and call me if you need me."

"Bitty," Chester called as she finished speaking with his daughter. "Bitty, Bitty, Bitty," his teeth were chattering, "It's almost more than I can understand, I am so cold." Bitty lay a hand on his forehead. "Chester, you can't be cold your skin is burning hot and the doctor gave you something for fever."

"Come lie with me," he groaned in trying to reach up.

New emotions were claiming Bitty, hesitating only a moment, she slipped under the covers and with what strength he could manage Chester pulled her close.

"Promise me, if I don't get better…you'll lie with me just like this when I die."

"You're not going to die, Chester Mayfield." She was adamant, confused and angry, but angry with whom? "You said we'd have a good life together. You can't die. I won't let you. You promised."

Tears welled in the corners of his eyes. "I'm sorry, Bitty. I wanted to give you the world but not all this worry."

ANDREW SAT CROSS LEGGED IN the floor with his son. They'd built a tower with the blocks Harriet found on line and Andy was ready to place the last one. "Easy, son," Andrew drew in a breath as Andy's small hand hovered. "Just let it drop, don't let your arm touch the others."

Andy beamed. "I did it, Daddy."

"Yes, you did, now if we can get up out of this floor without knocking it over, will be the trick."

Harriet stood in the doorway, grinning at their accomplishment. "Andy, Hattie has a batch of cookies, right out of the oven, if you want one."

"What about me?" Andrew made a fake pouting face. "Just kidding," he said as Andy turned back.

They had cleared the room, when they heard the sound of wood clinking on wood. The tower had fallen. "Just when we thought we had it made, now it's gone." Andrew sighed, "Well that one is."

"Like life, isn't it? You think you have a hold on it, everything's going along nicely and then…" Harriet's words drift away as she glanced out the window toward Bitty and Chester's home.

"Not good, today?" Andrew sat opposite Harriet. How many times had they sat there, sparring, until finally his love for Anne and her kindness in taking in the wife and child he abandoned brought them to friendship? He brought his thoughts back as Harriet sighed, a weariness that said more than words.

"Bitty called and his daughter will arrive tomorrow. I wonder how that will go? They haven't met and she will be staying with them. Can you imagine, her dad is sick and she's meeting the new wife for the first time? But, what about you and Anne? She told me you all discussed next month and that's only two weeks away."

"You mean the wedding?" Andrew sighed. "I told her we could just move in together. That didn't go over well." He saw her roll of the eyes. "We were married, what's wrong with that? Not acceptable?"

"Of course not." Harriet's expression scolded, even if she spared the words. "Anne has changed. She wants your new beginning, just that, nothing to remind either of you of the first time around. But with what's going on next door, I know she hesitates to move forward with plans, these are her friends."

"Mine, too, I'm just ready to live our lives together and stop this visiting our son."

"Andrew, with all you put the poor girl through, it's a wonder she'd look at you." Harriet's stern countenance softened, "And if I didn't see the change, myself, I'd encourage her to run away."

"So," Andrew rose out of the chair to pace the floor. "Where do we go from here?"

"GO HOME." DR. LONZO PLACED the last file of the day on the desk. He had studied the file thoroughly. There had to be a reason his patient with the new knee's skin was breaking out; only around the knee. "I study this mystery of the knee, all by myself. You have grander things to think on; your wedding day, almost here." Fatigued at end of day, Dr. Lonzo ebbed into the way of his native tongue, sparing the English words that tied his thoughts together and at end of day Anne did not correct his speech.

"I don't know. With the captain so ill, maybe we should cancel."

"Cancel? Olivia cannot wait for our daughter in love to marry and we celebrate dancing and all your friends together." His smile widened. "We adopt you, if you allow it. We have no child to leave our art collection to. Marry. Be happy and let us dance at your reception. We give you honeymoon, also."

"It may not be a time to dance, Dr. Lonzo."

"Tch. Tch." He clicked his tongue against his teeth. "Cherie, people are sick every day, life goes on. How sick can our Chief of Police be that sick, you cancel your wedding? He would not agree."

"What if he's dying?" The doctor's expression became more serious. "It's that bad, Dr. Lonzo." She blew out a breath of frustration. "They haven't found an antibiotic to curb the infection, but they are growing cultures. Our waiting to marry is a small thing compared to his life, isn't it?"

"I understand, but if the culture combats bacteria in his blood." He made a gesture of not knowing, as he shook his head, "Go ahead with plans, Cherie, I believe they will find antibiotic. Perhaps, my patient needs cultures run, also. Rash around the knee, unusual. Why no where else?"

"His wife told me, he tried helping her in the flower garden but he got into a patch of poison ivy."

Dr. Lonzo's eyes darkened. "What you mean poison ivy?" He snorted his usual, "Hmph. Did not tell me a word about flower garden or what you call poison ivy."

ANNE SAW ANDREW'S BATTERED OLD car in Harriet's drive. She encouraged him to find another, but with the amount of money needed for the home he found for them he said no, they couldn't afford another car. Remembering their first marriage when he purchased what he wanted no matter the strain on the budget, Anne wisely held further words. She no longer questioned every move Andrew made, nor second guessed his motives, even Harriet believed he had changed and had given them her blessing.

There were things she needed to discuss with Ellen. Christ Church's Young married class had scheduled a Bridal shower and she didn't know the people, thus far she and Andrew only attended worship service. Andrew wanted the wedding to go on as planned, but she couldn't; not with Chester ill. She needed Bitty present. Andrew had no idea the bond between women when they struggled through trial and she had struggled. With God's help she was able to fight back the insecurities of those days. For now, she prayed life's return to normal of the last year. Andrew's attention seemed focused on her and their son. She sighed, heavily burdened, knowing even in this time of sadness for Bitty, God was watching over all. Perhaps she didn't understand but she had placed her trust in the Lord.

The sound of a door shutting made her turn to see Ellen's car at Bitty's. Hurriedly she climbed out, calling, "Ellen, wait up." Huffing a bit, as she reached Ellen, she hugged her friend, "What's today's news?" One look told her, "Not good?" They hugged again. "Oh, Ellen, I can't bear to think of Bitty's sadness."

"He's got to hang on; the cultures should tell the story; just another day." Ellen sighed. "Bitty called. His daughter is here. I don't know how that's going but even in her stress, Bitty will do her part for his child."

"What's brought you to this conclusion, Ellen? Tell me. I know you've seen something."

"It's the urine, Anne. The fever and the chills and he is hurting all over, Anne. I'm wondering if his kidneys are trying to shut down. Nothing looks right." She laid a hand on her friend's arm. "We must pray more, Anne and it's up to the doctor to share what we are thinking, not me." She hesitated only a second, before adding, "But Anne, they would want you to go on with your plans."

HALEY ARRIVED HOME FROM WORK to find Ruthie helping her mother. "Mom, have you ever wondered what was at play, that a year ago you didn't even know Ruthie? Now, here she is in your kitchen with strawberry stain all over her hands?" Tweaking Ruthie's nose, she peered over her shoulder to see her mother's creation. "Umm, strawberry pie, with crème cheese filling?"

"I don't bother your Mother," Ruthie said. "When she does paper work, I'm real quiet. I read."

Dorothy hugged Ruthie to her side. "No, I can't imagine not meeting Ruthie. It reminds me of when you were little, except you and Grant ran me ragged running through the house playing tag." She was aware of her daughter's withdrawal but she continued to speak of her son. "I cherish those memories, Haley."

"But he's gone, Mom." Haley's voice broke. "I want to see him in this house. It hurts, Mom."

"You will see him again." Dorothy's voice was firm.

"You can't be that detached. He was your son. I know you grieve over him dying because I do."

"Let go, Haley. Grant would want you to get on with life. Find a beau, unless you already have."

Ruthie giggled. "She has. I saw her kiss his picture." She scoot out of the way as Haley came toward her, crouching menacingly, as though ready to pounce. "You know you did. I saw you."

Haley grabbed her. "So what if I did." She laid a wet kiss on Ruthie's cheek, again and again. "What do you think of that?"

"I think he needs a towel," Ruthie giggled, squirming to be free. "That's what Momma needs for the twins."

Dorothy smiled. It was good to have Ruthie in their midst. Truly, God planted her there to bring them out of the misery of the painful reminder, Grant was gone. Haley had returned home to have to face his absence three years after his death. Only time was making it easier for her and Harper. Haley's coming home had cleared the cob webs; they had to turn loose, life must go on with Haley. They'd tried, taking in Andrew and it had helped. Now Haley's resentment and attitude were changing, due to the young man in Tennessee.

Dorothy shuddered to think Haley was abducted. With that thought, she became aware her helper had left her and was now being chased through the rooms by her twenty three year old daughter. Life was good, finally, and Ruthie was a blessing in disguise. She would always carry her son in her heart, but with Ruthie's entrance into their lives, the ache of losing him had begun to heal. It happened in changing to Christ Church because Haley felt more at ease there, God blessed them with more Christian friends, among them a five year old. *And I thought my days of child rearing were over*, a lift to her spirits occurred and the song in her heart rose above heartache.

That sweet little girl came full blown into her thoughts. Something was troubling Ruthie and she would not share the problem. It could be she missed Bitty, for the two had a bond of love that would last *forever.*

❖

"FINALLY." ANDREW MET ANNE AT the door but immediately he saw her sadness. "What's wrong?" She came into his arms, willingly. "Is there word about Chester?"

"I spoke with Ellen. She checks on them every day. It's not good." Andrew was waiting. "Ellen says we must go on with our plans, that's what both Chester and Bitty would want and if there's opportunity she will discuss it with Bitty. Chester is in God's hands and we, his friends, must not forget to pray."

Harriet arose from the chair where she and Andrew had been in conversation. "Everyone is suffering. Anne, you must go ahead with the shower, I know you've thought otherwise and Bitty won't be able to be there, but life must go on. At this point all we can do as Ellen says is pray for Chester and Bitty."

Anne appeared very thoughtful, "Did you know Bitty encouraged me to use the song played at their wedding? Except I want the words sung. I love Bitty and Chester; why did this have to happen, Harriet?"

With a pained expression, Harriet replied, "I asked Ellen the same. She said God doesn't make bad things happen to his children but when it does he allows them to work through the problem. How they handle it becomes a witness to others. Maybe it is a test of faith, our job is to pray."

"I'm listening to that explanation, Harriet." Andrew's head was tilted, his eyes seemingly assessing her words, "But doesn't a Christian get tired of being used for that purpose? And that scripture Ellen uses, 'All things work together for those called according to His purpose.' Seriously I'm asking, does it?"

"Romans, eight, twenty eight," Anne said, pulling away, to go to Harriet's table and pick up her Bible. "And we know that all things work together for good to them that love God, to them who are the called according to *his* purpose." She had me to memorize that one, but I seem to turn the words around."

"Here is how Ellen guided me through that scripture, because she does use it a lot. She said when we come through the situation and we can look back without animosity, not blaming God, to ask our self, did the situation teach us anything."

A whisper of a smile came into Harriet's eyes. "You, my dear Andrew were nothing but a rascal when first we met and I wouldn't have given a tree leaf in a hail storm's chance for you and me becoming friends." Her eyes held his, "You've been through a lot, nearly going to prison if Mr. Gipson hadn't known the Judge and seen worth in you. Now, tell me how that scripture applies to you, Mr. Attorney at law?" She motioned toward the chairs. "Let's sit for a moment. Have any of your trials, helped you?"

Andrew's face wreathed in smile, mischief was in the set of his mouth. "Well, Miss Stone Cold, rich lady," that's how I thought of you. What about your sorry struggle to find Marigold? How's that working?" He sobered, "Not meaning to insult you, but in a way Harriet you were as detached from this thing we call Christianity, as I was." He reached for Anne's hand, pulling her forward as he peered into her face. "This woman has given me another chance," he paused, "If Chester hurries up and gets well. I believe according to the scripture, it's working out pretty good for me. Now, your turn."

"I seemed to have gained not only a daughter I'd longed for but a very talented son in law who calls me "ma." Don't you dare tell him, it warms my heart when he does, but I still don't see myself as anyone's 'ma'. He and I will work that one out through the years."

Andrew's laughter rang through the rooms, bringing Andy from the kitchen, "and there's my boy." His eyes twinkling, he squeezed Annie's hand. "Don't we need to keep the dates we planned? I know I'm getting ready for wedded bless and a chance to show you what a good husband and father I can be." Leaning down, he whispered in her ear and laughed when Anne blushed.

CHAPTER TWENTY ONE

MATT FOUND MARIGOLD SITTING ON a stool, her spangled tunic hanging limp against her body, her hair in spikes, not from gel he surmised but deep study and running her fingers through until she gave the appearance of Spock's friend, Jae, on Star Trek. She heard the door close but didn't look up.

"This is a stick up. Give me your money."

"It's over there, take all three dollars," she replied, and then giggled. "I know it's you."

"And just how would that be?"

"I smell you."

"Ouch." Matt raised one arm and then the other. "I don't think it's that bad." Stepping to the stool he draped an arm around her shoulders. "Perhaps you smell the brawn of a mighty man. Me."

"Truthfully, what have you been into? It smells like baby poop."

He drew away to sit opposite her on the other stool at the tall table. "You should be an expert on that. Want me to pick up Matthew John from Harriet's. I haven't seen Ma this week."

"She's going to kill you if you keep calling her that."

"She likes it." He grinned, "just like you like me to call you Tinkerbell. Terms of endearment."

"She won't like that smell coming into her house. So what is it, a new glue Harper's using?"

"I hate to tell you, Miz Nose of the Year. It's plain old cat poop. A cat got in the house and was locked in all night. The other guys wouldn't touch the mess. It has to be on my shoes, because Harper insist I wear gloves. I cleaned it up threw the cat outside, or vice versa."

"Where's the cat now?" Matt was silent. "Matt Langley, you didn't bring that cat home with you? Did you?"

"I did and guess what. I talked with Haley's boyfriend on the way home. He's bringing his charge to meet the group when he comes in this weekend." He leaned close to whisper, "I think it's a surprise for Haley. Did you know it's her birthday?" He smirked. "You should, she's your employee."

"I know. We're having a dinner for her. Me and her mother, if everything else is going all right."

"Why are you thumbing through the Bible? Shouldn't you be making orders or counting your money?"

"I told you, all three dollars are in the drawer." For the first time, she glanced up. "Someone was in today." She sighed. "I tell you, Matt, I know the Lord but I don't know how to explain the scripture. They were talking about forgiveness and forgiving people of horrible crimes committed against them and I wondered if I could forgive the person who broke into my store, not because anything precious was taken or damaged but because they took Haley, and for that matter, would Haley forgive the person."

"Isn't that behind us?"

"I don't know. Ruthie was here, on Tuesday. Mrs. Gipson brings her those days for dance class. Haley stays on the extra hour and Mrs. Gipson browses. Well, this elderly man came into the store. I saw Ruthie stiffen and then she just sat and observed him. At first it made me uneasy, but when she didn't get alarmed I just let it go and he left anyway."

"You are telling me this, because?" Matt's eyes held concern. "Anything to do with the intruder?"

"I don't think so; maybe that's what put Ruthie on guard. I don't know. We were busy and I didn't have a chance to ask and then she and I hurried off to dance class." She paused. "I'm going to have to give up helping Melissa. We are building a clientele' Mr. Langley, much to your surprise, I bet."

"No, I'm not surprised but I'm trying to fit this together, a nameless man came in, last Tuesday, Ruthie was here and paid attention to him, and now you are searching the bible on scripture about forgiveness."

"Oh, Farmboy, it is just too much for you." She rippled her fingers through his hair as he pulled her from the chair and clasp her to his body.

"Don't mess with me, Tinkerbell, or I'll let the cat come in to your place of business."

He was placing wet kisses on her neck, as she squirmed, until he turned her around to face him. "I love you, Tinkerbell," he whispered. And she whispered back, the same. "Guess I better go get Matthew John before I get in trouble," he said. "Reckon Ma would like a cat?" But before closing the door, he said, "I think I'll check on Chester, first. Is that all right?"

"You might better take your shoes off at the door, Farm Boy."

We are all trying to be normal, and life does go on, she thought, it has too. We can't all be sick at the same time. God didn't plan it that way. Again she thought of the women's conversation on forgiving. They didn't know about the break in. She was the one, wondering if she could forgive the man who entered her store. A chuckle issued from deep within her chest, like if he'd dare return. She glanced up at one of the last signs the supplier had brought; 'For as many as are led by the Spirit of God, they are the sons of God and the Spirit itself bears witness with our spirit, that we are the children of God.'

What did that have to do with what she was thinking? Maybe the supplier was getting a bit personal with these signs placed all over her building. The Spirit within, answered. *"You are a child of God, when you are tuned in, there is dialogue. You ask questions, the Spirit answers. You are concerned over the man's return, and if he does how you will handle it. I am feeding you scripture to allow you to know how to behave."* Thinking quickly, her sassy spirit replied. "Really?" and then, "I'm sorry." She was learning.

———◈———

"I HAVE TO SEE UNCLE Chester." Ruthie's eyes were ominous; the worrying thread in her voice had not lessened as she pleaded with Ellen to take her to Bitty's. "Momma, please, I don't get to see Bitty. I know she misses me because I miss her and I need to see uncle Chester."

"Sweetums, Uncle Chester is very ill. He wouldn't feel like your company."

"But Bitty needs me. I need her." Ruthie was near tears. "Daniel will be here with my brothers."

"I have to attend a meeting at the hospital, Ruthie. I'll be leaving in a few minutes."

"I'm ready. You can drop me off and pick me up later. I have to see Uncle Chester, Momma."

Ellen's patience was coming to an end. "Ruthie Elizabeth Anderson. Why are you doing this?"

Ruthie was hesitant. She had heard the discussion after the man broke into Marigold's business. They had not known she listened when they said *the world was not to know about Ruthie's gift, because someone would use it in the wrong way. Harm could come to Ruthie and they would not allow it.* Now she was confused, did God want her to speak to people or not? She had thought on it for days, but the need to see Uncle Chester had grown until she thought *the need* would burst right out of her chest.

"Momma," Ruthie's voice soft and full of question gained Ellen's attention. "Am I supposed to be ashamed of the gift God gave me?" A tear slipped from the corner of her eye as Ellen stooped to peer into her daughter's heart, her own aching. "I don't know what to do, Momma. I'm not trying to have things because God speaks to me." *They will use her gift for worldly gain, resounded in Ruthie's mind.* "I don't need anything."

"Ruthie. Ruthie." Ellen's arms closed around her child. Eternity held the answers. Ruthie had overheard the group talking on how to protect Ruthie. "Oh, Sweetums, you've been worrying." A contrite Ruthie leaned into her mother, crying her heart out, not knowing what God wanted her to do because adults had been overheard and the situation not explained to a child. *If she should fall into the wrong hands, God forbid.* "You are not the problem, here, I should have known. My dear little girl, God gave you a gift, you are to use. I didn't realize, until now, you thought otherwise."

"Then, please, Momma, let me go see Uncle Chester."

"Sweetums, he is restless in his spirit and his body is very weak. Uncle Chester is ill and close to dying."

"Then I have to see him, Momma."

BITTY EMBRACED RUTHIE, HOLDING HER close for a very long time and Ruthie was ecstatic to be with her very own Bitty. "I missed you. I like Mrs. Dorothy but she works on papers all day long and I try to be quiet. Momma says she is Mr. Harper's book keeper, but it's mostly papers and she has a computer."

Laughing for the first time in weeks, Bitty said, "Ruthie, there's someone here for you to meet. It's Uncle Chester's daughter."

"Is she nice?"

"Would Uncle Chester have a daughter that isn't?" They entered the house, to find a tall blonde headed lady sitting at the breakfast bar having a cup of coffee. "LeAnn, this is the little girl Chester was trying to tell you about. He had no idea she would be coming to visit him, today. Have you had breakfast, Ruthie?"

Nodding, Ruthie stuck out her hand. "Me and Bitty are best friends. Do you have any children?"

Leann smiled and shook Ruthie's hand. "Yes, I do, but they are grown and they aren't with me."

"Do you like my Bitty?"

"Ruthie." Bitty was taken back, "We don't ask such personal questions, do we?"

"Well I do," Ruthie was waiting for an answer. "I'm sorry," she said to Leann. "I love Bitty."

"Yes I do like your Bitty, very much," Leann replied, her smile growing broader and making Ruthie think of Uncle Chester. Leann was wondering what the next question might be. "Would you like to visit my daddy?" Ruthie shook her head and offered her hand.

"Come along, I think he's ready to see you." She wondered if she should prepare the child but Bitty told her the child's mother had called.

"Dad, look who came to see you." Her father lay curled up in the bed, huddled beneath the covers.

Chester tried to rise, but the weakness wouldn't allow it. "Where have you been?" He tried for the usual joy in his voice when he saw Ruthie, but that failed him, too, and he knew she was taking it all in. His eyes strayed to Leann and she understood he could not fake any measure of happiness.

"Come along, Ruthie," Leann was taking her hand again. "I bet those blue berry muffins are ready to come out of the oven in Bitty's kitchen."

"I need to stay here awhile, if Uncle Chester doesn't mind. I'll lay down right here, where Bitty sleeps and I won't bother him." She saw Leann's glance at her dad; he had a restless night, what should she do? But Ruthie was removing her shoes. "You don't feel like getting up, do you, Uncle Chester?" His eyes were trying not to close, "It's all right if you go back to sleep. I'm just going to lay here and hold your hand." Ruthie understood Leann's hesitance, but she waited to hear the door close softly.

— ◆ —

BITTY COULD BARELY HEAR THE humming. She glanced at Leanne. They tiptoed, standing in the hall listening to Ruthie's sweet voice singing words of praise. Barely audible they could see her holding Chester's hand sending the message of healing to Chester in the only way she knew.

Tears pooled in Bitty's eyes. "I don't know how to console that little girl if her Uncle Chester dies. I guess he will be the nearest she will have encountered losing in death."

"It won't be easy, for you, either, Bitty." They lingered only a moment, to return to the kitchen, where Chester's daughter said, "We didn't think of music, Bitty, to calm his restlessness. The little girl did."

"I thought by now, they would have an antibiotic, Leann. I can't believe we've come this far to find there are times the medical world can't help us." Sitting, staring across the table, Bitty found it unperceivable, "Your Dad, a big strapping man, reduced to this and to go so quickly because of an infection. Ellen warned me an infection can take a person down. I feel so helpless not to be able to help him."

"My regret, is that I nearly waited too long to see him. I thought life was too busy for a trip here." She reached out to touch Bitty's hand. "It was never that you didn't make me feel welcome. There was so much going on with my family," her words dropped low, "I thought I was busy."

From the window, across the lawn, Bitty saw stirrings at Harriet's house. "Life goes on, Leann, in spite of one's personal sorrow, those around you have to keep going. That's why it's called life, isn't it?"

ANNE'S NERVOUS LAUGH RANG ACROSS the morning quiet. "I can't believe it, Harriet. Pinch me."

Harriet's smile bestowed blessing on Anne. "You deserve this happiness, Anne, and if we hadn't checked this charlatan out by this time and believe he's changed then your friends deserve a good smack on the head, as Bitty would say. Andrew is a different man than three years ago."

Keying the engine, the purr of Anne's car and steam from the exhaust brought a semblance of order to both women but they still glanced toward Bitty's wondering how Chester had made it through the night.

"I feel guilty, going to find a dress for the shower and maybe for me to be married in and our friends going through such turmoil." She sighed heavily. "Thank you for coming with me."

They were passing Bitty's home now. "They would want you to be happy, Anne. Let's find that dress."

YAWNING, HALEY CAME INTO THE room, "Mom?" She called again, going to the sunroom to find her mother outside watering the flowers. Hearing Haley's call she came inside. "What's that wonderful smell, Mom?"

"I promised Harriet I would bring those little cupcakes. She and Dr. Lonzo's Olivia have planned the most beautiful setting for the shower. This morning is my trial run for the shower and the wedding. They have everything else catered, who knew they'd want my small offering?"

"You're pleased, aren't you? Let's try your *offering*. I'm starved."

"You are always starved." Dorothy tilt her head, staring at this daughter who was such a delight these days. "How can you eat as you do and never gain an ounce?"

Haley's laughter rang through the room. "Mom, I was hungry for two years. Food has this amazing appeal, sometimes I wonder if I eat just because I can." She grabbed her mother and did a whirl around the room. "Mom, I'm so happy." She ended the whirl around with a big smooch on her mother's cheek.

"I find it hard to believe my cupcakes are responsible. What's really behind this happiness?"

"Jeremy's coming in. Can he stay in Grant's room, instead of at the hotel, Mom?" A mischievious grin spread across her face. "You know, Mom, if I could get hold of that Caroline person that Miss Harriet brought in to cover for her at work that time, I'd do it, with Marigold's permission, of course, then I could spend the whole day with Jeremy. Wouldn't that be just about as delicious as these gift cakes?"

"I don't know if that would meet Marigold's expectations."

"Trust me. It would. Caroline has a way about her, kind of like Ellen. You feel her kindness."

DR. ANTHONY STUDIED THE REPORT. "Call Mrs. Gates," he said. "Tell her I'll meet her at the Mayfield home in one hour." He thought for a moment. "And call Home Health, this is too important for me to mess up, even if I am supposed to know everything." A slight smile in his expression, he admitted. "They will be much more skilled at this than me. It could be the difference in life or death for the Captain."

"You don't normally allow this procedure in a home, Dr. Anthony, what made the difference?"

"His immune system is beyond warding off anything else he might have encountered in the hospital. There's too much going on there. I hope fighting the infection at home has saved him from a plethora of other evils. And now there are other problems.

"I'll make that call to Mrs. Gates, Doctor."

He stood there, with the report in his hand, not only was there an infection, the cancer of the prostate had metastitized to the lungs. Shaking himself from the new finding, he realized you fight the first problem before you advance to the second. If they could combat the infection, then they'd battle the cancer. The Lupron had not been enough, those three month shots supposed to control the cancer in the prostate. At least it had not spread to the bone. Yet.

ANDREW STUDIED THE FILE. THE girl lived with her grandparents. Hers was the story of every teen he saw between age thirteen and twenty; that passage between being a child and adulthood and in his own case twenty had only meant more available vices. Here he sat studying yet another case because of the folly in his own life. But the Judges decree that he work pro bono for the city's poor was a blessing in disguise since it kept him from going to jail. No frivolities for this position, not even an intercom. He arose and stepped to the door. "Cynthia Simpson."

A young girl, he guessed to be fourteen or fifteen sauntered toward him. "Come in and take a seat." Leaving the door open, he sat opposite her. "Miss Cynthia Simpson, tell me why you think you are here."

"I didn't see you the last time," she said, her eyes straying to the name card on his desk. "I didn't like that surly woman, either." She was chewing gum and took her time in rolling it from one cheek to the other, working it to perfection. "She called me lazy, unappreciative and said she didn't care if she never represented another ungrateful kid in her life." Cynthia's eyes shot darts at Andrew, in the recall of her past experience. He was waiting. "Well," she blew a small bubble and let it pop between her lips. "I didn't shoplift, but I was with the girl that did, you've probably met with her already and I can tell you she's guilty as sin. I didn't have the guts to take home the things she did, besides they have those cameras. I told her but she wouldn't listen."

"It's your story that you did not shop lift but you were with someone that did."

"Exactly." Cynthia gave a great sigh. "My gramps is tickled to death the court assigned you to my case. He says I've been more expensive than any grandkid he helped raise."

"Your grandfather raises his grandchildren?"

"Most of us. His own kids aren't worth a…" She caught herself in time, hadn't gramps said no cursing? "You get the picture? Gramps is not well off, but him and Gramma have this, well, Gramma died last year, just before Christmas." She was working the gum again. "That leaves him to take care of a lot of issues. But I read the statistics; he's not the only grandparent raising his kid's children."

Andrew was studying the file again. Cynthia Simpson's father's name was William. "What's your grandfather's name?" Her mother's status was unknown; her father was in jail presently.

"I put it down at the bottom in case you needed to call him." She grinned. "He said if I'd keep my mouth clean and listen instead of talking you probably wouldn't have to, call him that is. It's Earl. William Earl Simpson but everyone calls him Earl."

Bingo. Andrew raised his head, staring at the ceiling. That name rang a bell. Hadn't he run enough lists to recognize it? "All right, Miss Cynthia Simpson, we will set your court date, you will appear with your grandfather, and we will see what the Judge decides about you."

"You believe me, don't you? I didn't take home anything but I was with the girl that did. Does that make me an accomplice?" She chewed the gum in frenzy. "They got cameras, can't you examine the film?" A crazy thought entered her head. "That takes a while to do, doesn't it? You don't think I'm worth it." A curse word escaped her mouth. "You're all alike. You don't think I'm worth crap."

Standing, Andrew leaned across the desk. "Cynthia Simpson, I believe you have an opportunity to turn your life around. I see you have working papers and that's good. If you get a job that looks good to the Judge, I will do my best in representing you but the rest is up to you. Keep your nose clean and appear on the arranged date."

Little would Andrew know, leaving the community office, Cynthia would climb into a Suburban driven by her grandfather, a vehicle derived through running scout for a shady business now defunct, the owner of that business ensconced in a nice home in another state's community while he regretted any association with such and wondered if his own money needing status had taken him into an association of sorts that would one day catch up with him and land him in jail to sit beside the son of his loins.

"How'd it go?" he asked Cynthia. "Did you keep your mouth shut?" One glance her way and he knew she hadn't. "Did you curse when I told you it would only get you deeper in your own problem?"

She squirmed. "I did and I'm sorry, gramps." She sighed. "What you gonna do about Dad?"

"Maybe let him sit in jail a few more days. I don't have the money for bail, kiddo."

"What happened? You used to have money when you worked for that guy, that owned that business right there." She pointed out the window as they passed the shop bearing the sign MARIGOLDS. "Can we go in there, Gramps? They say it has a lot of nice things. I promise I won't ask for nothing. Please, Gramps. Turn around. Let's just stop and look. This morning has been pretty grueling."

MARIGOLD WAS RIGHTING THE LAST table, something Haley normally did at end of each day but yesterday they'd both hurried out the door, wanting to arrive home in time to freshen and change clothes before attending Anne's shower. Smiling, she glanced up when the man and young woman entered the shop. Anne's shower had been a blessing; starting fresh with a host of new things and leaving behind the baggage of her and Andrew's first marriage, Anne had glowed with happiness and the joy had been infectious. It was a very good shower. She studied her customers, they appeared to be browsing, she had come to the point her impression of buyers was pretty accurate. Yes, these two were browsers.

"Haley, can you come out front?" She called to the back where Haley was opening a crate of dishes; hand turned Carltons from North Carolina, expensive but in demand by the young marrieds. She had to chuckle, she and Matt were using the left overs she had found in the cabinets when she bought the four square, all the while her mother's good china was packed away in the basement.

"May I help you?" She asked the girl, studying the two. "Is this your grandfather?"

Busy chewing gum, the girl nodded, "yep, he is my grandfather and daddy all in one, 'cause my father, he don't amount to much and besides that he's in jail, anyway. Ain't that right, Grampa Earl?"

The grandfather was shaking his head. "Cynthia, you offer too much information. I'm sure the lady isn't interested."

"How old are you?" Marigold was interested. "I need someone to unpack items and Haley here, needs to be out front waiting on customers." She saw a need for discipline in the young woman's life and she truly needed help. "Minimum wage starting out." Glancing around at Haley, she said, "Remind me to call Caroline. We will need her this weekend since I ran the ad in the paper more people will be in."

"He didn't want to stop." The girl pointed to her grandfather. "See, gramps? What if we hadn't? Who else you got working for you? Could you use, Gramps? He's not employed. He needs a job."

Marigold ran the thought through her mind; there were numerous loop holes in her business. Not only did she need someone to open boxes and barrels and do inventory, she needed a general handy man. "How good are you with a hammer?" She asked studying Earl. "Are you in good health?"

CHAPTER TWENTY TWO

EARL WASN'T SURE ABOUT THE new job. Maybe he was courting disaster. He couldn't renege, not with Cindy excited, telling everyone she and her grandpa would be working together. Could he use a hammer, the gal had asked. Yes, he could. In his list of employments he had once worked with a carpenter. That was before he fell off the ladder, rather was knocked off the ladder by a silly old fool, thinking to play a prank on Earl Simpson. The prank took away his livelihood for a good three months and by then they'd hired someone to take his place. He'd moved on to be custodian at a school. When the school consolidated, he lost that job to find one working for the city. Now the city downsizing jobs turned him loose, him being the oldest.

His, was the life of the school of hard knocks. He'd about given up. After Mandy died, a house full of grandchildren looking to him to be fed clothed and a few extra dollars along the way, he'd wished sometimes he could run off, but he'd never leave them kids. Maybe it was his fault his and Mandy's own hadn't turned out well. Mandy was an angel, Amanda Greer Simpson. That was what the obituary read and for once their three had shown up to pay respect to their departed mom, at first defiant as though he were the cause of their ugly lives, but by the time the funeral happened with spirits broken they became the children he remembered.

That hadn't last long either. They left after the funeral, taking whatever food the neighbors had brought in, in paper plates, uncaring their own children were staying and would have naught for supper. Not one mentioned helping pay on the funeral bill. That's when he agreed to the side business of his old friend. Now that one was living the life of Riley in Tennessee, with the money Earl had confiscated beneath the boards of this gal's business and here he was, Earl Simpson, trying to figure out if there was any way that Haley girl recognized him. He was fairly breaking out in hives to think she'd accuse him and whether he could lie his way out of it. Well, that was all behind him. He'd give it a try, keep his head down and act like he didn't know the place.

"LET YOUR GRANDPA HELP YOU open the boxes and barrels. Be careful not to cut the merchandise inside, and you, Cindy, stack the dishes on this table. Don't stack too high. And Earl, when you finish opening the containers, I need several shelves assembled that we are going to hang on the wall." She turned to go to the front. "You have already met Haley. The other lady working today is Caroline."

They made it through the weekend's onslaught of customers. There was some kind of activity in town which brought visitors by Marigold's shop. Several times, Earl had been called to help load merchandise into vehicles. Marigold had praised his ability. "I didn't know how much I needed your help, Earl."

The other woman was a curiosity. Earl wasn't sure how to take her. She eyed him up and down. "Come, Monday," she said, "we are going to work on you." Those were fighting words. What did that uppity gal find wrong with him. He asked Cindy and she sputtered and laughed and said, "I think I know. Let's just wait and see."

He returned to work, on Monday, anxiety creating an uproar in his stomach. There she was, that Caroline woman. He heard his new boss say, "Its fine with me. Tread carefully." Well, if it were him they were discussing, maybe it wasn't fine with him.

"Come with me," Caroline said. "By the way, how old are you?"

"Fifty three." He wanted to say, 'what's it to you?' but he didn't. "Where are we going?"

"To the barber shop. It's just across the street."

They made it across the busy intersection, Earl practically dragging his feet except for the traffic.

"He needs a cut. Not a crew cut, and not too long. He's already scraggly. Just shape him up."

Like a lamb to slaughter, Earl submitted. His whole body was sweating and his mind in turmoil. He watched as she handed the barber the ten dollars touted on the front window and waited until they were outside to have his say. "You got no right to do what you just did. If I like my hair long and as you said, scraggly, that's my right."

"You want to work in Miss Marigold's shop with that granddaughter of yours?" He nodded, his eyes darting fire. "Then follow me and I don't need to hear you complaining. I went through the same mess."

"Who as you said, shaped you up?" The anger subsided a bit. "And how old are you?"

"I'm thirty three. Got kids. My husband died and I have learned a lot since then. But its people like Miss Marigold's mother took an interest in me and helped me get a fresh start. Now, I'm passing that on to you."

"Well, thanks a lot. If I'm working in the back what does it matter what I look like?"

"Did I see you hanging shelves and following Miss Marigold around the shop area?" He nodded. "Then I rest my case. All right, we're here. What's your waist size? Pants length? You do know that, don't you?" They had walked through the doors to Good Will and she was already digging through men's clothing. "Here, try these on. There, behind those curtained areas."

In little more than an hour's time, Caroline Hawkins had her new charge back to Marigold's. His granddaughter was grinning at him like a banshee, the Haley girl seemed to like his new look and Marigold was pleased. She laid a hand on his arm. "Earl, you look like a forty year old and I thought you were ready for retirement. If I hadn't seen your age on the papers I couldn't have guessed it." With that she turned to Cindy, "Do you have your paper, today?"

"What kind of paper is that?" Earl asked, immediately suspicious of a set- up.

"Relax, Grampa." Cindy felt his anxiety; maybe the morning had been too much for him. "If you are between fourteen and seventeen or eighteen, I forget which, you have a blue paper that tells the employer you're still in school and can't work too many hours and not in a factory, I think, at all. Something like that. That lawyer checked it out and told me to get a job."

Earl's heart sank. Cindy's mention of a lawyer raised the owner's eyebrows. He didn't think his stomach would take much more. Cindy had hold of his arm. "You all right, Grampa?"

Marigold was studying the two. There was an obvious love between them and she gave the man credit for taking the granddaughter under his wing. She needed them and from what she'd seen they were good workers but she had to chuckle inwardly, Caroline Hawkins had reconstructed a younger looking man out of the Grandpa. *Wonders never ceased.* She could only wonder what Caroline looked like before Harriet Becker got hold of her. Rolling her eye, Haley's direction, she signaled *back to work.*

Haley studied Caroline's transformation. The man resembled someone she'd met before.

RUTHIE WAS QUIET. BITTY INQUIRED, "You all right, Ruthie?" Ruthie nodded. "Your Momma is on her way to pick you up."

"I need to stay. Will you call Momma and tell her? You don't care, do you?"

"Mercy, no. I want you to. I'll call her but if she says no, we'll just have to accept it." Bitty returned the call to Ellen. "She says she *needs* to stay, Ellen. She's really quiet. *You know what I'm thinking?*" Bitty listened and returned to where Ruthie was sitting. "She says if you need to, you can spend the day."

"Uncle Chester's doctor will be here soon."

Chester's daughter wasn't certain if it was a question or not, "Yes, I believe he will," she replied.

Bitty was busy placing a vase of fresh roses on the dining room table. "Are you praying, Ruthie?"

"Yes, ma'am."

Home Health people arrived as Dr. Anthony's car pulled into the drive. They weren't there long. A new bag of antibiotic was hung on the pole. Chester Mayfield barely grunted as Dr. Anthony saw his vitals were taken. He thanked the nurse as he leaned down and peered into his patient's face. "All we can do is wait and see, Captain." Turning to Bitty, his expression was grave. "Call me if you need me, Mrs. Mayfield."

"Few doctors, make house calls," Chester's daughter remarked. *She thought, my father is going to die.*

⟡

HARRIET'S LAUGHTER WAS AS JOYOUS as rain after drought. "He's not out of the woods but he is not bowed in that death curl, as Bitty called it. Chester Mayfield is too tough to die, but he almost did." She was slipping her cell back into her purse. "Bitty thinks the antibiotic is working. Can an antibiotic really work that quick, two days?" She turned to Anne. "Can it?"

"Well, we know we can see a visible difference in most cases, but evidently, for Chester, yes."

"Ruthie sat with them all day, that first day of the new antibiotic." Harriet's voice lowered, considering God's blessing on that little girl. "Bitty told me she actually lay on the bed and held his hand and hummed that song we hear her singing. And it certainly isn't a death dirge, it gives hope."

"She's precious. Harriet, have you ever stopped to think, if we hadn't met Ellen, so willing to share her Christ with us, we would still be stuck in our own misery, not once stepping out on faith?" She grinned remembering Harriet. "Anyway, I would, I was pretty insecure and scared of life."

"I saw that. You know I wanted someone to know I had more in me than being considered that rich old woman." Harriet laughed, "But I certainly hid it from the world. My heart was hardened and my spirit bitter. Then, I find Natalie…" She paused, "I mean I found Marigold." A smile covered her face. "Anyway, I found my child. We know what life was like before Jesus came into our hearts, as Ruthie says, and now here we are ready for your big shower. Two days until the shower and a week away from the wedding. Looks like you have nothing to fear. It's a good thing, Andrew was growing impatient."

"You are sure you don't want to stand with me?"

"Anne, I've been through this wedding stuff, with Ellen and Bitty. I'll pass this time, since Olivia and I will be busy overseeing the reception and you can call on someone else for the honor."

"Ellen and Marigold have agreed. Since it's the second time for me and Andrew, we thought to keep it low key, but Olivia," she grinned, her eyes holding Harriet's, "and you, have made it an extravaganza."

"What's Andrew doing today? He didn't show up for coffee."

"He is meeting with Marigold later, and the rest is as usual, work for Harper, appease the Judge."

"CAROLINE, ARE YOU AND EARL becoming a *twosome?*" Marigold was curious.

The question rang in Caroline's mind as she faced the situation. It was a big surprise to confront the question and find the answer yes? She couldn't believe the man she'd walked over to the Barbershop and down to Good Will, would have become a friend. He was pretty hostile after that, but with his granddaughter's help he simmered down and over time had forgiven her.

"Yes, ma'am. We're friends." She was aware that Marigold was waiting for more information. "That's all. Just friends."

"I heard you went out to dinner with his family."

"That won't happen again. Those grandchildren got the manners of a goose. He needs help. His own kids leave theirs with him and now that he's working they run roughshod over the neighborhood." Caroline sighed. "I got my own to corral. Earl needs to make their parents straighten up and take care of their own or send them to the Y or something while they're out of school. I don't know."

"Does the age difference bother you, between you and Earl?"

"No, ma'am. Fourteen years doesn't mean a thing when two people compare hard times and understand each other. But there is the matter of whether our friendship develops beyond that. I think we both have been through so much, it's just good to have someone to talk to."

Haley arrived during the conversation. "You know, I like Earl, but for the life of me, he reminds me of someone I've met and can't remember where, exactly." She began to fold an assortment of napkins.

"Maybe on one of your trips to Tennessee," Marigold teased with a southern accent. "I hear you and Jeremy are pretty tight these days. He's coming in pretty regular isn't he? How's that going, staying at your parents' home?"

"My parents amaze me. They like Jeremy. Mom's made him feel at home in my brother's room." She caught Marigold's question before it was asked. "I know. I resented Andrew being in Grants room. I guess I should apologize for slapping him, huh?" She giggled. "But that was before I had my attitude adjustment. Riding in the back of a truck with your arms and legs bound is a good stabilizer. I realized I had to ask God to help me and if I was asking Him to do that I had things I needed to face up to."

"We're not all saints, are we?" Marigold moved on to dust the porcelain' figurines. "I tell you that Earl does a good job installing this hardware for the shelves. Matt could, but Mr…" She grinned, "Your Dad, Haley, is keeping him busy. Not to worry, though, he loves it. He may never go back to the farm."

"How's that situation?" Haley raised her head, from lifting a stack of place mats from a box. "I've been around long enough now to hear the story about your mother in law not liking you."

"Sadly, she still doesn't like me. Can you imagine the poison it must create in her, thinking I took her son away from her? But I didn't. Matt and I met through the Art Gallery, because of his paint-ings." She hung the duster behind the counter and eyed the clock. "Five minutes til opening. Thanks for coming in early. I'm always glad when we have a few minutes to know what's going on in your lives." She heard the door opening in back of the shop. "Well, Earl and Cindy have arrived, let's unlock the door."

ANDREW FINISHED HIS DAY'S WORK, leaving early for the City Complex. "What's your plan for that teenager?" The Judge had barked his question over the phone. "She's to appear before me, tomorrow and I want to know your thoughts. Do we keep her or send her off for a tweak of the character?"

"I'm checking on her today. I'll get back to you." Troubled, he stared at the scarred table top he called a desk when he was doing community penance, aiding the less fortunate who were in need of a lawyer and had no means to pay. Yep, that was his job. Appearing with them, advising them before hand to keep their thoughts to themselves and those derogative comments they were prone to utter, to themselves. He had seen Marigold and Matthew on Sunday, but the conversation had been lively, in view of Chester's recovery com-ing along now, the group was in high tone, happy for their friend.

He had spent hours considering Earl Simpson's plight. His own past could be branded the same. They'd both made mistakes, the dif-ference being Harper Gipson had taken a chance on him, taking him under his and Dorothy's wing, albeit into their home, no less. Here was a man who had made a wrong choice but in his sessions with the granddaughter he gleaned information that made a difference in his own personal thinking and as a lawyer should never enter in. If the Judge found out, he might throw the book at Andrew and not Simpson.

What to do? He placed the file back in the cabinet. Both grand-daughter and grandfather worked for Marigold now. She was satisfied. Haley, seemed unaware her abductor was actually working under the same roof; and it was his understanding the women had shaped him up and he looked like an up-standing citizen these days. There was no doubt the granddaughter and a few more siblings looked to the man for guardianship in the absence of their own parents. This was a tough one! Did he go it alone; trusting his gut instinct the two would better themselves with Marigold's willingness to hire them? Or, was it his duty to tell Marigold the rest of the story and let the pieces fall where they would, out of his hands into the jurisdiction of the court?

Then what? Who would care for the other children? Left alone they would become wards of the court and Cynthia? He sighed, heavily burdened. *There but for the grace of God, went my little boy. What do you want me to do, God,* he questioned, his eyes closed. Shocked. He opened his eyes. If he was calling on Anne's God, maybe it was as Harriet said, "I'm not giving up on you, Andrew, there's hope."

He thought he heard laughter. Maybe Jesus had a sense of humor, but he'd always imagined God as a stern deity, if he had to judge the sins of all the people he couldn't be humorous, could he? Then he remembered Anne saying, "*God loves us, Andrew. His compassion and mercy are the stepping stones where we realize His grace is sufficient, for us, no matter how grave or irregular our problems.*"

Harriet's words rang in his head. "There's hope for you, Andrew." Maybe there was. He promised Anne he would attend church on a regular basis when they married but it would be more enjoyable if he truly believed. As Harriet said, maybe God was doing a work in him. And yes, she always added, "*wonders will never cease.*"

Leaving the building he stepped out to the curb and climbed into the old clunker. Gone were the days of fast cars, loose women and all night stands. Andrew Graves was finally growing up, leaving behind the selfishness of thinking only of self. He would become a family man Anne would be proud to call her husband and Andy, his heart swelled with love. There, he had no shadow of doubt, God loved him and gave him a son. What must he give in return?

Andrew drove, taking the long route, passing by Daniel and Ellen's home, considering their life together. His mind flit to Harriet's distinguished home front, next door to Bitty and Chester and down the street, Marigold and Matt. Someway, God had brought them all together; people with mixed and unusual problems. He could list a law suit in every one of their lives but they had handled their problems under the umbrella of God's mercy and grace. Could he learn to trust as they had? When they'd almost lost Andy, he'd promised God he'd change and he had changed but he hadn't fully committed himself. He kept those parts of his life he wanted to control. What he had done was renege on God because he hadn't given himself completely. Now, here he was handed a situation similar to his own, a man who made a mistake and now when life ahead looked good there was a penalty to pay.

The Gipsons filed through his thoughts; Dorothy who looked him in the eye and said, "Don't try pulling anything on me, Buster, I've got your number." He had to laugh. The months under that couples roof had been an eye opener. Their reason for taking him in, if possible, was to save him from himself because they had lost their only son and saw perhaps a glimmer of worth in him. Then came their daughter, at first resentful and mean hearted, insulted by his presence in her brothers room, but when her own problems escalated he had seen a changing in her attitude and he suspected in her heart.

He was almost there, what was he to do about Earl Simpson; turn him in to the authorities and wash his hands of the whole situation or keep the knowledge, forever, that this was the man who abducted Haley.

Lord, help me, weight of the problem made sweat break out on his brow. Was he actually asking God for help? What would Harriet think about that? Well, until this matter was settled, he couldn't tell her. He heard laughter as he entered. Marigold was in the middle of a story, hands active as she talked, telling about her and Harriet's animosity to each other. "Who knew she was my birth mother?"

It was Cynthia Simpson noticed him standing inside the door, listening. "Why Mr. Graves, surely you didn't come down here to check on me, did you?" Her brave voice belied the anxiety in her eyes. But it was the gentleman next to her, interested Andrew. Cynthia wasn't missing that either. "Come meet my Gramps," she said. "Miss Marigold needed a handy man and my Gramps is very handy. Aren't' you, Gramps?"

"Cindy," the man reprimanded quietly as he stepped forward and offered his hand. "Earl Simpson."

"Andrew Graves, your granddaughter's attorney."

"Yes, sir, I want to thank you for helping Cindy." Their eyes met, their hands unclasped and Earl stepped back as Marigold came forward. "I'll finish this stand, Miss Marigold and then unload your van."

"What's in your van?" Andrew was following her toward a small side office, very elite but very small. Typically Marigold, a feathered ink stand, glass fringed drape across the small window and a deep rose velvet chair she motioned he sit in. An elegant frame showcased Marigold, Matt and Matthew John on the wall opposite the window with a huge mirror stretching behind her desk.

"I have a couple antique pieces of furniture I brought down from the attic," she grinned, "With Matt's help and we are going to use them to display jewelry and small gemmed cases that look as though they came from that era; good stuff but not authentic." She laughed, "You get my meaning?"

"Not the real thing?"

"What is the real thing?" Marigold shifted, as she sat on the edge of a gilded desk, staring at Andrew. "You and I have access to a host of people and I don't believe there's a bad apple in the barrel, do you?"

"How about your staff? How's that working out?"

"If you're worried about Cynthia, we call her Cindy because that's what her Grandfather calls her, well, Cindy just needs another woman to guide her and Earl is a gem." She sighed, "I don't know how I got along without him. Matt doesn't have time to hang pictures and assemble shelves since Harper put him in charge of another project. You know that." A smile formed, "Those two have lightened not only my load, but Matt's, too. If his mother would accept me, he'd be one happy man."

He left Marigolds, his mind on Earl Simpson. With Marigold's glowing report resounding in his head, "Earl is a gem. He lightens my load." Headed toward the old car, deep in thought, the first blow caught him off guard; the second dropped him to the ground. Later, he would recall being dragged across the pavement and thrown into Marigold's feathered van. Two men had appeared as out of nowhere and now here he was, gagged, feet tied and handcuffs around his wrists.

The sound of vehicles moving through traffic came to his ears. "Hey." He tried to call out. Whatever was tied around his mouth taste of oil and grime, a grease monkey's rag. "Hey." His voice was lost in the street noise. Now, he gagged, his mind coming awake to the taste and smell. It was a dream, wasn't it? Hadn't this story been played out? It was Haley's situation all over again. He had to pay attention.

"Walden said we're not to mess up pretty boys face. Just give him a good ride, question him to see what he knows after we've scared him up a bit. Whether we get the info or not, we toss him in the river and let the ME decide what happened." Listening, Andrew detected a Southern drawl to the man's words. "He seemed to think no one would miss 'em for a good while. In Walden's mind he's worthless."

"What'd he do to bring on Walden's wrath?" A huge belch followed the second man's words. "Not that it matters. I can stand the extra dollars. Old lady says we need to buy our Rosie a bicycle for her birthday. She knows I ain't worked for months. Whadda's she think, I'm made of money?"

"Maybe she'll let up after this, when you produce the dough." Number one gave a deep sigh. "Seems this one double crossed Walden, got 'em sent to jail. He was the PR man that stole Walden's car, the one the drug money was hidden in. When the car come back, Walden claims the money was gone and life's been goin' downhill for Walden ever since. A man can't do much behind bars."

"He's got us, ain't he?" Another belch followed Number Two's words. "Man that bologna has to be tearin' up my stomach. That was lunch and I'm already hungry." He was quiet for a while thinking. "I heard Walden's deranged. Him all set to run for office. His wife kicked him out, said he shamed her and she'd tired of his ways. My buddies, there, say he's practically foamin' at the mouth but there's some young blonde visits him pretty regular."

"You do have your contacts don't you?" It was plain number one was in control of this situation.

"Where do you hide money in a car?" Number two asked.

"Walden said it was sewn into the upholstery, so as not to rattle."

"Money rattles?" Number two gave a guffaw of a laugh. "Mine don't stay long enough to rattle."

"Remember, Walden said this one's smart. Be careful. But he didn't see us coming, did he?"

Listening, Andrew considered Walden thinking he was smart. Well, obviously not smart enough.

"So we're going to dump him? How long you think 'til the girl misses her van?"

"It's near closing time. We'll get the van off the street; leave it at the station then around midnight after we question him we'll take a little drive down by the river." They drove on silent for a bit, hitting red lights and passing one patrolling police car. Then the station came into sight. "Let's pull in, go get a bite to eat before we do our business with Graves."

"Yeah, the manual labor." Number two's voice held elation. "I hate that part." His laughter was exuberant. "Makes a man feel good to land a few punches on those who think they're above them. Graves had an uppity way about him, a pretty boy. We're kinda what they call a poet's justice ain't we?"

"Remember, no marks on his face and let go before you did last time." There was warning in Number One's voice. "You don't want anyone knowing you ever seen this guy. Now, close the doors. No need locking them. We got him tied and taped. He's not going anywhere. Should that happen; he gets loose it's only a matter of time. His days are numbered. You don't double cross Walden."

Truth told, Andrew's head was buzzing. If he could feel it, he was certain there was a lump the size of a goose egg on back of his head. If he could see, he just knew his vision was blurred. Nausea was hitting hard but that could be from the rag in his mouth. He tried to swing his arms up, let his hands feel the rag and found tape over the gag. Able to pull that away, he tried to turn the rag to untie the knot. His hands were fumbling all the while but he managed to turn it inch by inch.

Listening, he heard an air compressor come on, the hiss and lurch of the motor. It was a service station. Closed. Dark, he supposed. If he could pull the tape away from his eyes maybe he could see. He wondered that they hadn't wrapped tape over his nose, too. Peeling it away, he saw the eerie shadows of the shop, a car to one side, the grease rack, tool boxes and rubber tubing used for one purpose or another. He had to get out of there.

They must have wrapped the tape around his feet twenty times. Digging in, he tore and stripped until his feet were free and he could rise, but something held him back, a rope around the middle of his body was attached to a hook on one side of the van. He supposed Marigold used the rope to stabilize Matt's larger paintings in transport. He swore; another knot to undo. When the task was finally finished he run his hand alongside the wall of the van searching for the door handle; slid it to one side and stepped out onto concrete. Clumsy, his feet aching, his hands in the cuffs, he tried the door to the passenger side, leaned in toward the console and searched for a key to the cuff. It was empty.

In the dim he searched for the shop's entrance, nearly invisible to one side behind a large barreled object. The smell of grease and cleaning agents combined assaulted his nose. There was little time now. He had to get out and find a place to hide out while their search was on. Praying there was no alarm system he opened the door. The air smelled a bit cleaner. He breathed in, deeper. Maybe his head would clear and his vision steady.

He felt his shirt pocket. No cell. Patted his trousers. Nothing. Then he remembered he'd stuck it in the rear pocket when he was sitting on the stool at Marigold's discussing Cynthia Simpson and her gramps. Fumbling again, he dialed the number from memory. His guy came on in his usual nonsensical way. "Can you come get me? Now? I'm stranded at this station. Let me see where I am." Leaning back he read the name off the building. "I need you, like yesterday." This time he returned the cell to his shirt pocket, in case Pookie called back. His and Pookie's association had been lawyer- snitch friendly. Pookie knew the people on the street because Pookie had in the past dealt a few of the street *happenings* himself. Now the waiting was hard. Walden's goons could return at any moment.

MARIGOLD LOCKED THE DOOR, WATCHED her employees climb into their vehicles and drive away as she headed toward her van but *it wasn't* there. She left it right there with the keys in the ignition. Harriet was always warning her one day the van would turn up missing. Glancing around, she saw Andrew's old car still parked in front. A relieved chuckle grew inside her chest. Now Andrew was in on the game. Thinking to scare her, no doubt, Harriet had enlisted his aid. He'd taken her van and she was to drive his car, *if he left the keys in it.* Wait until she saw Andrew Graves, again. Now, here was a novelty; she pulled away from the lot, into the mainstream of traffic, for an old car, Andrew's car fairly hovered as it moved along.

IT SEEMED AN ETERNITY. ANDREW moved on down the street standing beside a huge trash can, his cuffed hands appearing to the world as casually bent while he watched traffic. The small green car glided to a stop. He climbed in. Sweat was dripping from his brow and his heart was thumping wildly in his chest.

Pookie eyed the cuffs with interest. "Man, what you done gone and got yourself into this time?"

"Thanks for coming. You got a key to fit these things?"

Pookie drove with one hand, reaching into the pocket on the passenger side, riffling around to bring out a string of keys. "Here. Have a blast. Try until you find one that fits."

"You amaze me." Andrew was trying the keys, one by one. "Awkward," he said. "I'm so tired I can't think, unless it's the hit on the head." He explained the situation to Pookie. "How about we circle the block and maybe my attackers will come out of that restaurant and I can have a look at them?"

"It's your party. Just put that pair of sunglasses on and we'll take a spin."

"Man, it's dark. I don't need sunglasses."

"Trust me. You need them." Pookie reached under the seat and brought out his own and slipped them on. "They're cover, you need to see them but they don't need to see you." He gave a short laugh as Andrew complied. "There's two dudes coming out of the restaurant. See? Over there. One is tall and thin, the other with the shirt sleeves rolled up, either on steroids or built like a bull, low to the ground, muscles."

"I need to hear their voices."

"Sink down into the seat." Pookie pulled over, rolled the window half way and stuck his head out. "Hey, there, gentlemen, can you tell me where Austin and Main Streets intersect?"

"Ain't heard of Austin, have you Rick?"

"No, don't believe I have." The second voice drawled. "Sorry, can't help you."

Pookie pulled away from the curb. "Where to, Bro?"

"First to Marigold's. You know where the car dealership used to be that has a new sign?"

"Sure thing. Old man got his tail in a crack, didn't he? Story goes he was money laundering."

Considering he had checked it out for Marigold, Andrew only nodded. His mind strayed to his and Pookie's talk from long ago when he caught Pookie in his own apartment and they'd formed a strange alliance. Pookie had even taken care of his personal items while he was jailed thinking he faced prison. "How's school? You remember our plans to go in together some day and build our own law firm?"

"I'm working on it. Getting all legit and more. Gave you my word, man." Pookie laughed. "You won't believe how smart they say I am. I don't even believe it." His laughter held a joyous ring. "So tell me what's next in this little fiasco of yours." Pookie was viewing Marigold's empty parking lot. "She's not here. There's not one car. So what's next?"

A bit shocked, Andrew considered Marigold driving his car. "Marigold must have taken it. She's the kind of girl thinks nothing of oddities. Yes, she would certainly do that." He had to move on to the next problem. "I need you to make a call, right now, to the police. Let's just say it's poetic justice."

"What must I say?"

"You observed two men driving a van with strange paintings on the side, when it pulled into a service station something didn't seem just right. So when they went in a restaurant you tailed them and listened to their conversation and it seemed the two were planning a heist. Don't give your name. Just give them the info and hang up. But do tell the person on the other end that "these are Walden's men.""

"What makes you so sure they are Walden's men? I thought he was locked behind bars."

"Bars do not a prison make. He has contacts everywhere. For the right price, they'll do his bidding. I heard bits and pieces. Evidently there was money hidden in the car I stole. Walden thinks I have it. He pays well and he promised he'd get even with me. Besides, I heard those two use his name."

"Because of money he wants you." Pookie gave that some thought. "They impounded the car. I could take a look; maybe check it out for the money?" He was dialing the Police station, hiding his number. He delivered the message, turned off his cell and made a private decision to check out the car. "It's a wonder the Feds didn't move on that car, by now, but they haven't. I see it every day."

"Perhaps it's a ploy."

"Since your wheels are gone, man. What's next?"

Andrew was seeing the world through a hazy fog, his head was spinning and he was trying to think fast. "I don't feel good," he said. "Take me to my apartment and I'll try to figure out something."

"I thought you were getting ready to get hitched and here you are playing cops and robbers."

"I was. I mean, I am. Don't breathe a word of this to anyone, you hear?" He sighed. "It could mean life or death, anytime you deal with Walden."

POOKIE WAS IN HIS ELEMENT. Cracking cars and taking what he wanted was pretty much a career. He climbed the fence as daylight slid into dark, that time of day moving objects become an illusion. There, sitting off to one side, Walden's prized sports car sat alone. He wondered why they hadn't already checked it out. Padding quietly to the car, he tried to open the door. It was locked. He used the tool he'd brought.

Once inside, he ran a gloved hand over the upholstery examining the sewing. No one had opened a seam. He knew how the side panels of the door fit together. Quietly he removed the panel, laying it aside, his heart skipping a beat at what he was seeing. That small shield wasn't supposed to be there. He produced a screw driver and went to work admiring the hand work of an unknown brother. Anyone would think the shield was part of the door's inner workings. He pulled it off. Now let's see what's behind it Pookie was thinking. Ten to one there'd be one in the other doors. When all was said and done, the inner lining of his jacket was protruding unnaturally. His heart was thumping like a cannonball and the elation he felt beat any high he'd ever known. Maybe he'd keep this bit of evidence for a later date with Andrew. There was no reason to tell everything you knew, was there? The panels went back on. He wiped everything carefully and left the lot a heavier man than when he arrived. Climbing the fence would be a bit more of a problem with his bulging jacket and he wondered why he hadn't brought a bag.

<hr>

COMPARABLE TO A DEFLATED TIRE, Andrew let himself in, walked straight to the bedroom and fell across the mattress. He had set his phone's alarm while Pookie was driving him home. His head was pounding and he was dizzy on his feet. He was getting married if he could pull himself together. Nothing better get in the way of his and Anne's day.

In his frazzled state of mind it was all he could do to comprehend Walden sending his goons after him. He hadn't known there was money hidden in the car and if there was what other person had access to Walden's vehicle to remove the money?

Then it came to him; the same person that drained his bank account Walden's step daughter. He tried to think logically. She was back in with Walden? Together they would plot anything; a drive by shooting, an accidental drowning, a car exploding; all reasonable unpredictable incidents. He couldn't think any more. He had to get himself in shape. If he didn't marry Anne this time she'd never have him.

Andy's little face, precious and small loomed in his memory, always trusting his daddy. I love him, Andrew thought as his mind closed down and sleep crept over him like a warm blanket. Then he saw the picture; Walden holding a gun to Andy's face, Andy crying. "Oh, God, no. Please. Please no."

Against the fatigue of his own body, Andrew found himself jumping from the bed, a scream issuing from his throat. It was the sound of a dying man. Walden had killed Andy over money? Disbelief grabbed his conscience. His body was shaking and the sobs he heard were his own.

It's a dream. It's a dream. He reached for the phone. Dialed. Listened.

"Hello." That soft whispery sound he loved to hear. "Andrew, is that you?"

"Yeah, it's me. I just needed to hear your voice."

"I hope you can say that after fifty years." Anne's laugh was soft and gentle.

"I will. I love you, Anne girl." He struggled to be normal. "How's our boy?"

"He's sleeping. Too much attention today." Anne sighed. "He's going to miss Harriet."

"I love you, Anne."

"Are you all right, Andrew?" Concern edged her words.

"Yeah, I just had a bad dream. Needed to hold you in my arms and let the dreams go, I guess."

CHAPTER TWENTY THREE

"HOLD STILL, SWEETUMS." ELLEN WAS tying the sash to Ruthie's dress. "Miss Flower Girl, of the year."

"What does that mean?" Ruthie tossed her curls. Haley had come after lunch to style Ruthie's hair and after all was said and done pulled the pins that held the curls on top of her head and said, "Ruthie, you are much prettier with your hair in curls down your back. Let's forget this up-do. You're still a little girl."

"Well, you were a flower girl for your Daddy and me."

"You mean, Daddy Daniel. My other daddy didn't like me and left me, and we got a new one."

"Something like that." Ellen agreed to prevent further discussion. "This daddy loves you. Right?"

"Right." Ruthie raised her arm, "High five," giggling as she and Ellen did the motions. "I'm so happy."

"Remember, we have to watch your brothers, now that they are walking, they are fast to get away."

"Me and Andy will keep our eye on them. Did you know he's wearing a sash, too?"

"No, Sweetums, that is called a cummerbund. Men don't have sashes that tie."

"They should." Ruthie whirled around, the blue dress puffing about her knees. "I love this dress. I love you and Daddy and Sammy and Danny. I love everyone, and Momma, I love Jesus and His father, God." But suddenly, Ruthie stopped, the dress swooshing in the air as she studied her mother's face. "Mommie, are you all right? Jesus just whispered to me that I must take care of you and help you."

Ellen laughed. "I'm fine, Sweetums. You've just been moving too fast. Sometimes we have to slow down."

"That too." Ruthie was perplexed. "Jesus said you needed to slow down."

THE WEDDING WAS TO BE in Harriet's garden because Anne said many of her personal problems had been settled there. She was beautiful in an off- white, form fitting lace dress, striking simplicity at its best. Hope had created subtle streaks in her blonde hair and Andrew told her she looked like a million. She would wear the pearls Ellen had given her when Ellen and Dan married and her shoes were matching. Harriet had accompanied her to St. Louis where they found what Harriet considered a divinely perfect dress. Anne smiled, alone in Harriet's room that had been her refuge for nearly three years, her heart filled with gratitude. This night she would start a new life in the home Andrew found for them on a shaded side street, two blocks away from Harriet and Bitty but within walking distance when they chose to visit. This was not goodbye; the bond between them was too strong. This was new beginnings.

Ellen arrived, Ruthie bouncing along by her side, to find Andy and take him to a corner to read a book. "You look beautiful." Ellen stood on tiptoe to place a kiss on top of Anne's head. "That's what Daniel used to do, kiss me on the forehead or the head; so many times as if to reassure me, all was well." She sat gingerly on the bed, so as not to muss the dress Anne ask her to wear, light blue, Anne's favorite color; Dark hair around her shoulders, her own pearls, Ellen, serene, beautiful, Anne's true friend.

"And it is, well." Anne beamed. "Oh, El, who would have thought? Did God know Andrew and I would finally live together in peace with our son?" She grinned. "I know what you are going to say, he knew me before I was formed in my mother's womb, before the foundation of the world. Oh, El, I invited my mother but she's so far gone, Olivia and Harriet stepped in to fill that void." For a moment her voice broke, "It's not the same, but the years have helped to diminish the hurt of my own mother's absence in my life. I have to put that situation in God's hands and be thankful for Harriet and Olivia."

"No time for sadness, today, my lady," Ellen rose from the bed. "Your groom waits."

"If only Chester and Bitty could be here."

Ellen smiled. "It's all right, Cherie." Anne laughed, knowing Ellen was imitating dear old Dr. Lonzo.

Daniel met them as they entered the side garden where Harriet had placed a latticed barrier for Anne to wait until the music began. Marigold had entwined roses and baby's breath. Light blue bows the color of Ruthie's dress were tied on each end of the rows of chairs, where at least a hundred people were waiting. The Harpers, Haley and her Jeremy, Caroline Hawkins and Earl Simpson and his granddaughter; the list of names went on, Andrew's mother had been seated on the front row where the Lonzo's and Harriet would sit after being escorted down the aisle and honored by Anne; several from Christ Church and Jonathan, who had befriended her when Andrew had stripped her dress from her body at Hutson's Grand ball, was there with his new wife, Angie. Peeping through the lattice, Anne saw the people who mattered most and wished for Marigold's sake, Matt's parents had accepted the invitation to come and share in this moment. She had come to love Marigold as the sister she never had and Marigold's heartache of not being accepted by Matt's parents had touched her heart.

It was Bitty and Chester she missed the most. Two weeks had passed since the antibiotic was begun. Chester's body had suffered the effects of an infection that raged out of control, not one to be squelched in a day and the group had prayed unceasing for fear of losing him. Then she saw them. Harriet had found a secret place for Bitty and Chester, away from the crowd, lest he in his low immune state take on another risk to his body. No one would know, and when the ceremony ended, two of Harriet's confrères from Becker Steel would whisk them back home. It never ceased to amaze Anne, the authority Harriet Becker held, though she remained low key, using that authority with discretion.

Anne smiled remembering the ordeal with Andrew at the ball and learning later, it was Harriet took charge of a volatile situation and kept the community at large from knowing. She searched the crowd to find Harriet with Doctor Silverman by her side, conferring with Dr. Lonzo, not only her boss but the father figure in her life since her step father died; Dr. Lonzo, who tried to give her a car and continually insisted he and Olivia had adopted her. She was all they had. Anne laughed as Ellen poked her and said, "Laughter is good on your wedding day. Now, there's the organ. Listen, Brother Joe has begun."

"This is the day the Lord has made, let us rejoice in it," Pastor Joe's voice rang out. "May we all please rise in honor of our bride, Anne Graves and our groom, Andrew Graves. Our ring bearer is their son, Andy, and for you who do not know, this is a second marriage to each other and this time it will last."

Laughter filled the garden, as the organ pealed victorious note. Another feat, Harriet and Marigold managed, Anne was thinking, watching the Lonzo's and Harriet and Dr. Silverman being seated, followed by Dan and Ellen leaving the latticed cove, knowing Marigold was sending Ruthie and Andy ahead of them, Ruthie strewing rose petals and Andy carrying the two gold rings on a satin pillow.

Anne stepped from behind the rose twined barrier to meet Andrew's gaze upon her and her heart filled with thanksgiving. *Thank you Heavenly Father, he loves me.* She saw Andrew's eyes fill with tears and her heart nearly burst, for there they stood, Andrew, the man she had always loved holding their son's hand.

Andrew's heart ached to think he had almost missed Anne walking toward him. Bittersweet, he considered the danger he'd experienced in the dream of Walden hurting Andy. Now his joy mingled with sadness knowing in the deranged state of mind Walden was in these days, he might turn that anger toward Anne, too. He had to keep them safe and he had confided in Harriet, remembering the night he attacked Anne when he was in a drunken stupor and *Harriet's men* had come for him and carried him out. Their warning rang in his ears, even now. With Walden's men on his trail, Andrew had reached a decision, not only did he need the Lord on his side; he needed God's protection on his family. For Anne, he would do this. When he said his vows he would publicly proclaim that intent. God had to know he meant it. Andrew Graves had been running long enough for himself. God could have the rest of his life.

Pastor Joe's sister, Lauren Hill began to sing. Anne reached the circle of flagstone where Harriet had chosen for the wedding party to stand and Andrew reached for her hand. Ruthie and Andy moved in front of Ellen and Daniel. Anne, listened, to words she had chosen, thinking they spoke words of assurance to their future. She had heard the song played at Bitty's wedding and searched for the words.

"Oh, promise me that someday you and I will take our love together to some sky, where we may be alone and faith renew, and find the hollows where those flowers grew, those first sweet violets of early spring, which comes in whispers, thrill us both and sing, of love unspeakable that is to be, Oh, promise me, Oh, promise me."

Anne's smile, serene, calm and beguiling, held Andrew's thoughts that she had waited for him through painful encounters only he had the power to thrust upon her. He didn't deserve Anne's love but he would cherish her and make amends for the rest of their lives together.

"Oh, Promise me that you will take my hand, the most unworthy in this lonely land, And let me sit beside you in your eyes, seeing the vision of our paradise, hearing God's message while the organ rolls It's mighty music to our very souls, No love less perfect than a life with thee, Oh, promise me. Oh, promise me."

"Dearly beloved," Pastor Joe began, "We are gathered here today to reunite Andrew and Anne in Holy matrimony, that whatsoever God joins together, no man can put asunder. As the circle of life has a beginning and for believers has no end, today, Andrew and Anne are promising each other to live life together fulfilling the plan God has for their lives with their son, Andy."

Sitting on the third row, Jeremy squeezed Haley's hand. "I like that," he whispered. "Will you marry me?" He squeezed her hand harder, to know if she heard him. "Will you marry me?"

Haley's eyes filled with tears. "Yes." The last song was in progress before Haley's heart settled to a steady thrumming. She saw Andrew kiss Anne and heard the words they had chosen to bind their lives; From the bible, the great love story of Ruth and Boaz, the words Ruth replied to her mother in law. "Whither thou goest, I will go, whither thou lodgest, I will lodge; Thy people shall be my people, and thy God my God."

"IT WAS BEAUTIFUL," BITTY SAID, as Chester settled into his favorite chair. "It gave me hope."

He motioned she come to sit on his lap. Bitty's face flushed. She still held reluctance for public display of affection. "Come over, here, Bitty." Chester's smile was filled with understanding. "There's no one here. I want you by my side. We've experienced the renewal of our friends lives together and in a way our own. I guess sometimes in the dark hours of night I wonder if you would leave me because of this. It seems there are times you pull away."

"I don't mean to," she said as she came, timidly resigned to this big statured man that had lost so much weight through his sickness his clothes nearly fell off of him. He pulled her onto his lap.

"Bitty," he said, "We are not too old to care about each other and I know I've failed you, getting sick like this, losing body functions that no one would ever believe can happen, but Bitty, we can make a life together that will bless us both. I know that's what God wants; us to go on and do the very best we can and when I regain strength I don't think it will bother you so much. There's just something about a man being able to work." Chester sighed. "If he can. I know there are those who can't and I don't envy them trying to reason it all out." She moved, gingerly as his arms drew her near. "Relax Hon."

"I can't," Bitty whispered. "I have such a fear of hurting you."

"The doctor says when the infection has completely left my body, Bitty, there are tests to see if my bladder will function again. I don't think I'm going to have this catheter the rest of my life, but if I do, there's a lot to be said for companionship. Marriage is many things. I found that out after losing Mavis. There's the intimacy of lives shared; the simple appreciation of having each other, to hear a voice, to feel someone touch you because they care." He leaned down to peer into her eyes. "We have to learn, just because our married life has taken an unforeseen turn, we have each other and it is not all about sex." He grinned. "I said that, didn't I? You may find this hard to believe, but these last years since Mavis died, when I wished for someone to talk with, have a cup of coffee or take a walk, I wasn't thinking of sex, I was hoping for a friend. I had so many lonely hours and now it's hard for you to talk with me about our future and I need you to, Bitty. Help me through this."

"I always hoped to be able to discuss anything with anyone but not this, even the doctor discussing it made me uneasy. I feel resentful that someone would cause you unnecessary pain." Bitty turned her face away, it was all too much. She didn't want to talk about it. Ellen had tried but it embarrassed Bitty and she told Ellen the doctor had explained it all. "I don't understand why God let it happen."

"At the hands of an experienced physician," Chester agreed, "But she didn't know what she was doing." For some reason one of Pastor Joe's messages came to mind. "Do you remember Pastor Joe's sermon, when he said, *'Sometimes, God allows things to happen to good people to benefit others. Imagine an unsaved person watching how a Christian handles an illness, a loss, a tragedy. That may be the only Christian witness they will have. People who have no hope really don't know where to turn when hard times strike, Christians know who to lean on.'* What if people had no one to make them think?"

"But, your urologist thinks you may have to wear a catheter that sits above your waistline that runs into your bladder. I don't understand how that situation could keep from being prone to an infection, and here you were doing what the doctor said and got an infection before that procedure even happened." She saw in his eyes, a pleading to understand. He did need her to listen. She was his wife.

Bitty tried to relax, to lean back into his arms. Not for the first time, she questioned this big person loving a small wag of a woman such as herself. Love had seemed out of her reach. When Ruthie was kidnapped she had thought his attention meant he suspected she was culprit to the kidnapping but his reluctance to give up on her had persevered throughout many denials on her part. No, she wouldn't give up on him. Losing her first husband had been painful but life alone at times was nearly unbearable.

"I love you, Bitty." Chester's own insecurities flailed in his mind. "I never meant to disappoint you."

She felt his sadness. "Chester, we have so much together, I thank God daily and if He wants to give us more, then I'll accept that too, but marriage should begin as a friendship, people doing things together, why don't we trust our love to the Lord, and let Him do the rest."

"That sounds like Ellen talking," Chester replied. "I declare, the two of you speak God's love like an evangelist."

Bitty's laughter rang through the rooms. "As you have just seen, I have to work things out in my own way, and it isn't my intention to grieve you or the Holy Spirit but it hurts me more than you know to see you struggle with normal body functions," She shook her head remorsefully, "I guess I was being rebellious. That Ellen, she taught me different. She has no idea how many lives she touched. And you know her usual expression, "God works in mysterious ways, His wonders to perform."

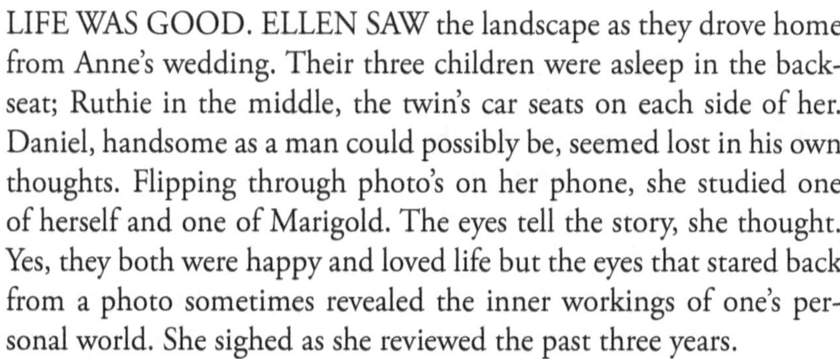

LIFE WAS GOOD. ELLEN SAW the landscape as they drove home from Anne's wedding. Their three children were asleep in the back-seat; Ruthie in the middle, the twin's car seats on each side of her. Daniel, handsome as a man could possibly be, seemed lost in his own thoughts. Flipping through photo's on her phone, she studied one of herself and one of Marigold. The eyes tell the story, she thought. Yes, they both were happy and loved life but the eyes that stared back from a photo sometimes revealed the inner workings of one's personal world. She sighed as she reviewed the past three years.

So much had happened, not to mention her happiness. The group had grown closer through the situations life had presented, Chester's illness not counted as least because he had come close to dying. Bitty had renovated the old house and it stood as prestigious as Harriet's. Then there was the friendship between all, even Marigold and Harriet reaching an understanding as mother and daughter and Andrew gaining trust. Ellen's heart was full, she thanked God Daniel had adopted Ruthie and if Ruthie's birth father were alive he had not contested the adoption. Coming out of her reverie, she saw Daniel was staring at her.

"I love you, Mrs. Gates. You, my beauty, have blessed me a thousand times over." Reaching for her hand, he lift it to his lips and kissed it. "God is so good. I thank him every day." The usual chuckle accompanied his words. "I think, anyway I hope, all of our lives have reached a point of peace. Aren't all accounted for in that department. But I have noticed this whole thing has left you looking a bit wan."

"Wan is it?" Ellen's smile was mischievous. "Haley could not contain her excitement. It seems Jeremy proposed, today, right in the middle of Anne and Andrew's vows."

"What about the boy Jeremy had with him? I understand he has guardianship over him."

"Glenn? Rumor has it that Dorothy and Harper are taking him in, even considering adopting him."

"That leaves one little item, doesn't it?" They said it together. "Matt's parents accepting his wife."

"God works in mysterious ways," Daniel. "I believe that is going to happen, in God's time."

For a moment his eyes held hers. He had no idea why the thought came to him at that moment. "You've got to take care of yourself, Ellen. The twins are a handful and I'm busy at work. Sometimes I worry about you." He gave a deep sigh. "I love you, Ellen."

"I love you, Daniel." Ellen glanced to the back seat. "And our three little munchkins." It was then Ellen noticed the car behind them, practically on the bumper of the Escalade, but it was the driver fairly visible through the windshield made her shiver as her spine tingled in alarm.

Daniel heard the gasp. "What's wrong?" The car behind was coming around.

She felt foolish saying it. "Oh, Daniel, the person driving that car reminded me of Jeffrey."

"The devil has a way of robbing us of happiness and securities, Ellen, especially at times like this when we are happy for others and our world finally feels right." Still, Daniel gave the car a quick check.

<hr>

"TIRED, BABE?" MATT SLIPPED HIS arms around Marigold's waist. A feeling of content washed over him as she relaxed against his strong body. He nibbled at her neck, feeling the long strands tickle his cheek and remembering the spiked haired gypsy she resembled when they first met and he had loved her, wondering in his silent way if there were a chance she would possibly ever return the feeling.

"I was thinking of all that has transpired in our lives, Matt. Our little Pumpkin. Harriet really trying to be a mother to me and I know Mom and Dad would be happy that I have all of you, even Harriet."

"Hmm." He turned her around to face him. "I want to see you as you talk. Go on."

"Have you considered how strong Ellen's faith has always been?" Marigold let her cheek settle against his chest. "There were times in all our lives, we panicked. Struggle was our middle name and yet, she would tell us those stories about her grandmother, "my mimmie, she would say. And it makes me think how we have to learn how to impart the faith we have to our children."

"Child or children?" Matt felt a quickening in his heart. "Are we going to have another baby?" His laughter rang through Harriet's garden. They were ready to gather Matthew John and his belongings but had side-tracked to the garden, a moment alone, before the family progressed to their own home. "You remember I had to take matters into my own hands, last time. You were keeping a secret from me."

"I was so worried over your mother's acceptance of me, Matt."

He heard the tears in her voice. "I know, Babe. I'm sorry for that. If it helps to know, I love you, Tinkerbelle and I will love you forever. Just don't ever keep things from me again."

"I try not to keep secrets from you, Matt, but you know that painting you did of the couple in the garden and you painted the little boy running toward them? I knew you had your parents in mind when you painted the couple. Their shape betrayed who they were and no one could deny it was our Pumpkin."

"It sold, didn't it?" Matt sighed, kissing her forehead, her nose and finally her lips. "Yeah, it was them." His heart seemed to dull down when he thought what they were missing and he wanted to see his son running down a path to his parents with their arms opened wide. "Yeah, I miss them, Tinkerbelle."

Marigold's eyes were damp. In his arms she felt heaven on earth. "It didn't sell, Matt. I sent it to your mother." She felt his body tighten. Now as he positioned her to stare into her eyes, she said, "I received a short hand written note from your mother. This morning."

Matt wasn't certain where this was leading. But he couldn't get excited. His hopes had been dashed too many times. "Maybe one day she will come around."

"She invited us to come see them, Farm boy, as soon as we can." The next thing she knew he had picked her up, holding her eye to eye level as his laughter sounded through the garden and the expression of joy in his eyes would be remembered forever. "I love you, Farm Boy."

"I love you, Tinkerbelle." The end.

EPILOGUE

B ITTY STOOD AT THE WINDOW, one hand touching the woodwork painted less than a year ago. The trials had been many during the time of the old house renovation. Now she stood pristine as Harriet's, not that that was the goal, Bitty had not known with skilled carpenters the house could gain such privilege to be placed on the city's touring guide, alongside Harriet Becker's antebellum.

Sighing, Bitty turned toward Harriet's home. It seemed no one was stirring. Since Anne married Andrew, leaving with little Andy, the rooms were quiet with Harriet and Hattie moving daily through the midst of antique furniture and multitudes of memories. But there was no sadness, Harriet's own daughter was still on the block, though there were unconfirmed rumors that Matt's family had asked him to move back and take control of the farming operation. Bitty wondered how that would sit with Harriet. She could just hear her say, "Take my Matthew John away?" That incredulous voice and disbelieving face would give both Matt and Marigold something to think about.

So much had happened in their lives. They had welcomed the Gipson's' as part of their group, on behalf of Haley returning from prison not favoring returning to the Gipson's home church due to her way of thinking, "the people will be so caught up in discussing my whereabouts the last two years, we won't be able to worship." Haley had been a bit reserved and perhaps rebellious of nature in the beginning but Ruthie had helped to soften her heart. When Bitty asked Ruthie how that happened, the five year old said, "I told her, Jesus loves her and she needs to talk to him, and then listen."

"How old are you?" Bitty always asked their long time joke, knowing the reply.

"I'm five but I feel like six."

Laughter always followed and now Ruthie was six, ready to enter school, probably to disrupt the system knowing what to do with her as she could read any book she wished. Whatever they decided, Ruthie would be happy and content. Her name changed from Anderson to Gates had surrounded Ruthie's aura, blessed and assured she was Daniel's child just as surely as the twins, Daniel and Samuel, Ruthie seemed to have an inner glow. That glow sometimes concerned Bitty but her group of friends were resigned to protect this child with the *gift*.

Bitty turned from the window, found her favorite chair and settled in for her daily commune with the Lord as she reached for her Bible and let the pages fall open where they should. For the love of a child the group had come together, lives and marriages intact. Ruthie seemed to move in their midst discerning things beyond comprehension with knowledge of the Lord; accepting the mysteries. And all those who loved her could do was trust in the Lord that she would not be misunderstood in the world, nor misused.

"Bitty," Ruthie's voice spoke through her memory, "If Uncle Chester dies, he won't be gone forever." Bitty's heart quickened, as she thought *but I will miss him. I don't want to live in this big old house alone.* "Jesus prepared a home for Uncle Chester in Heaven, already, Bitty. If he can't get well, then we have to let him go. Jesus decides, Bitty." *I cannot bear this again, I lost Larry and now God wants Chester. She knew she had struggled with trusting the Lord at that point and perhaps a bit of her own rebellious nature had returned, the Lord was asking too much. Give up the man she had just married, try to reconcile her own emotions, it wasn't fair.* But Ruthie had held Chester's hand and in the end the Lord had given Chester more time to live and Bitty more time to understand whatever happened God would be there to see her through.

Glancing down to see what passage she was to read, Bitty's heart felt joy, *You are the God who performs miracles; you display your power among the peoples.* Psalm seventy seven, verse fourteen. Yes, God had performed miracles in the lives of all. Daniel found Ellen. Andrew straightened up his life and remarried Anne. Harriet's search for her daughter could not have been more divinely orchestrated. Marigold moving two doors down the street had to be as Bitty often heard a *God thing*. The Gipson's daughter, Haley, met her gentle friend from another state and would be marrying him soon and that had to be another of God's works, that he could move people from state to state in order to find the person He was choosing for them. Now that Haley accepted her brother's death, the Gipson's were reliving hallowed memories of their son. Sometimes grieving was a horror but with God in charge the promise of heaven and eternal life brought peace in those times of sadness and they realized eventual joy as the family would reunite. Matt's family was being obstinate and selfish, but now that they wanted him back to run the farm, Bitty just believed Marigold had a fighting chance with the family.

Life was good. God was blessing them and when there were trials they knew who to look too. Chester was strong enough to keep his job as Chief of Police. He would be coming home, at the end of the day, his energy bursting into the room as he lift her off her feet and kissed her. "I'm thankful for every day the good Lord gives me, Bitty. Let's make the most of it. What if we hadn't found each other?" Bitty realized she had come a long way. Theirs was a love story. Truly it was a blessing to love again.

Laughter filled the walls of Bitty's old house and at Ellen's the walls were fairly rocking with sweet little Ruthie and those rambunctious twins. Ellen's news flooded Bitty's heart with happiness. "God works in mysterious ways, Itty Bitty. We're going to have another little babykins."

www.ingramcontent.com/pod-product-compliance
Lightning Source LLC
Chambersburg PA
CBHW061434150726
47987CB00001B/215